I0665919

War of Shadow and Bone

Of Gods and War, Volume 2

Olivia Gold

Published by Olivia Gold, 2025.

Cover designed by Getcovers

Published by Olivia Gold

ISBNs:

Ebook: 9798991937726

Paperback: 9798991937733

Table of Contents

To all who have faced death and come away unafraid

Pronunciation Guide

Meiora (M-eye-or-uh)—Darci's cryarsh

Ryuzio (Ree-you-zee-oh) Darci's primary dragon

Myzonia (my-zone-ee-uh)—Adrian's world

Oria (or-eye-uh)—Darci's world

Amenir (ah-men-ear)—Luna's world

Leasia (lee-see-uh)—Araina's world

Mount Eirlo (air-loh)—(location of dragon army)

Plains of Okira (oh-keer-uh)—a stretch of land between the capital of Myzonia and Zaiven

Yeeri (year-ee), a tiny village along the plains of Okira

Faolan (fay-oh-lahn)—boy

Stygo (sti-go) -pink fruit, a cross between an apple and berries

Zaiven (zi-ven)—a small village near Adrian's house

Rizyrk (ri-zirk)—capital of Myzonia

Novundo (no-voon-doh), capital of Oria

Khitaen (kite-en)—God of War and Peace

Araina (uh-rain-uh) Goddess of Light

Luna–Goddess of Wind and Sky

Markyr (mar-keer), God of Fire and Ice

Cryirz (cry-irz), God of Night

Endelio (en-dell-ee-oh) universe of the divine in which all things exist

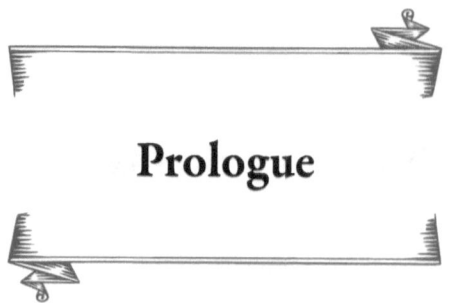

Prologue

"Humans are prone to greed and malice. Seeking their destruction, then blaming the deities for their lack of involvement."

—Supposed quote from the Death God to Araina, *Scrolls of Markyr,* passage 391

35 Years Ago

Making a deal with a goddess is a nasty business. Kings and queens of these worlds are usually not foolish enough to try; however, that hasn't stopped this king from meeting with me. Greedy and afraid, he doesn't think he betrays his motives this easily, but I see the monster in his eyes. I hear the beating of his frantic heart and smell the terror on his skin, observing the hints his body gives away.

This will be fun.

"You want me to empower him? You think I would give so freely of myself?" I purr the words, predator that I am, longing to see him flinch, to make him cower.

"I am willing to pay whatever you want. I am not afraid of the cost you may require from me." His voice wavers, but disappointingly, he remains steadfast in his posture.

"And why would you do that? Why do you not ask me to empower you?" I squint my eyes, suspicious of this human's motives. Most people want power for themselves, wanting to exist forever in control of their destinies. Yet, this man asks for power for another.

I have an idea of his desires. There is something about him that is wrong, broken, and irreparable.

A shadow flickers in the corner of the room, and I smile.

"I—-I am dying," he stutters. "I only ask that you imbue a piece of my soul within him, too. You—You can take me. Whenever you please."

I notice the pallor of his skin. A sickly tinge to his dark brown that shouldn't be there. Yes, he would need me soon anyway, and perhaps his current state is the reason I was drawn to his presence in the first place. Death calls to me.

"You wish to gain immortality through him, for you to endure in your son. Is it because too many oppose you now? If you return as him, do you think your critics will simply let you continue your plans? If I give him power, he will be deadly in all the ways you hope him to be, but he may not allow you to control his actions."

He stares at me, silent and trembling, but he holds his tongue.

I tilt my head, observing him and watching his odd behavior, thinking about his request. He wants to corrupt what is new and gentle. I was not always dark and jaded. I used to love. Perhaps there is an opportunity here for me—a chance at redemption. A flutter of excitement awakens in my chest. He interrupts my thoughts before I can fully immerse myself in the potential outcomes.

"I need a strong ruler to take my place. I need to ensure we do not fall prey to those who would destroy us, who would make us weak. Take whatever you need." He draws in a shaky breath.

A plan forms as I reflect on his words. "You will not die today, king. Not even tomorrow. I will grant you this one gift. You will live to see what he becomes. I will give you thirty years. On one condition."

"Anything," he breathes.

"You will give me the northern half of your kingdom to do whatever I wish to do with it."

I see the objection in his eyes. He wants to protest, but it's an easy bargain. He's probably more concerned about the lack of taxes than anything—greedy, selfish man. I'm being far more generous than I should be. I'm granting him thirty more years of life in exchange for what? A partial kingdom? Seems fair enough to me. I don't tell him the northern part of his kingdom will be taken from this world if he agrees to this deal.

The battle he wages with himself concludes. "Yes," he murmurs.

He holds his hand out. I take my dagger and slice his palm quickly. He startles because he was expecting a handshake, no doubt. I make an identical cut across my palm before grabbing his hand, pressing our bloody palms together. He spasms and screams. Shadows swirl around us, engulfing our hands and sealing the bargain between humanity and the divine.

He wants eternal life. I'll give him a taste of it before I steal his soul for good. He is a monster after all. I am one, too, but there is a good part of me I can share. I see a vision of a baby with dark brown eyes and deep brown skin. He will be more than this king could ever be.

When the bargain is complete, I release his hand and glance down at my shadowed fingers. He'll regret his decision, no doubt. Not all monsters destroy everything. Not all monsters are me.

It's a nasty business—making deals with a goddess.

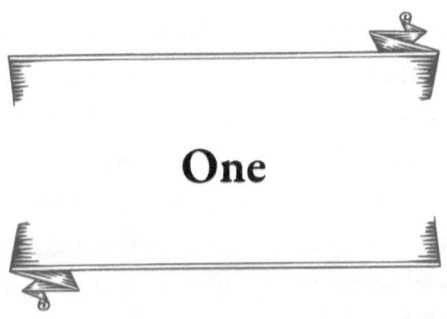

One

"The God of Death fought against his natural place in the worlds. Each god was entrusted with one world to guard and protect, except for him. He created one that never should have existed. The Goddess Araina destroyed the abomination and exiled the God of Death."

—"Account of Death and Life"
Scroll of Myzonia's Origins

Marcus
Present Day

All I feel is agony, like a part of my soul has been ripped out by the discoveries in this room. The house creaks and whines with the wind howling outside, and the windows are cracked, letting slivers of cold air slip in unwelcome.

She lied. I knew we couldn't trust her, but the twisting pain in my stomach protests the information. I want to throw up; I want to rage and destroy and unleash my magic on something or someone. Everything about this place is wrong, a shrine to her lies. Why do I feel like someone stabbed my heart? I shouldn't feel this betrayed or broken by the truth. Adrian stands frozen in the room with shadows and death all around us. The cryarsh slithers along the floor again and slips out of the room.

"This is them, isn't it? Her family—she killed them." Adrian's words are strained, whispered declarations too painful to hold in, but are they the truth?

Did she kill them? Of course, she did. The God of Death works closely with her. The walls are marked with monsters. Great, winged dragons are painted everywhere, and shadows swirl constantly around the emblem of death itself. I'm transfixed by the skeletons on the floor in the corner—the large one is wedged between two smaller ones. The churning in my stomach intensifies at the sight.

Shadows swirl across them, an unnatural glow emanating from their deathly pallor. Are those tiny fractures across all the bones, as if they have been shattered and put back together again? Black flowers rest across them, a symbol of death, looking strangely beautiful. An eerie black light glows around the entire display. I don't understand how they can exist in this temperature, other than to assume magic holds all of it in place.

A thought sparks to life in my mind.

"What if the God of Death has control of her? Maybe she's trapped as a part of some plan he has."

I'm grasping at anything to explain away this terror. I know I am. I want her to be who I thought she was. I want her to be my Darci.

My thoughts screech to a halt. *My Darci.* When did I start wanting her to be mine? This is madness. None of this makes sense with what we know about the God of Death. He is an enigma because we don't learn his history, and drawing attention to a monster is shameful. I've never heard anything in our stories about him controlling or possessing another person. How did she end up tangled with him?

While I'm here, drowning in my thoughts, I don't notice that Adrian hasn't answered me yet, that he never even reacted. "Adrian, that has to be what it is, right? Dark Lord Daemon must be in on it, too. Adrian?"

Adrian doesn't respond. I tear my eyes from the skeletons on the floor and the dragons on the walls to scan my friend. He's trembling.

Not in fear—-more like he's desperately clinging to his control. Sweat beads on his brow.

"Adrian? What's wrong?" His hands are clenched tightly; his nails are probably cutting into his palms. Something isn't right. There's a heaviness about his presence that I didn't feel until now.

I pull my magic from deep within, letting it flood to the surface with the electric power of a thunderstorm. Dark, swirling shadows seep out of my friend's skin now, familiar in an unsettling way. Darci. The same magic she carried in her veins is showing itself in the Sovereign of my kingdom. My chest tightens with anxiety and adrenaline.

"Adrian, I think we need to leave. Now." I reach for his arm. This is my friend, my brother. I don't understand what's happening here, but it feels wrong. It feels like another presence is here with us. Before I can grab his forearm, one of the tendrils of shadow magic lashes out at me, burning my palm, and I swallow a scream.

Pain blinds me momentarily, but I need to get him out of here. I remember Darci struggling with her power, and a memory resurfaces of our time in the temple. *Please, still be here.*

Without hesitation, I scream, "Meiora! Meiora, I need you to help me."

Adrian's breathing increases, and my heart races in response. The trembling grows in his body, and his knees begin to buckle under the strain.

I'm about to make another dive for Adrian when the cryarsh swarms the room. Its shadowy form fills every crevice and corner, engulfing Adrian. I hear him gasp and groan.

"Adrian!" All visibility is lost, the room vanishing under a blanket of shadows. The cryarsh wouldn't hurt him, would it? Darkness smothers every tiny flicker of light trying to dispel it.

As quickly as the shadow creature comes, it drifts away, vanishing like smoke on the air. Adrian kneels on the ground with his hands pressed to the floor, head hanging. He's sucking in air like a man saved from drowning. I've no doubt he most likely was.

I rush to his side, dropping to one knee beside him. "Are you okay?" My fingers shake as I reach to touch his shoulder. Will it hurt again? The shadow magic vanished. Surely, it's safe. A thread of tension releases when I make contact and feel no pain, relief flooding my system. He's okay. We're okay. A spark of rage grows inside of me, mingling with my despair. None of this should be happening, especially not to Adrian. He's too good, too necessary for our world.

He shakes his head and swallows before answering. "I think, I think there's a monster inside of me."

Connections. Adrian kept saying that he felt connected to Darci. Something drew them together. Her magic is obviously in his blood. If I hadn't recently spent so many days with her, teaching her to control her magic, I might not have known what it looked like. Those shadows I saw emanating from him were the same as Darci's. The pain I felt touching his arm was the same pain I felt when I carried Darci to the Chamber of Silence at the Temple of Markyr. Dread settles in my chest.

I lock eyes with him, and the blood running in my veins turns sluggish and cold. A faint rim of glowing green that wasn't there before surrounds his dark brown irises—a green reminding me of Darci. It's as if I'm seeing a piece of her soul embedded in his.

Their connection runs deeper than any of us could have imagined.

"Okay, it's okay. We'll figure this out." I hold out my hand to help him up. His grip is tight, yet weak. He seems drained after fighting whatever was trying to get out only moments ago.

We stand side by side momentarily before I turn and lead the way out of the room. Once we're safely outside, I close the door and immediately feel a weight lift off my shoulders. Adrian looks frail. He's never looked frail in his entire life.

"What happened? What were you feeling when you froze up in there?" I wait, not wanting to rush an answer out of him.

He stares down at his hands, and I notice the red half-moons from where his fingernails bit into the skin.

"I don't know. I felt this surge of power like I've never felt before." His voice catches. "It burned from the inside. I... I had to hold it in, and I thought it was going to kill me."

He looks up again, and those green rimmed eyes make my heart skip. He doesn't look like himself. He looks possessed.

"I could feel the weight of it. It was heavy and dark. It—-" I look away.

"What? What did you notice about it?" He implores. I can't lie to him.

"The magic coming off your skin was the same magic I saw on Darci. I trained with her for long enough to recognize it. Your magic was the same." I make myself look him in the eye.

"But you said—you said the magic she had was given by the God of Death somehow. That it was his magic. That it was too powerful for a mortal to contain." Twisting, aching fear swirls in my gut.

"I know, Adrian. That's what we learned from the priestess." I pause to regroup. "Maybe you've both been cursed by him. You said you felt connected to her somehow. You sensed each other's presence when you were apart." She doesn't have to be evil. This could be a targeted attack by the God of Death himself.

"But what if I can't contain this power either? It was strong, Marcus. Stronger than anything I've ever felt. It wanted out, like it was alive." He shudders, then opens and closes his hands like he can't feel his fingers properly.

"We'll find an answer. We'll travel wherever we need to go." Because the alternative isn't acceptable.

"I need to find her, Marcus. I need to know what is happening and how she's connected to him."

I nod because what else is there to say? I want to find her too. I turn and walk back to the front door where we'll enter Myzonia.

"Marcus?"

I stop and face my friend, knowing exactly what his next question will be.

"I'll need you to end this. If I can't protect our world anymore..." He doesn't look away from me. He stares intensely, pleading for me to do what he needs me to—to be his obedient commander.

"You can't ask this of me." My voice is tight; anger creeping up my back.

His eyes widen in surprise for a moment. I don't wait to hear what else he'll say. I walk to the door, sliding a dagger across my palm and applying my blood to the framework. When I open the door, swirling shadows greet me instead of the wintry world of Oria. Adrian comes up behind me, both of us remaining silent as we step into the shadows.

It's time to find out who Darci really is.

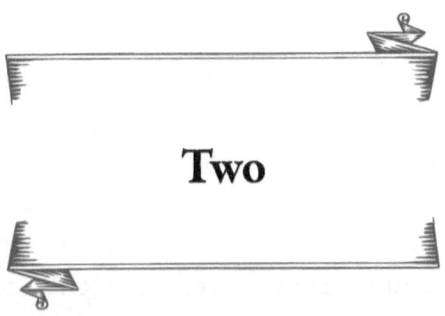

Two

"The great Goddess of Light, Araina, holds all things together."
—Opening prayer recited by priestesses
every morning at the temples
across the worlds

Darci

Power feels good. I had forgotten how good it could feel to let loose the magic that courses through my veins and to unchain the monster within. It's been far too long since I tried to be something other than myself. I wanted to be good and gentle. I wanted to lean into that part of my soul that creates life, but the burden of my past and the way the others have always treated me has made it feel impossible.

My skin vibrates with magic now, and I waste no time lingering in my world. I think my sister is expecting me. If she isn't, she's an even greater fool than I thought. When I left the supposed dungeon that Khitaen placed me in, I brought myself to the forest in Oria. The shadows from the trees and the darkness calling to me from the avgrunn bring comfort to my restless soul, if I still have one. A brief image of Adrian appearing in the snow-covered woods fills my mind, and a twinge of guilt pinches my chest. The feeling passes quickly enough. I saunter in the direction of the avgrunn that will take me to Leasia, where Araina spends most of her time.

Such a strange thing, these worlds. You'd think one would be enough to satisfy the egos of the divine, but obviously, Khitaen wants more than just his world. All of them want to be loved and adored in every world. That's why their temples dot the landscapes of any place mortals walk. Ever the outsider, I have no temple and no place to rest. I call them all mine, because they all come to me in the end.

The snow is deep and wet. The wind whistles through the treetops, and a stillness about the woods keeps my senses alert. I breathe deeply, letting the crisp bite of the winter air pierce my entire body. The forest thickens the deeper I go, but the avgrunn is not far now. The deep, black pit in the center of the clearing churns up ahead. In the corner of my eye, a shadow shifts almost imperceptibly behind some trees. A sad smile graces my lips, but I don't look toward the movement. I don't interact with it.

Instead, I step forward into the clearing, the power of the darkness in the avgrunn reaching for me across the untainted snow. This time, I willingly walk into the shadows and the writhing black mass. My magic swirls around me in response. Shadows and black light drift through the air until I move into the center of the abyss and close my eyes.

ARAINA HAS DONE QUITE well for herself here. After I walked into the avgrunn, darkness consumed my senses like a familiar friend. When I opened my eyes, I found myself in my sister's disgustingly lovely world. A lush forest of deep green and blue trees and pale pink vines stands behind me. A vibrant, teal river flows in front of me with flowers of such variety and color embracing its banks that I imagine my sister vomited a rainbow to make them. In the distance, great, white-peaked mountains guard this basin of life, appearing both majestic and ominous.

A cacophony echoes through the trees as birds and other creatures sing and chatter to each other, showing no regard for the blight that has just appeared in their land. I sigh because, as much as

I want to despise this world overflowing with life, I can't. It's a world I would have loved long ago, before everything fell apart.

Now that I'm here, it doesn't take much magic to shift myself to the capital where my sister's temple is located. I breathe in, breathe out, and vanish only to reappear on golden steps before an exquisitely designed temple to the goddess of light. Two human guards dressed in golden armor withdraw their swords at my sudden appearance.

"Don't move." A stern voice commands. "What is your business here?" The first guard to speak has tanned skin and blue eyes, reminding me of another pair I knew intimately. I force myself to swallow the knot suddenly forming in my throat before speaking. The other guard appears younger than this one, probably a recent recruit to the service. His hand holding the sword trembles slightly, and his gray eyes betray his fear. If it's possible, his pale skin lightens a shade more when he sees the wisps of shadows moving across my arms.

I pull back my cloak's hood and roll my sleeves up. It's ridiculously hot in this world. My reticence frustrates the first guard. He tightens his grip on his sword and steps in front of the doors in a vain attempt to block them.

"I asked you what your business is here. Magic wielders are not allowed to bypass the gates into the temple." I like this guard; he's brave. His eyes cast a glance toward my shadow magic before returning to my stare.

"I don't want to harm you, soldier. Especially your young companion. He looks quite terrified. Not a fan of shadows, I take it?" The guard audibly swallows.

"State your business." This one won't give up.

"If you must know, I am here to visit family. My sister, to be precise. I find it a bit rude that she hasn't told you about me. Although I've been finding that she hasn't told many about me. Not truthfully, at least, for the past one thousand years." I mumble this last part so that they cannot hear me.

"Who is your sister? I think you're confused."

I smile and let the magic flow to the surface again. The brave one's eyes widen, and the young one shifts back a step.

"I'm not confused. Most of history is a lie for you people here, too, I expect. My sister is Araina. Now, if you don't mind, I really don't want to dispose of you." I unclasp my cloak because the heat here is getting to be far too much, and drape it over my left arm. I'll give Araina this—she has chosen noble guards to stand at her doors.

"You—you need to wait until I confirm whether you are welcome here or not." He never lowers his sword, but the frightened one standing next to him trembles even more as I move up the golden staircase toward the doors.

Flowery vines coil around the white pillars on either side of the opening. I don't want to do this. Maybe a small part of the goodness in me still lives because I decide to give these two one more chance.

"Do you know who Araina's sister is, soldier?" I nearly whisper the words, but I know he hears me. His grip tightens, and I see the calculation in his eyes, determining when and where it will be best to strike me down.

I lift a hand and blow across my palm like I'm blowing a kiss toward the pillar to the right of the door. It's wrapped in vines with deep purple and blue flowers dancing in the breeze. Shadows stretch out from my hand toward the vines, and in a matter of seconds, what was once beautiful and alive has turned to ash. The puffs of their existence carried along the breeze.

The younger soldier stumbles backward, cursing. The brave one startles at the sight and meets my emerald gaze for only a moment.

"Please, stand aside, soldier."

I see the moment he chooses not to concede. I sigh. His bravery is honorable, and he deserves an honorable death. I can at least grant him passage to Arawnia, but that's the most I can give him.

The guard lunges forward to plunge the sword into my torso while I raise my hand and clench my fingers into a fist. Instantly, he drops to the ground—his heart silenced by my unspoken command. I could have turned him into ash. At least, I left his body for another to bury and say their goodbyes if he has a family. I kneel next to him to fulfill my duty, placing my palm gently on his chest. A gentle tug and a filling up of the space inside of me occurs. There is more to me now than there was before. I inhale, letting my mind envision the land of rest, the place beyond all our worlds, which I have watched over for eternity. Exhaling, I release his soul into it.

A clatter of steel on stone jolts me from my reverie. The young soldier has fallen to his knees before me, hands spread wide in supplication. Tears course down his cheeks.

"P... pl... please. Please don't kill me."

Perhaps I'm not as hardened as I thought I was. I stand and step over the fallen guard and walk to the large oak doors, dropping my cloak on the ground next to the other guard. He cowers as my shadow passes over him, and I don't give him another look. I push the doors open and step into the great hall of white stone that embodies my sister, Araina—the Goddess of Light.

THE EMPTY HALL IS OSTENTATIOUS to a fault. I want to gag at the extravagance of it all, but I don't have time to waste. I stride toward the dais at the end of the hall. The skylights in the ceiling let the sun dance across the golden details of the throne. More flowers, more vines woven around the base and up into the back of the monstrosity. The only thing missing is my sister.

A few priestesses scurry into another room, fearful of the stranger who has entered their midst. I pause at the foot of her throne before stepping up and sitting down unceremoniously. She knows I'm here, and she probably knows I killed someone to get in. Oh well, there's nothing to do about that now, is there?

"What do you think you are doing?" Her cold voice echoes through the hall, the soft shuffling of her feet drawing my eyes toward her sudden appearance from a door hidden by tapestries. Seeing her lovely face, a tendril of jealousy unwinds in my chest. Araina's mahogany skin is complemented by an ethereal blue gown that glows slightly with the residual effects of her power. She is beloved and adored by all who call on her name, while I am a lie whispered behind closed doors among those haunted by my constant appearances.

"Sister, didn't you miss me? I know it's been a while. Considering all you and your friends attempted to do to get rid of me. It's a bit ridiculous, though—-the idea that you could get rid of death." I lean back into her throne and cross one leg over the other.

Her eyes reveal nothing. No worry or fear. No concern either. Interesting.

"Arawna, you have taken everything too far."

I hold my hand up to silence her, allowing wisps of shadows to move across my pale skin. "Please. I prefer to go by Darci, if you don't mind."

I gesture for her to continue, and the lovely Goddess of Light rolls her eyes at me. I wonder what her adoring acolytes would think of that.

"Darci, then. You were never meant to have more than what you did. You were never meant to have a world all your own, yet you've always been a bit selfish."

"You see, I disagree. Why should death be kept from having anything good? You send all your subjects to me anyway. Why not let me have a world all to myself?"

Her jaw tightens in frustration. "Because you are supposed to guard Arawnia and protect those in the afterlife. You're not meant to exist in the present. In fact, the worlds would probably be better without you at all."

I narrow my eyes at her. "Do you think that death will simply stop because you wish it were not so? Did not our mother and father, Goddess and God of Light and Dark themselves, perish? Did they not entrust me with the power of death?"

"They chose to return to the stars. They wanted to be united. They never entrusted you with life in the worlds. We were supposed to work together, sister."

"Wrong. You were only supposed to bring light to the worlds. Not life. I was given death that I might rule life too. Shepherd it and guard it. Only I was meant to extinguish it. The humans destroy and kill only because you took my place from me after our war. But do you know what I really wanted? Do you know what I saw when I looked at the mortals? Love. Life. Companionship. I saw everything I had ever been denied because of you and your band of Gods."

There it is. A momentary flash of regret and fear in her eyes. I smirk, feeling a bit more victorious than I probably should.

"The worlds don't want death, Arawna. They will never want you."

"They ask for me, though, in the end. Without me, no one is there to guide them to peace. Do you know how many were left waiting—-lost, scared, forgotten while I was gone these thirty-five years?"

She says nothing, but I see her swallow and clench her hands into fists.

"I didn't think so. I have work to do, but I'm done letting you and yours rule with an iron fist. I'm done being kind and good. It's time for a new era."

"You would start a war that would kill millions of innocents? All because you're too proud to step away?"

I launch to my feet, feeling rage build in my veins. "I'm not the only one who is proud, Araina. If you won't concede, you'll be as responsible for their demise as me. Welcome to the death war, sister."

With that, I shove past her on my way to the doors. Not turning back, I shout over my shoulder. "Oh, and if you want to keep magic wielders from shifting into your temple, you should probably make it impossible to shift to the front steps. Fewer guards die that way!"

I open the doors with unnecessary flourish, allowing them to slam shut behind me. The poor, frightened guard flinches and backs into the wall next to the door but avoids looking me in the eye. I reach for my cloak on the floor and swing it up around my shoulders again. Clasping the front, I peer toward the guard. His companion's body is gone. At least someone came to do their job.

If I weren't so angry, I would probably say sorry, but if I speak now, I'll probably do something I will regret. Instead, I salute the soldier, unleash my magic, and shift back into the woods near my avgrunn.

I hesitate briefly, closing my eyes to let my other senses reach out and enjoy this enchanted space. Then, I step into the darkness and let my magic lead to colder places.

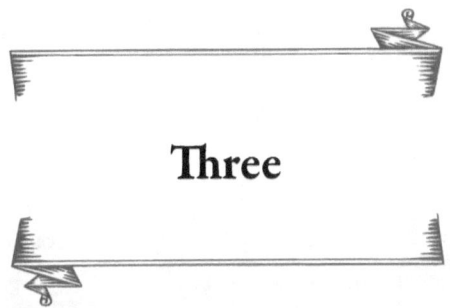

Three

"Dark and light work together to bring life, but Death supersedes all. This is why the gods and goddesses worked to destroy the God of Death and banish him forever."
—Quote from High Priestess Clodina
Discussing the creation of worlds

Adrian

Marcus won't look at me. Ever since we stepped back into Myzonia and Gennet's study, he keeps his icy blue eyes focused on the wall or the window or anywhere but me. As much as I wanted to ignore it, I can't deny that what I asked him to do is too much. We're brothers after all—not of blood, but of something deeper and richer. I can't ask him to kill me when he has lost so much, but he'll need to, because what if I can't end it first? What if I become the danger to the world that we believed Darci to be?

Gennet stares expectantly at us both, waiting for one of us to speak. My skin tingles with strange power. It's suppressed, but for how long? Meiora's presence smothered the magic coming out of me, keeping the power from overwhelming me with its weight on my body. But the creature disappeared shortly after, and I haven't noticed it here yet.

"Well, is one of you going to explain what happened?" Gennet's piercing gaze makes my skin crawl.

I glance at Marcus, but he's frozen. He holds himself solid and immovable as a statue. He looked utterly betrayed when we discovered what was in the room. I think he may still be in some form of denial about Darci.

"We didn't find her. But... we did find her house." I hesitate.

"And? What was in it?"

I look at Marcus again, but he stands rigid, anger seeping from him and tainting the air like smoke from a fire. Gennet's eyes dart to Marcus before returning to me.

"There is a room in her house. It—-it was a shrine to the God of Death. And..." My voice trails off. Gennet's eyes reveal nothing. Her face is calm and receptive. She isn't surprised. This isn't news to her.

"What, child? What did you see?"

Marcus swallows audibly, but he remains silent otherwise.

"Three skeletons perfectly preserved by magic. Dark magic. And I think they are her family. I think she killed them, and she must belong to the God of Death, himself." I stop myself from revealing what happened to me in the room, how the magic Darci possessed wanted to erupt from my veins, too.

"She doesn't belong to the God of Death. He forced her. Destroyed her family." Marcus breathes like he just ran through the mountain trails. Gennet offers him a sad smile.

"Oh, faolàn, we have discovered something since you both left. You were not gone long, but..." Her voice trails off. She steps into the hall briefly before returning with little Risa.

The child looks scared, wringing her tiny hands together and shuffling her feet closer to Gennet. Then, I understand—seer magic.

I kneel in front of Risa, careful not to touch her because I don't know what this power inside me might do.

Trying to keep my voice gentle, I ask, "Risa, did you learn something you want to share?"

She nods and looks up briefly at Gennet and then at Marcus. The sight of him standing there, looking ready to strike down an enemy, frightens her.

"It's okay. Marcus is a little upset right now. But he's not mad at you. You can tell us. You won't get in trouble." I reassure her.

Her big, round, brown eyes lock onto mine, and a sheen of unfallen tears gathers in them. I reach to touch the hem of her tunic, still afraid to touch her hands. Nodding, I try to look encouraging and confident.

"I... I had a dream." She hesitates and looks down at her hands before continuing. "I saw Miss Darci, but she wasn't herself. She looked different. There were shadows, and it was scary." She stops, closing her little eyes tightly while a few tears escape down her cheeks. Gennet gently rubs circles on her back.

"Did Darci look scary? Or just the shadows?" I don't want her to clam up, but she also might not understand enough of her magic to interpret this well for us.

"She wore armor with a picture of two black dragons and a black sword between them. And everywhere around her was red and watery. Her eyes were glowing. Just..."

She pauses before locking eyes with me in a way that sends shivers down my spine.

"Yes, Risa?"

"Her eyes were glowing just like yours."

I shift back, pushing to my feet quickly. Something stirs in my chest, and Marcus grabs my arm to steady me.

"Thank you, Risa. You can go out now." Gennet pats her gently on the head before facing me again.

"Adrian, tell me the rest of what happened in the room."

Marcus steps back, eyeing me. I nod my assurances.

"Gennet, I was overcome with power wanting to explode from my veins. It felt like Darci. I mean...I could feel her. My skin..."

I pause, trying to gather my jumbled thoughts into something cohesive. "Black light and shadows were coming out of me. I knew if

I let go, the magic would destroy anything nearby." I shut my mouth, clenching my jaw at the memory of the pain.

"It was the same magic Darci had. The same power. I saw her battle it for weeks. She was struggling, but it looked the same on Adrian. I couldn't." Marcus turns his back on us before continuing. "I couldn't do anything to help him, Gennet. It was like being in the presence of a god." He stops, and I see him contemplating what he said.

"The cryarsh stopped it. For now. It... it helped me."

"Interesting." Gennet steps over to her chair and settles into it. "I know Risa's vision is not clear, but I think there are truths about our histories we need to delve into. I think there are things we got wrong. But I do believe a part of Risa has known from the start there was something different about Darci." She hums as she turns her attention to the fire.

"Do you think our history is wrong?" Marcus questions, appalled.

I jump in before Gennet can answer. "Something has felt off about all of this. Regardless of what the history scrolls say, I need to find Darci. I need to find out why we are connected and how. I need to end this."

"What exactly is *this* that you must end? Yourself? Her? Why not the Death God himself?" Marcus snaps at me, his anger building with each question.

"We don't know what needs to be done! But we can't risk our people, Marcus. Our decisions have to be for them. Not just our feelings. Not just what we want!" I'm tired and frustrated. I want to lie down and sleep for days. My body feels ragged and worn.

"I know we must do what's best for Myzonia, but I won't kill you in the process. There has to be a way to make it right without killing more people." He crosses his arms and scowls.

"Peace, you two. We cannot fight amongst ourselves. Risa woke up terrified from her vision. I think there are things we need to discover about our world. And yes, I think it is time to find Darci. But first, we need to get everyone else moved into Zaiven and protect our people there. Or did you both forget that we've been under attack?"

Marcus and I both have the decency to look ashamed. She's right. Once we get Zaiven protected, I can go to the capital, where I'll have more access to the histories and Araina's temple.

How do you find someone who has vanished with a dark lord that has been seeking the destruction of your kingdom? There are multiple worlds out there. More than Oria and Myzonia.

I sigh, feeling defeated already. I walk out of the room and into the foyer to see what I can do to help. Marcus moves stiffly behind me but doesn't speak. There is a wall between us, a barrier I didn't intend to erect.

Where are you, Darci? What did you do to me?

"EVERYONE IS SETTLED into homes. The villagers were quite welcoming. I have soldiers in pairs creating a perimeter around the village, but we don't have enough to give sufficient rest intervals. Not if we want to keep the town safe. We need to call in more from the capital." Aella, a fierce warrior and commander of the soldiers here at Zaiven, stops her report long enough to give Marcus an irritated look.

"We can't afford to make the capital weak," he snaps back.

"We can't afford to condemn our weakest who cannot escape to the city for refuge," she retorts.

"Who said we are condemning them? We have them protected the best we are able. I can summon another company, but we are also risking weakening one of the districts of the capital, which is where your Sovereign will be going shortly."

Aella wants to protest again, and while I understand her concerns, I'm exhausted by the constant bickering between her and Marcus. No one can claim she doesn't care for these people, but Marcus is concerning himself with my safety over the people of our land, and I can't let him do that.

"Enough. Marcus, order another company to come here. I will not have these people harmed." I raise my hand to silence his protests. "Yes, I am going to the capital, but I am strong enough to protect myself well. I don't need to be extra guarded when there are children here. I'll be surrounded by wards when I'm in the temple of Araina. We've wasted enough time debating this."

Marcus refuses to respond at this point. Aella's pale cheeks flush in shame, but I don't rebuke her. Both simply want to do what is best for our world, and Marcus is being more unreasonable than usual thanks to the terrible mood plaguing him since we left Oria.

"Aella, you can go. I'll be leaving for the capital soon. Please, don't hesitate to send for me if you need to." I pause. "And if the woman returns? Darci? Call me right away. Do not engage with her."

Marcus's jaw tightens, but he doesn't argue. Aella nods her head and marches away without another word.

I turn my attention to the surly commander at my side. "Quit fighting them on everything. Quit taking your anger out on them. They're only doing what you trained them to do."

Marcus releases a tight breath. I see the way he tries to relax his shoulders. It's futile, but at least he's trying.

"I'm going back to the house to get changed and gather a few items. I want you to stay here for now. Make sure the other company settles in and makes camp properly. You can join me at the temple when you're done."

I can see how much he hates this plan. He doesn't want me to go alone, but he will obey my orders.

"Be careful, Adrian. Especially at the house. No one else is there now, and the forest might not be safe anymore."

I laugh cynically. "When have the trees ever been truly safe?"

Without another word, I draw from my magic, allowing myself to focus only on the house. Everything around me turns to shadow for a moment before I find myself standing in the foyer of the house, staring into brilliant green eyes.

I startle for a moment before recovering and clearing the gravel from my throat. A hum vibrates beneath my skin that wasn't as noticeable before. Familiar and warm.

"Hello, Shadow." I breathe out.

"Hello, Adrian. Did you miss me?"

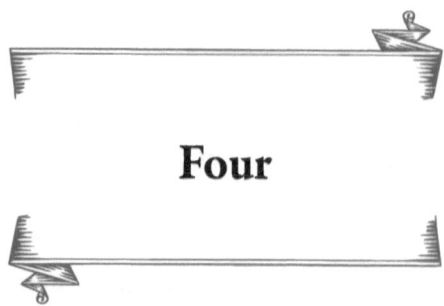

Four

"Those who leave this world are welcomed into the next, where peace and prosperity reign and death greets them no more."
—the scroll of Arawnia,
passage 47

Darci

Trying to soften my eyes, I force my features to relax and paint a gentle smile on my face. I'm not as unkind as I appear to be, and Adrian looks haggard from everything I've unintentionally put him through. The caution and distrust I see in his eyes reveal what I already knew to be possible. He's found the room in Oria, and now he believes he knows my deepest, darkest secrets. Meiora's wispy tendrils slip under the door behind him and gather at his feet. The appearance of my shadow creature brings a more genuine smile to my lips.

The calculations happening behind his eyes intrigue me. I wait for him to answer my question, to see how he intends to react to my presence. His magic pulses off him and into me with each heartbeat. I hear his heart, the steady thumping beginning to mimic mine.

"Of course I missed you, Darci. Where have you been? What happened with the Dark Lord?" He stands unmoving and makes no attempt to approach me. His wariness causes a strange pain in my chest.

I ignore his questions. "Did you come looking for me in Oria?" I keep my eyes locked on his, barely blinking.

He doesn't miss my avoidance of his questions but chooses to let it go regardless. "Yes, we did. You weren't there, Darci. Where did the Dark Lord take you?" He shifts his weight from one foot to the other. He looks exhausted, and I can't deny I feel the smallest twinge of guilt because of it.

"We?" My foolish heart quickens.

"Yes, we. Marcus and I came to your house in Oria."

"Is he okay?" I curse myself for letting this emotion slip into my heart, but I'm more frustrated that I revealed this feeling to Adrian. The bond between us tightens, feeling strained.

Surprise splashes across his features briefly.

"He's as okay as one can expect him to be. Given the circumstances."

"Adrian, what is it you want to ask me?" I twirl my pointer finger, and Meiora glides across the floor and twines around my arms and legs. If I'm not mistaken, it seems reluctant.

He takes a tiny step forward as if against his will, his eyes following Meiora. Is that fear I see there with the absence of the cryarsh? Odd. Silently, I reach my thoughts out to the cryarsh, feeling its response and gaining some clarity.

"Who are you really? I saw the room. I felt the magic. What did you do, Darci?" Anger flares in his tone.

"I'm simply a person who wanted to be loved and to love in return without conditions, Adrian. A person who wanted a family and to be someone else for a change."

His house, standing empty, is a sad picture. I want to see life in this place, to feel it and hear it, but I know Khitaen has been sending his monsters to attack innocents throughout this world. This home has lost the sense of safety it once offered. The God of War and Peace will pay for that someday. I move around the foyer to trace my fingers along the beautiful wood walls.

"Are you working with the God of Death? Tell me who you are!" His body trembles with repressed rage.

A bright green magic begins to glow on his hands, but it's different now. The magic has a shadow tainting its edges like snakes writhing together. It's then that I notice the rims of green on the outside of his beautiful, dark irises.

Me. Inside of him. I didn't expect our bond to be this strong. I didn't expect us to be tied together this intimately. My mistake for making unprecedented deals. This complicates things.

"No, I'm not working with the...death god."

"I feel like you're lying, but you've done it so much, I'm not sure how to tell the difference anymore."

"I never lied to you. There were circumstances I didn't remember. Things about myself I had forgotten. But I didn't lie, Adrian. I told you what I knew about myself."

"The room in your house disagrees."

I close my eyes briefly and sigh. "With great magic comes great sacrifice. I helped you. You don't realize it, but I did. Without me, you wouldn't be who you are."

"And who are you, Darci? You won't tell me. You won't answer. You keep avoiding the truth like it is death itself."

His hands clench tighter, and the desire to soothe his fears grows stronger. I can't, though. Not yet. Not entirely. He wouldn't believe me if I told him. The truth about me has been altered over millennia. Twisted and torn from its original nature to become a weapon used against me.

"I never avoid death. Do not pretend to think that I do." My words carry a bite now.

He doesn't say anything. He simply watches me and waits.

"Adrian, what if everything you believed turned out to be false? History is often distorted and changed. The truth of it rarely comes out unless one is bold enough to stand against everything ever written. You don't understand the Death God at all. Maybe you should investigate that more."

I'm trying to help him. If I plant a tiny seed of doubt, will he seek out answers instead of believing the lies he's been fed?

"If I knew you'd believe me, I would tell you exactly what you want to know this minute. But you know as well as I do that anything I say now, you will deny. It's easier to believe the history we are told is infallible. It's harder to confront it and our deities head-on."

There. Another tidbit of truth, if he's willing to see it.

He stiffens and opens his mouth to speak but shuts it again. He doesn't believe me. I know he is afraid for his kingdom, his world. My magic in him terrifies him just as it did me before I remembered. I don't want him to fear himself.

"You think you understand the worlds, but they are more vast and more complicated than even your high priestess can comprehend. I'm going to change them. I'm going to make things new and different. Maybe even better."

I consider turning my back on him and walking toward his study, but I decide he might lash out given the chance. Instead, I raise my hand and allow shadows to swirl around me.

He finally breaks his reticence. "What are you doing? Where are you going?" He unleashes his magic in a stream of green light expanding out from him in all directions. It cannot penetrate the darkness around me, though.

I leave him with one encouragement if he's willing to accept it. "Don't be afraid of your magic, and don't be afraid of mine. I think you can control it if you don't resist it. It belongs to you more than you realize, and it is not your enemy."

He gapes at me, but I don't watch him for long. Darkness eclipses the room, and the next moment, I find myself standing in the woods near a hole in the ground, spewing shadows. I waste no time walking into the avgrunn and willing my mind and body to Oria. I need to begin preparations for what is coming.

Inhaling the crisp air of this icy world, my eyes close, and I allow a few shadows to slip from my fingers, soaking into the earth. Meiora winds around my body before it moves ahead of me.

"Meiora." The cryarsh hesitates; its wispy form waiting for me to continue.

"I'm sorry for all of it. I know what the cost will be if you lose me, but I also know what it will cost to keep things the way they are. I don't think I can be as good as you want me to be."

The shadow creature reaches a tendril toward me in reassurance. A pain tears across my chest—a reminder of what it will mean if I fail and who I will lose if I cannot wrest control from my sister. Meiora's velvet touch warms my skin. It's clear what must be done.

"Go. He needs you more than I do."

The cryarsh doesn't hesitate before vanishing from Oria completely. Sighing with relief, I rest in the knowledge that ultimately, I might not be as horrible as they all think I am.

I plod up the hill, stepping out of the shadows of the trees. With a thought, I summon the darkness that is never very far away. In the distance, I hear the beating of great wings and the roar of a beast of my own creation.

As I approach the house, its shadow passes overhead, and I smile. A dragon twice as large as my house lands as daintily as a bird on the ground before me. Its black body ripples with wisps of shadows coming off it, standing in stark contrast to the snow beneath its feet. He beats his wings twice, stretching them and allowing smoky shadows to spread out from them along with a rush of wind.

"Hey, that's cold." I laugh, reaching my hand up to touch his great head. He shakes it briefly before lowering it to my meager height. "Ryuzio," I breathe out.

He feels much like Meiora, velvety and solid, made of shadows given form. I think he and the other dragons are my greatest contribution to creation. They need only my essence to be alive. They feast on the lifeforce my magic pushes out into the world. Their existence ensures my magic doesn't become too great. I need an outlet, and they grant that to me.

They are deadly. The black fire they can breathe is as destructive as I am, but they are completely at my beck and call. Perfect soldiers ready for war. Like Meiora, he doesn't speak, but the sensation of his thoughts and desires cascading through my mind gives me plenty of understanding.

"I need you to bring the others. I don't want a war, but if I cannot convince Adrian of the truth...if Khitaen moves sooner than I anticipate...we must be ready."

The dragon snorts a plume of shadows into the air before spreading his wings and launching into the sky. There is a lot of work to do, and I don't have enough time to do it all.

I continue toward the house, thinking about my next steps. I'll need to assemble an army. Again. One as vast and complex as it was in the Thousand Years War. It's been a long time since I created anything. I cast a glance back toward the woods and the shadows dancing along the snow. Well, it's been a long time since I created anything on purpose. Desperate times and all that.

I keep my back to the forest now, but I know they are gathering there. Shadows sliding through the treetops, watching and waiting—-summoned by my presence to this place yet again.

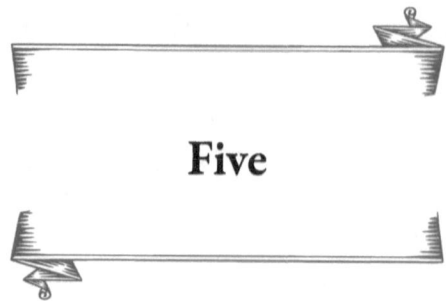

Five

"The Thousand Years War was fought between the gods and goddesses of old. Victory came when the God of Death fell to Araina and Khitaen. Forever banished."

—*A History of the Thousand Years War,*
page 973

Marcus

I hate that he left without me when everything feels more dangerous than ever. Too much hinges on the truth about Darci, and I'm afraid of what we will discover. The ache in my chest never goes away. I didn't imagine everything between us, did I? I catch myself rubbing the skin over my heart, trying to extinguish the constant pain there.

"Commander?"

I startle at the interjection, not realizing that one of the young arrivals had been standing next to me. Stealing one more glance at the tree line, I focus on the task at hand.

"Yes? What did you say?"

"I asked if you wanted us to set up camp along the road into the village or keep more of the soldiers between the homes and the forest." He shuffles his feet before catching himself. "Sir."

"Did the provisional group arrive with the company? We can't expect the villagers to provide food for all of us."

"Yes, sir, they arrived together. There is enough food and supplies for one week. We can always send the group back to begin preparing another shipment."

I nod, pleased with our progress.

"I want us to focus on the forest. Set up primarily between the village and the forest. Place at least sixty percent of our men and women there in tents. The rest should be spread out around the other borders. I want whatever comes for us to face our warriors before it even thinks of entering the town."

"Of course, Commander."

"You're dismissed. I'll be around shortly to see how things are going."

The young warrior offers a curt nod before returning to the awaiting company. I may not agree with Adrian and Aella, but I know their intentions are pure. There wasn't a best choice in this situation either. I only hope Adrian remains vigilant when he returns to the capital.

Walking toward G&G's pub, I can't seem to soften the scowl on my face. Most of the villagers bustle about trying to help where they can. Some appear to be packing, deciding they are better off traveling to the capital for a stay. The forest is close to this village, and it suddenly seems far more ominous than it used to be.

Is this how Darci felt about the woods outside her home? That there was always danger waiting for her? Or was she the only dangerous person there? I rub my fingers along my temples, trying desperately to relieve the tension headache building.

The former sounds of laughter and life are gone from the pub. The only customers are somber or whispering urgently with each other about the attack on Adrian's house. Pots clang in the back where the kitchen is. Ginger must be scrambling to prepare extra food. I should tell her not to worry about it.

"Don't you come in here with that scowl on your face, scaring off the few customers I have." Gwenyth glides up to me and stops with her body close enough to mine that I can feel the heat coming off her. I shift backward a step and don't miss her raised eyebrows in response.

"I'm not scaring anyone away. I wanted to inform Ginger that she doesn't need to worry about preparing extra food. We have a provisional group that came with the company." I rub my forehead again. This headache won't go away.

"Oh, well... good then. We didn't want to make a bunch of money feeding another couple hundred warriors in our midst, anyway." She smirks. I can't muster up the energy to respond to her sarcasm.

"The soldiers are welcome to come here, but we want the residents to have access as a priority. I've no doubt you'll have plenty of admirers who venture in here regardless."

"Oh, I'm sure we can manage." The mischief in her eyes would normally have me annoyed, but I'm slowly going numb.

"Is that Marcus?" Ginger's voice rings out from the kitchen. I don't know how she is so loud.

Gwenyth chuckles, "Yes, it is! He's as grumpy as ever."

Ginger pokes her head out through the door. "Oh, but I love when he's grumpy. Is he trying to make sure we behave with all the fresh blood recently settling in?" She disappears again, but I'm sure she plans on giving her opinion on the matter.

"Yes, he never lets us have any fun, and he is trying to scare the customers away." A few of the patrons chuckle before nervously returning to their meals when I shoot a glare their way.

"I'm not trying to ruin your fun. I just want to make sure everyone is safe and taken care of. I don't want the company stealing all your good food when others could use it more."

Ginger's offended face appears again, "I was going to experiment with a new recipe involving radishes and rabbits. Get it? Alliteration!"

Gwenyth shakes her head subtly, eyes wide. Damage control is my best option.

"I won't keep them from coming here to try out your recipes, Ginger. I just want most of their meals to be provided for by the capital, not you."

This doesn't fully satisfy her. She narrows her eyes at me before vanishing once again. Gwenyth lifts her hands in exasperation.

"I was trying really hard to prevent her from creating anything too outlandish, and you couldn't help me out? You couldn't have told her no food from us at all? No strange recipes that might make your warriors sick?"

When she puts it like that, maybe I should have discouraged Ginger more, but the deed is done. I shrug and move to a table in the corner. The same table I sat at before with Darci and Adrian.

"I thought you said you wanted to capitalize on all the...fresh blood that's come in."

Gwenyth scowls—a strange sight on her face, but she softens when she notices my distress despite my efforts to hide it. She gives me a sympathetic smile.

"I heard she disappeared unexpectedly."

"Hmmph."

"I liked her. Wish she had stuck around." She rambles.

A tight squeeze in my head forces my eyes closed. When I open them, I see the knowing look in Gwenyth's eyes.

She looks at me coyly, "Can I get you some cider?"

"No. No cider. I need to be alert, and knowing you, I wouldn't walk out of here with a clear mind. Just—-get me some water and something quick to eat if you don't mind."

"Alright, I can do that." She saunters away without another word.

I'm not actually hungry, but I need my strength if I'm going to face whatever is to come. I focus on not letting my thoughts drift to Darci. The mere act of remembering the room in her house filled with bones and shadows makes my stomach churn.

When Gwenyth returns, I offer a weak smile that feels more like a grimace before I pick at my food. I drink most of the water, but nothing that enters my stomach settles well. I use my time in the pub to listen to the conversations surrounding me. Everyone is talking about the recent attacks on the house.

I'm about to leave when I hear snippets of a conversation, intriguing me enough to make me stay. Two men sit at a table behind me. They came in after I did, and with my back to them, I don't think they realized who I was. They aren't familiar to me. Perhaps they came with the company from Rizyrk, though they aren't dressed like my soldiers. Most of their conversation had been about what to eat, with a few crude remarks about some of the women in the village. A shift in their demeanor has me paying closer attention.

"I heard he's making his move tonight."

"Shh... You don't know who could be listening." The older of the two whispers.

"There's no one important in here. Besides, what can any of them do to stop him now?"

"We shouldn't speak of the Dark Lord. You don't know what you're talking about."

"I heard he plans to destroy the house. A few of the soldiers were saying the Sovereign had returned to the house alone. Everyone else has left. If he doesn't leave soon, the Dark Lord is bound to capture him." The younger man draws a deep gulp from his cup. Most likely Gwenyth's famous cider.

"You don't know what you're speaking of. The Sovereign is powerful enough to escape harm."

"Powerful enough on his own? With the Dark Lord of Daemons coming for him? I say good riddance." The older man pulls a dagger quickly from his belt and presses the point against the young man's hand.

"You dare to speak ill of our Sovereign?"

His eyes widen. "I didn't mean any harm, but what good has he done for me? His father destroyed our lands to the north. We have nothing left."

I want to intercede. I want to attack, but I remain still, waiting, listening for whatever the fool is willing to spill. My heart pounds in my chest, and magic sparks to life on my fingertips. Adrian is alone at the house. If there's any truth to this man's statement, I need to investigate it.

The older man moves the dagger away before sheathing it at his hip. "Boy, you don't know all that has happened and all that will. Death is coming for the world."

A strange pulse of magic spreads throughout the room—there for a moment and then gone. I know it well enough, though. Seer magic. I've only met one other seer in all my years in this kingdom, and she is a child without enough understanding of her power to do much with it yet. But when her power moves, a strange wave of energy emanates from her.

The old man possesses the same energy.

I need to get to the house right now. I launch to my feet, my chair scraping loudly on the floor. Gwenyth looks up from where she stands next to another customer with a question in her eyes. I waste no time explaining myself before I push through the door and into the street.

Trying to maintain some semblance of control, I force myself to walk briskly but not run in the direction of the house. A few people stare, but most ignore me, too occupied with worries and fears all their own. The snow has turned to mud and has made my path a bit more treacherous. The woods loom off to my right, the setting sun casting more shadows along the ground.

As I leave the homes behind, I pray to Araina that Adrian has already left the house for the capital. The darkness creeping across the land echoes the seer's prediction. *Death is coming.*

I break into a jog as I see the house come into view. I'm ready to breathe a sigh of relief because it is still standing when movement from the shadows of the forest catches my eye. Dread builds in my chest as a dark, shadowy creature prowls out of the woods. I've never seen anything like it, but I know the Dark Lord's work.

Magic springs to life on my hands, and I'm ready to attack when, without warning, a multitude of the strange, shadowy monsters pours out of the forest and heads straight toward the house. *No.*

They are all teeth and claws with golden eyes. None look toward me, but their large bodies race for the only place I've ever felt safe, the only place I've felt at home, and straight for Adrian.

A scream of agony and rage leaves my lips as I send my magic out in a flash of lightning for the monsters. At the same time, their bodies dissolve into a black fire that strikes the house with such force, I'm certain people miles away can hear the explosion. I'm too late. The shockwave of power knocks down trees and slams into my body with such vehemence that I'm not sure if the cracking I hear is the branches of surrounding trees or my body breaking.

The force lifts me before slamming me down again. Black dots fill my vision, and the last thing I see is the absence of the house. Nothing but shadows and ashes drifting along the air. The monsters vanish with the impact, sacrificing themselves for the mission set before them. A numbness cascades over my limbs, and the taste of blood lingers on my lips.

One thought comes before the darkness consumes me.
Adrian.

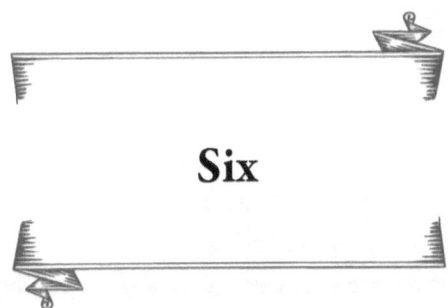

Six

"War is a friend of no one yet welcomed by all the offended."
—Orian proverb

Two Thousand Years Ago

"This has to end, Arawna!" Araina's voice cracks—-a combination of fury and sorrow. "You have to stop before there is nothing left."

Stop? *I* have to stop? What about them? When were they going to stop pushing me away and lying to their creations? Just because death brings sorrow doesn't mean it is evil. They created the monster. Not me.

Lightning flashes in the sky as rain pours down on the battlefield. Blood and death surround us. My creatures of night and shadow cut through the ranks of men deceived by their goddess to believe they are on the right side of history. My power sweeps through the armies more than once, leaving ashes behind. No bodies to bury this time. Screams of agony echo with the peals of thunder overhead.

Araina stands drenched, her tunic clinging to her body and mud smeared across her face. Yellow magic dances over her rich skin. Her eyes glow with power. Behind her, the other gods battle. Khitaen moves only because he thinks he will gain my powers and authority over the worlds. More lies, more bargains made amongst them to undermine my existence. No one likes to admit weakness, to lose the power they are already given. Luna frantically moves from body to body, attempting to save some lives before my dragons eradicate any trace of their existence.

"You led them here, Araina. You lied to them. You brought these men and women onto the battlefield to fight your war. I created my army, but only because I had no other choice." I scream over the sound of the storm raging around us.

"You cannot have the power you want. You cannot keep it. It is too great. Too uncontrollable."

I scoff, "Uncontrollable? Then why does Khitaen think he will get it? Why does he want it? Why do you think I made them!? Only I can control it, Araina! They gave this power to me, this work to me. They didn't leave it for you!"

I hold my hand up, signaling down the many bonds I've formed with my creations for them to stop. To wait. To no longer decimate. Luna looks toward us, standing on the cliff overlooking the battlefield below. Cryirz and Markyr hesitate, noticing that their fellow soldiers no longer fall to the ground. My shadows—-creatures of my heart—-pause. Only the wisps of their smoky existence shift on an unseen breeze—the life breath that brings them into existence.

Khitaen doesn't stop, though. His magic attempts to charge through my monsters. Some falter, but they won't die completely. Not as long as I live.

"There is already too much death, sister." Her voice is hard, unfeeling.

"Too much death? Or is it because the humans didn't fear death enough?" I whisper the words, but I know she hears them.

"You cannot be trusted with this power anymore. You created monsters that shouldn't exist. You allowed the people to seek out your favor. You let them start wars over things as foolish as trade and land."

I smile, unamused. "I let them start wars? Maybe I let them become the monsters they already were because I didn't create them. You did. What does that say about you, sister?"

She sucks in a breath, and I notice the muscles along her jaw tighten as she clenches her teeth.

I continue. "You lied from the beginning. You hated that I was given a place to lead them to peace. To grant them goodness when the worlds left here were not enough. You wouldn't let me create anything in this realm. You're jealous. Jealous that they weren't afraid until you made them that way.

"Maybe I did let them go to war. Destroy themselves and each other. Maybe I got tired of fighting for anything good in these worlds."

A trickle of blood slips down my cheek from a wound at my brow.

"No more, Arawna. Our parents would have hated you."

The blow stings. I wish it didn't. She knows her words struck true, though. The corner of her mouth tips up in triumph.

"Okay, Araina. But if you think that the worlds will be better with me gone, you're wrong. No matter how many lies you spin, how many times you twist the truth, or distort history. I'll be waiting. It will all crumble around you. Someday, there will be nothing left but what I have created for them."

She opens her mouth to speak, but I twist my wrist, and instantly my shadow creatures vanish. Drawn away to another place. She gazes around us, dumbfounded. Perhaps, she was right. Perhaps, I am a monster.

But I'll wait. I'll watch. These creatures she has, these men and women, they will not be everything she hopes them to be. And where will they rest, if I am not there? I see Khitaen jerk his gaze toward us, a snarl forming on his lips.

I smile before my shadows envelop me, taking me far from this battlefield. Leaving behind the many souls lost and wandering—-the ones seeking only rest. Forsaking the work I am given to do. Khitaen's roar of frustration brings a sliver of joy to my cold heart.

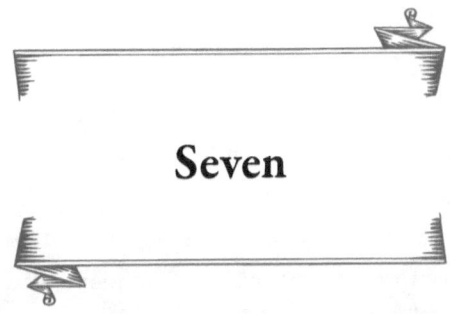

Seven

"Death isn't only the end. It is also the beginning."

—Unknown

Adrian

Present Day

Murmuring reaches my ears as I walk through the halls of the castle in Rizyrk. Everyone casts their eyes toward me in concern and confusion. Word of the attack on my home in Zaiven has reached the capital, and the recent movement of part of my army to the town for protection has caused expected anxiety among the servants here. I arrived only moments ago, and I waste no time in preparing to go to Araina's temple.

In my rooms, I change quickly into a new tunic and pants, washing my face with cold water before pressing my hands onto the sink's edge, letting the excess water drip from my skin into the basin. Darci is lying about her involvement with the Dark Lord. She must be. Seeing her again filled me with anxiety and tension. This balance of longing to draw her into me and wanting to destroy her is wearing me thin. Our connection is strong—stronger now than it was before, if I'm honest with myself.

The bond tightened in her presence. The magic belonging to her pulsed to life when I stood there in my house. How is it possible for us to be deeply connected and for me not to be aware of her until recently? The magic running through my veins is powerful, but hers feels stronger. It battles with me, leaving me exhausted and worn as I fight to keep it down.

What did she say about not being afraid of it? But how can I not be afraid when only a short while ago we were worried about her possessing this same power?

She was different—her face, her eyes, even the way she carried herself. She was more self-assured and confident, and no longer the frightened woman scarred by her past. The memory creates an unwelcome fear in my chest.

I close my eyes and rub my face with my hands, not caring that my skin is still damp. I'm about to step out of the washroom when an explosive pain takes me to my knees. I must cry out because two of my guards who had been posted outside my chambers burst through the door. One of them scours the room for the intruder who must be attacking me. The other rushes to my side, checking for injuries.

I clutch my chest, feeling a tearing sensation. It becomes hard to breathe.

"Your Majesty! What's wrong?"

I can't answer him. The pain consumes my every thought.

"Anthony! Anything?" The other guard steps back into the main room after searching my chambers.

"There's nothing. Should I get a healer?"

"Yes! I don't think he can breathe!"

I hear footsteps, but other sounds in the room become muffled. The pain spreads to my back and courses down my spine. I fight to stay conscious, but something is horribly wrong. Magic flares to life on my hands, and I imagine my eyes look strange because the guard at my side recoils slightly before stopping himself.

Before anyone else arrives, I exhale one name. "Marcus."

I'M NOT IN MY ROOM. I stand in a forest with stark shadows slashing across the ground all around me. It's strangely quiet. Almost eerie. I can't hear birds singing or leaves crunching from life. Where is the snow? Did I accidentally shift to another place, somewhere warmer? I don't feel warmth, though. The air is cool, crisp like harvest season.

Turning slowly, I absorb as much information as I can about my surroundings. None of it is familiar. In the distance, a new sound pulses, and the hair on the back of my neck stands on end. Wingbeats. They sound large, belonging to only one creature I know of—dragons.

I breathe slowly in through my nose before exhaling and forcing my heart to calm. A shadow dances in the corner of my eye—-familiar and strange. Have I seen this before?

It feels like an old friend.

I turn my head toward the shadow, but when my eyes drift over the trees in that direction, nothing is there. Just branches and shadows cast on the ground because of them.

"Hello?"

No one answers, but the sound of a branch cracking from behind startles me. I spin to face the direction it came from. I can't see anyone, but that doesn't mean someone isn't watching me from the darkness.

"Who's there?" I let magic seep into my fingertips, a soft green glow building on my skin.

The shadow appears again off to the right, barely visible in my peripheral vision. Whispers drift along the breeze toward me in a language I've only heard once. Words spoken by Darci when she dreamed at my house.

My house. The thought sparks concern in my chest. Something happened to the house. I need to find it. I need to go back. I try to shift myself there with my magic, but nothing happens. Am I dreaming? I squeeze my eyes shut, trying desperately to remember what happened before I woke in this strange wood.

Pain? Stabbing pain. Guards yelling. Marcus. No, not Marcus. He wasn't there. Where was Marcus?

"*Shhh... your heart beats too loudly.*" *A breath tickles my ear in a strangely familiar voice. Goosebumps rise all along my arms. Real fear nestles down into my core. I pivot, preparing to face the owner of the voice, but no one is there. Only trees and shadows and whispers.*

The beating wings grow louder. The shadow in the corner of my vision moves again, coming toward me, or not. I can't tell. I squeeze my eyes shut. When I open them, only darkness greets me.

"YOUR MAJESTY." SOMEONE presses their hands against my cheeks. A warmth, like the first spring day after a long winter, seeps into my skin. The residual pain fades, and the weight on my chest lightens. Air rushes into my lungs, and blessed relief brings a sigh to my lips.

"It's okay, Your Majesty. Everything is okay."

But it's not okay. Something is bothering me, something is wrong, and was that a dream I experienced? It felt familiar—-the voice like someone I had spoken to before, long ago.

I blink my eyes open slowly feeling the sting of the brightness of the room. A woman's face comes into view. She is clothed in white robes, standing before me with concern etched into her features. She must be one of the healers from the temple. Anthony and Jacob, the guards who entered my room earlier, stand at attention behind the healer.

"There you are. How do you feel now?" Her voice is soft, slightly accented. I don't recognize her, which is unusual. I know the primary healers who work within these walls. She must be new.

"I..." I clear my throat and try again. "I feel better than before."

I push myself to a sitting position and wince. Overall, I feel normal, though.

"Sovereign, what happened if you don't mind my asking?"

I rub my forehead, willing my mind to clear. "I'm not sure."

A sense of urgency floods my veins, and I seek out my guards.

"I need you to send word to Zaiven and check in with Marcus." As soon as I finish the words, footsteps pound down the hall, drawing closer.

Anthony and Jacob both draw their swords and step to the door, prepared to protect me. I rise to my feet, trying to dispel the fuzzy feeling pulsing through my head.

A voice I don't expect to hear reaches me through the doorway. "I need to see the Sovereign. Immediately."

Aella.

"Let her in."

Aella bursts through the door looking haggard and filthy. Is that soot on her tunic? Her face is dirty, and ashes speckle her disheveled blonde hair.

She sucks in a deep breath. She must have shifted here only moments ago.

"Your majesty, the Dark Lord attacked."

"What? Where did he strike?" My stomach churns. Why is Aella here telling me and not Marcus?

"Your house is gone. We think he believed you were still there. There were monsters I had never seen the likes of before. They moved through the forest behind the village and went straight toward your home." She swallows and casts her eyes away before turning them back to me. "There is nothing left. Sir."

My throat feels tight. I swallow, trying to loosen the muscles there, to find a way to speak. I know Aella sees my fear, and I don't miss the wetness building in her eyes.

"Marcus?" My friend. My brother. Why isn't he here telling me this news? Why is she doing his job?

She shakes her head. "Marcus is unaccounted for. The last anyone had seen him was when he left the pub in a hurry. A few noticed him heading in the direction of your house." Her words come out stiff and halting. "We haven't found him."

My mind races. They haven't found him. They haven't found a body. He's probably okay, going after the Dark Lord. Doing something stupid, no doubt. Why is she looking at me this way?

"Well, we have to keep looking for him, then. He must be somewhere. Perhaps he saw the Dark Lord and went after him." Rushed, stupid words. Hopeful words.

Aella looks at her feet.

"Why are you still here? Assemble some guards to go look." Anger creeps into my voice. Denial. I felt...

"Adrian."

My name on her lips creates a buzzing in my head. *No.*

"Everything—-trees, the house, a few unfortunate horses—-they were turned to ash. If Marcus..." She stops, licks her lips. A single tear slips down her cheek. "If Marcus was close enough, there is a possibility that he was in its path too."

She doesn't say it—the reality too horrible to breathe into existence. My soul cleaves. Anger roars inside of me. A horrible, raging beast, no longer left to slumber, awakens. My skin burns with black fire—-Darci's magic, and it feels powerful. It feels like too much, yet not enough for what I want to do.

Anthony and Jacob pull Aella back away from me. The healer I didn't recognize is noticeably absent now. I see their fear. I feel it caressing my skin. I smell it in their blood. What sort of monster am I becoming? I breathe out slowly, forcing my mind to let go of it. Rage will not bring him back.

As it ebbs away, I'm left with the wrenching pain of loss. A fist clenched tight around my throat and heart, squeezing till nothing but death would give me relief. I turn away from their wary eyes and scream, feeling the shadow magic erupt around me and mingling with the creation magic of my blood. Streaks of green and darkness twine together. I close my eyes to the sight.

It builds and strengthens seeking an outlet. I could let it go. Let it end and be done with it, with this world. Tears streak down my face. If I end it though, who else will I destroy in the process? I think I hear Aella screaming my name. Anthony or maybe Jacob calls for help, a healer, anyone.

Suddenly, a velvety warmth wraps around my body. The magic in my blood cools; and comfort, peace become all that I feel, all that I am. I open my eyes to find only darkness—-a swirling mass of shadows all around me. All sound is muffled. I hear only the beating of my broken heart.

It takes a moment for me to realize what has become of me. Then, as if I knew it would come for me—-knew that it was meant for me—-I realize what shelters me from the pain inside. Meiora. It came. She sent it. I know she did. I don't know how I understand this feeling, but I know that Darci sent Meiora to me. She somehow knew I would need it.

Sweet relief floods my veins, the magic a calming presence in my body. It doesn't change that Marcus is gone. Or does it? Is he really gone? Wouldn't I feel his absence? But that's the horrible part. I felt it. I felt the tearing, the agony in my soul when I collapsed to the ground. I knew something was wrong, that something happened. Did his soul reach out for mine one last time?

I don't fight the sorrow. I let it wash over me like a wave that cannot be stopped—-that has no end. Deep crying out to deep within me. Friend. Brother. I whisper a prayer to Araina, not knowing if it's the right thing to do. His name escapes my lips—-a plea to death to give him back.

I fall to my knees, protected by the shadows of the cryarsh and hidden from view. Sobs constrict my throat, and I want only to hear him one more time.

To Arawnia, my friend. To Arawnia.

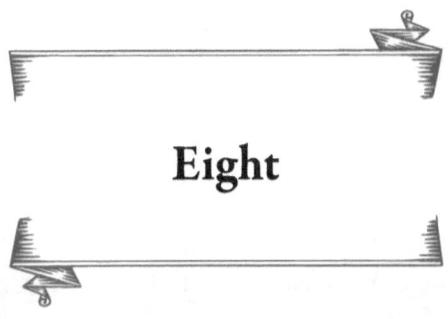

Eight

"It is believed that the gods were successful in banishing the God of Death because we hold no record of his reign or his powers beyond the disastrous effects of the Thousand Years War."

—**High Priestess Jaden
on Myzonian history**

Darci

The fire crackles in the hearth, warm and lively. It conjures up my days spent here in this house with Kiran, and I smile at the memory. I haven't welcomed any other cryarsh into my home, though I see them assembling in the forest. Meiora was different. I hope it comforts Adrian.

I sit for only a few more minutes absorbing the heat from the fire for as long as possible. The ache in my chest has dulled enough that I can breathe easier, but I still wish I'd told Adrian the truth in a clearer way. I need him to believe me, although I haven't shared everything he deserves to know.

I stand and walk to the table in my kitchen, picking up my dagger and sharpening the blade on a stone. I have grown used to holding a physical weapon since my power was nonexistent for so long. There's a beauty to it I enjoy, as strange as that may sound. More wingbeats echo overhead, and I stretch my neck side to side before slipping the dagger into its sheath at my hip.

I twist my wrist, and the fire dies. I have some unfinished business I need to attend to with the McClanes. I think it's time that I visited them. My lips twist into a smirk. I grab my cloak off the hook next to the front door and step out into the cold, wintry landscape.

Ryuzio stands restless in the snow. Shadows and smoke drift from him. The dragon delivered. With him are several more of my dragons exploring the snow drifts along the hillside.

"They need to remain in the forest for now."

Ryuzio looks at me before turning his focus to the other dragons. I sense their communications. Like phantoms that were never there, they turn into mist and shadow and vanish among the trees. Present, but hidden.

"Good. You're coming with me. We have neighbors to visit."

The great dragon breathes out a plume of shadows before bending one front leg, allowing me to climb up onto his back with more ease. This will be far more effective than only my arriving there. I need to know why Khitaen used them, and what he offered them in exchange for their betrayal.

Ryuzio launches himself into the air, and I allow him to see the path to their house through my connection to him. He turns effortlessly and carries me the short flight to their home. He lands as quietly as Meiora in front of their house. Their dog, Rust, lifts his head before launching to his feet, unleashing a somewhat determined bark. His wide eyes dart between me and the dragon, but despite the fear evident there, he doesn't hesitate to bark a few more times, alerting the McClanes to my presence.

"Rust, shh, it's me." The sound of my voice calms the old dog, and I pat his head as I climb the steps of his porch. He is close to the end of his time on this world, but I smile at all I can show him in Arawnia.

"Rust! What are you going on about?" Mrs. McClane freezes as she cracks open the door. Rust plops back onto the porch, keeping a wary eye on Ryuzio in the yard.

"Hello, Eleanor."

She swallows and glances behind me, noticing Ryuzio on the lawn. Her face pales, and tension spreads across her shoulders and neck. I wait for her to say anything, to answer the unspoken questions that lie between us. But she holds her tongue and swallows again.

The smell of fear permeates the air. Humans are rather easy to read.

"Eleanor, what is it?" Rick, her husband, steps up behind her.

His eyes widen when he sees me. I can't help the smile that tugs at my lips.

"Darci, what are you doing here?"

So, they're going to pretend they don't know who I am.

"Hi, Mr. McClane. I figured it was time for me to stop in for a visit." I cross my arms and rest a hip against the railing on the porch.

He pulls Eleanor away from the door and pushes her behind him. How sweet that he wants to protect her now.

"We don't want any trouble." He starts but stops when I narrow my eyes at him. We're not playing games anymore.

"What did you get?"

Confusion passes over their faces for a moment. When it's clear I'm not going to elaborate, he speaks.

"What do you mean? We didn't get anything from anybody. You know what it's like living in this world."

"See, I don't believe you. I gave up quite a bit to create this world and to make it better for those of you who were caught up in the transition, so to speak. Yet, the one who was never supposed to find me, did."

Eleanor gasps lightly and covers her mouth with her hands. He slams the front door, sliding a dead bolt into place. I sigh and shake my head before flicking my wrist and shifting into their living room.

A scream escapes Eleanor while Rick swears.

"Now, now... settle down, you two. I don't have time for all these games. Tell me. What did Khitaen offer you?"

"I don't have to tell you a single thing. You're supposed to be gone." The way his voice twists sparks my magic to life. I hear Eleanor's panicked whispers for him to stop—-for him to be quiet. Don't aggravate the monster.

He should listen to her.

"It's funny how everyone wants me to be gone. Even your gods and goddesses. But no one thinks about the consequences of my departure. Who would lead sweet Rust home to rest? Hmm?" My eyes glow a bright green while tears stream down Eleanor's face.

"Please, please don't. We just wanted to see our boy again."

A mother's pleas always tug at my heart. Their boy, who survived. He ended up in another world, isolated from his parents and all he grew up around. I understand their pain.

"What did Khitaen offer you?" I speak the words slowly, emphasizing the importance of the truth.

They look at each other—-the wife's eyes pleading with her husband to see reason.

"He offered to take us to Coty. He said he created passages between the worlds and that he would help us leave this one to find our son again." Rick's voice shakes slightly.

"You would betray me in exchange for a lie? Do you think Khitaen would take you from one world to the next because he is benevolent? He would have used you for his gain. I am the creator of the pathways of the avgrunn for the divine to easily travel among the worlds. Believe me when I say Khitaen would have led you to destruction if he ever came back for you at all."

They exchange a look before focusing back on me.

"Do you know what exists in all realms and in all times?"

I stroll around the room looking at the knick-knacks scattered about the place. I stop in front of the window, looking out at Ryuzio resting on the lawn with his head down. Rust has ventured over to investigate the strange creature on his lawn. Ryuzio blows a plume of shadows toward the old dog, who flinches and then snorts in annoyance. I want to smile, but I need to stay focused on the goal here.

Neither McClane answers me.

"Death."

Their pale faces lose the rest of their color when I turn to face them again. Shadows swirl in the air around me, dark light glowing on my skin. Terror. Everyone is always afraid of me.

"Please, have mercy." Eleanor clutches her husband's shirt at his back, trembling in the presence of my power.

"You spied on me when I was vulnerable. Khitaen found me and used me to get his way. But you both reported to him everything about me. You watched me. You threatened me." The anger boiling in my skin seeks an outlet. It wants to erupt. I force it back down, breathing deeply through my nose.

The swell of my power brings the McClanes to their knees, begging for something I don't want to give them. I flex my fingers, relishing the power on my skin.

"He promised us a world without you," Rick whispers the words. The sting I feel is unexpected. Interesting.

"Death is a beginning. Only through death can I be eliminated." I exhale slowly, letting my magic settle. I hear a snort in the yard outside. Ryuzio felt the disturbance. Without me, there is no him.

"Do you have anything else to offer me? Anything useful?"

They look at each other knowingly. I want to strike out, but I find that waiting tends to result in more answers.

"When I saw you at your house... the last time... I felt what he wanted." Rick avoids my eyes.

"And?" I hate waiting for answers.

"I think he plans to attack someone named Adrian? I saw an image of a house near a forest. I don't think he meant to show me. He was angry, and I saw more than I would usually see when he was in my head."

My suspicions were correct about him. His eyes were strange-looking, possessed at the time. Khitaen was using magic to possess a human's mind. Something the gods and goddesses never condoned.

"What-—is-—his-—plan?"

He shakes his head like he's trying to forget what he unintentionally saw.

"Shadows and monsters and ashes. Like small glimpses of his thoughts slipped into my head. Images that he didn't mean to let through." He swallows again but forces his eyes to lock with mine.

A cold dread grows in my stomach. The cabin. The monsters. He's going to destroy everything. My thoughts drift to Adrian and Marcus and finally Risa.

I stride for the door, pulling it open and trotting down the stairs into the snow. Ryuzio senses my urgency and bends for me, allowing me to climb easily onto his back. Rust scrambles as fast as his old body can to get out of the way.

Part of me wants to destroy their house. Destroy them and leave no trace behind. I can find a home for Rust. I hesitate only because of their son, and maybe a little because I don't have time to give rest to anyone. Shaking my head, I think to Ryuzio what I want him to do.

His wings stretch and beat at the air, lifting us off the ground and sending plumes of snow and shadows all around us. It takes no time for us to arrive at the forest and the avgrunn hidden there. I pat his neck before sliding down and landing near the darkness.

"Wait for me at the house in Myzonia. You know which one."

I step into the shadows of the avgrunn, allowing the darkness to sweep me away into another world. Ryuzio will arrive there soon, but it takes time for a shadowy dragon to travel the worlds. He has other work to do for me before he comes anyway.

I open my eyes to see a snowy wood not belonging to Oria. I run past branches, shoving them out of the way as the house comes into view.

I breathe a sigh of relief before I notice shadowy movement off to my left. Strange creatures are emerging from the trees. Abominations. Another figure draws my gaze.

Before I can react, an explosion of power shakes the forest around me, and it takes only moments for me to realize the other figure I noticed was Marcus. My mind screams as several cryarsh sweep into my field of vision. I command them without spoken word to find him, to find Marcus and pull him from this catastrophe.

I send a tendril of my magic toward him, but I don't see him. I see nothing but ashes as the beautiful house explodes into dust.

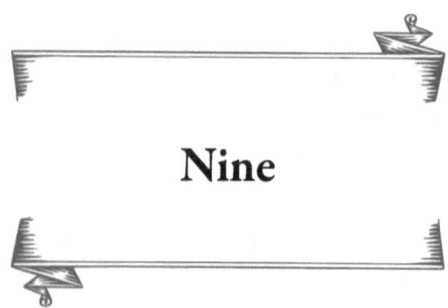

Nine

"Beware the shadows that creep at night,
Beware the darkness that doesn't flee the light."
—*The Book of Stories and Poems for Children*
Poem 125

Darci

S creams and breaking bones and shadows. My magic pours out of me with ferocity, sweeping across the landscape, passing by trees and searching for the monsters that destroyed Adrian's house. Searching, searching, searching for life and death-—souls I should lead home. In front of me and slightly off to the left stands Khitaen. His dead, white eyes lock onto mine. Monsters awaken for less than this.

Cold fury latches onto me, and I release my power toward Khitaen in a burst of black shadows. He disappears, but I sense his presence in the air. I shift, moving through space to land where he had been standing. The trees smolder around me. Some are completely gone, while others bear burn marks from the shadow monsters he made.

No sign of the God of War and Peace.

"Khitaen!" Magic seeps from my pores; shadows spread out from my body in all directions, looking for him. A tingle spreads on the back of my neck, and I whirl around, facing the dark woods. A flash of movement is the only warning I have.

A burning silver beam of magic smashes into my raised shield. The force of it makes me slide backward, trying to keep my balance on the slick, snowy ground. I take a chance and pull one hand away from the shield to send out a sliver of darkness toward Khitaen himself.

He sees it coming and sends his magic toward the shadows instead. Which works out perfectly for me. The reprieve is enough to allow me to shift next to him, pulling my dagger out of its sheath and slicing quickly across Khitaen's face. He roars in anger, grasping his cheek to staunch the silvery blood that flows from the wound.

A quick flick of his wrist, and I feel the smash of a branch colliding with my back from behind. I cry out but resist the urge to fall forward. He backhands me while I'm distracted, and blood floods my mouth. I cross my arms before me, and shadows envelop us. It's enough to halt his attacks and get me off the defensive. I slip the dagger into its holder so both of my hands are free. My back aches, and I feel my face swelling from the impact of his hand. But I refuse to back down.

Risa. Marcus. Adrian. The house—a mantra that resonates within my soul over and over again.

The beauty of darkness is that not all of us are blinded by it. Especially not me. I focus my eyes toward the space I sense Khitaen to be standing. *There you are, you monster.* I send a burst of my magic toward the god. He stumbles but doesn't go down. His eyes become slightly frantic, though, searching for me in the shadows.

He haunted enough of my memories. It's time for me to haunt his. He scans the shadows before locking into my general direction. The divine can always sense themselves in others.

"You dare think you can survive another war, Arawna?!" Hate and longing meld together in his stare.

I slip silently up to his shoulder. "Do you think you will?" His eyes widen as I reveal myself to him.

The mask has dropped. I hide nothing from him. He reaches up as if to strangle me, but the beating of wings vibrates the air. I grab Khitaen's wrist and shift us quickly onto Ryuzio's back. Pressing my hand to the back of his head, I send a sliver of magic into his mind, causing his body to go slack.

"To the avgrunn, Ryuzio."

The dragon breathes smoke and shadows into the air as he flies away from the aftermath of divine battles. I glance back over my shoulder, feeling a pang of panic and sorrow at the damage done. My shadows will search for those who were unfortunate enough to be in the middle of all of this. I have to believe they will find Marcus.

We arrive at the avgrunn, and I drop Khitaen to the ground amid the swirling darkness. I say nothing else before landing next to him and kneeling to press a hand to his chest. Darkness wraps us in its arms as I focus on where I want us to travel.

"I HATE THIS WORLD."

Heat and humidity bombard us the moment we arrive in Araina's home. Feels a bit weird appearing here again so soon after my confrontation with my sister. I yank my cloak loose and stride away from the prone Khitaen. It's dusk here. The sky is a dazzling combination of blue, purple, and pink.

Okay, I can admit there is something beautiful about this place, but it's always unbearably hot. Why does it have to be hot?

A rustle of movement through the trees draws my attention. Four soldiers step into the clearing with the avgrunn and stare open-mouthed at me. The leader of their group draws his sword. He hesitates a moment when he notices Khitaen and the silvery glow of his power pulsing around him.

I stretch my neck before turning my attention to the river flowing in front of me.

"State your business here." He finally got the courage to speak, and I have no more patience for this place.

"Tell your goddess I brought her a little surprise." I face the soldiers and pull my dagger out to clean dirt from under my nails. The soldier who spoke steps backward nervously when he notices my eyes.

"Who are you?"

Always with the questions. Always with the people, not knowing who I am.

Khitaen stirs on the ground.

I ignore his question. "Tell her I won't wait forever. She needs to come here and deal with the consequences."

Shadows gather at my feet, not dispersed by the beam of setting sunlight streaking through the trees. The men stumble as they cluster together for protection. I send the tendrils of shadows across the forest floor, allowing them to twine themselves around the branches and eventually the legs of the frightened soldiers.

Terror soaks the air. Pounding hearts and ragged breaths fill the silence. The first soldier tries again.

"Who are you?" He asks, voice shaking now.

His eyes dart to the ground where Khitaen pushes himself up to his hands and knees. He spits silvery blood on the dirt before rising to his feet.

My annoyance grows at this man's disobedience, at the audacity he displays.

Khitaen answers the question for me. "Death. She is death."

The three other soldiers scramble back the way they came. The other stands frozen, mouth opening and closing like he wants to say something but can't think of the words.

I smirk. "You better hurry. Before I decide that being gracious isn't worth the trouble."

He flees into the woods following the path his comrades took. I'm sure Araina will arrive shortly.

Khitaen eyes me warily.

"If you have something to say, just say it." I roll my eyes at him.

"Would it have been that bad for you to work with me?"

"Yes." There's no hesitation on my part.

"Why?" He does seem confused by my response. Is he blind to his faults?

"Because you seek only to destroy. You wouldn't have been merciful to anyone." You wouldn't have loved me.

"I am also the God of Peace, you know?"

I can't help the laugh that escapes. "You would only get peace through destruction."

"And you would only allow peace through death."

I say nothing else. My mind wanders to Adrian and Marcus. Adrian must be safe because I can feel his life tied to mine still. I wish I could be as certain about Marcus and Risa.

"What have you two done?"

Aww... she's here.

"You have a mess to clean up. I'm not going to take care of him for you."

Khitaen's eyes flash with fury at me.

"Arawna, what have you done? Why did you bring Khitaen here?"

She always pretends she has no idea what happens in other worlds. She can't fool me, though. She has many ways of keeping tabs on all of us.

"Khitaen broke our laws. The humans were not to be harmed by any interference of the gods. Yet, I watched him destroy a human's home. There's no telling who died in the process. My shadows have yet to report anything to me."

Araina's eyes dart to Khitaen. "Is this true?"

Khitaen shrugs, "I had good reason to believe Arawna was there. I was only fulfilling my duty, you and the others assigned to me. Or did you forget that you prefer having someone else do your dirty work for you?"

Her eyes narrow at him, but I don't hear her response.

A tearing in my chest makes me gasp. A cleaving of my soul into pieces. I grasp my cloak, trying to find something to do with my hands. Araina and Khitaen turn their attention to me, but I can't react. I can't respond. I stumble toward the avgrunn while the searing pain eats away at my oxygen.

One thought enters my mind. One name. Adrian. Something is wrong with Adrian. The pain he feels surrounds my entire being. My eyes blur with tears, and I end up on my hands and knees crawling toward the darkness I know so well.

The shadows creep up around me. The sentient nature of the darkness consumes me inch by inch. Adrian cannot die. I cannot let him go, but this feels like death.

I focus on where I want to go as the darkness shrouds me. One word comes through our connection as clear as if Adrian is kneeling beside me.

Marcus.

A scream tears through my throat into the nothing all around me.

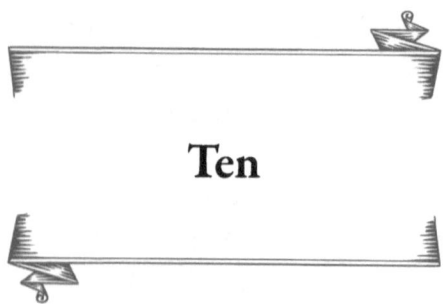

Ten

"Creation and destruction often go hand in hand. What was beautiful can die. What was dead can come back to life."

—Passage 392,
Scrolls of Markyr

35 Years Ago

In the entirety of my existence, I have never felt wanted. In part, I understand the sentiment. Who wants death? But what if death could be beautiful? What if death could lead to something better, something more lovely than what these worlds have to offer?

I created that. I made a beautiful place where rest could be found. A gift for mankind, a place to no longer endure the trials, the suffering, that the worlds bring. Instead of beauty, my sister saw only darkness. She saw only turmoil, and she wanted what I had made. Two thousand years of her twisting the histories of the worlds to create a picture where I no longer existed, where I was viewed as the enemy of all living things.

I'm tired.

I'm tired of fighting, of trying to prove myself. For once, I'd like to find a place to settle—a place that feels like home.

She can win this one, but I'm taking something for myself this time. Something she won't expect. Something she might even forget for an eternity.

The king of Myzonia is a monster. He doesn't deserve the world he's been given. He wants to be a god. What a fool! He doesn't know what he asks for, but I can use his folly to my advantage.

He's willing to let me have a part of this place—-foolish enough to surrender a northern realm to me. He doesn't realize that I'm taking the entirety of that realm and making something new. Five worlds don't seem to be enough for six gods. I think I'll make a new one.

I glance at the mark on my hand. The blood has cooled and coagulated into a thin reminder of the debt this man now owes me. I don't care, though. He sold his soul, whether he realizes it or not. It's a nasty business making deals with Death. A sardonic laugh escapes me.

He doesn't deserve the rest that I offer, and when the time comes, his kingdom will be torn from his hands, and he will be sent away into nothing at his death. I don't feel even a tiny bit of remorse at the fact. Our deal gave me the northern part of his kingdom. I plan on separating it from the rest and creating something unique.

A world of my own design. Perhaps I'll find something beautiful there, too, some place to settle into the earth. We parted ways only moments ago, but I won't forget my role in this deal. I gave him a sliver of magic that would kill him but sustain the one it was intended for. Part his blood, part another's, part mine. Little does he know the magic I gave him won't make a monster like he wants. Everyone thinks only darkness comes from me. They forget that I once held life as easily in my hands as I hold death now.

My skin vibrates in anticipation.

I step out of the avgrunn into a peaceful wood. It's cold, but not bitter. Winter hasn't fully made itself at home. In the distance, I hear the click-clack of horse hooves on stone and the whine of wagon wheels creaking. I must be near a village. I summon my magic, envisioning the world I want. When the image is clear in my mind,

I breathe out and cast shadows over the land. They sweep across the trees, the creatures, the villages, and soon, a blanket of darkness consumes all things.

When the shadows disappear, no one will remember anything other than what I've planted into their minds. A history and a world created to be void of all magic, even my own. I picture a kingdom where magic can't disrupt or destroy.

Magic draws the attention of the gods and goddesses. It seduces them the way a light deceives a moth. Without magic, the divine won't realize we even exist here. My shadows may even erase my existence from their memories.

I trudge through the forest, observing everything and soaking up all the sounds and wonders of my new home. Shadows reach out from me, slipping through the trees and hills and passing unnoticed through homes and towns. Their essence resonates in the darkest parts of my soul, a song of creation calling out to the one singing it. I run a hand across the shaggy bark of a hickory nut tree, smiling at the pulse of life that answers. The landscape shifts upward, and I notice trickling streams of water running down the hill, meandering around logs and rocks on the forest floor.

A clearing appears ahead of me. The trees thin, and my heart hammers steadily in my chest. At the top of the hill is the most beautiful flat expanse—a perfect place for a home. I need to see what's up there, what the view looks like from the hill. By the time I reach the top, I'm slightly out of breath—in part because of the climb, but also because the magic is slowly draining from my veins. It won't be long now.

A slight intake of breath is my only response to the view. Rolling fields are dotted with houses and barns; trees eclipse the land to the east of this plateau. It's stunning. This stretch of land overflows with life and goodness. I can barely make out a cluster of structures in the distance. It must be a town. A few wagons roll down the road at the bottom of the hill.

I've found the perfect place to finish this.

My dagger feels heavy in my hand, and I hesitate for a moment. Shadows flood the land in the far distance. They'll travel until they reach the northern territories' borders with Myzonia. I need only to wait for the coming rumble of confirmation.

My only regret is losing my shadows when the magic is spent. This world can't hold them. They'll be forced to remain in other worlds where the magic is alive and active. I won't be dead, but they will be severely weakened by my absence. Wings beating in the distance make my chest feel heavy, achy. I squeeze my eyes shut against the unwelcome sting there.

Let there be only light here. Not darkness. Not magic. *Oria*. I think the word and know this is the name of my new world. A deep rumble reaches my belly. The vibration of the earth beneath my feet awakening my senses one more time to the birth of this place.

I drag the blade across my palm where the deal was originally made. Blood spills onto the ground, and I clench my fingers into a tight fist, forcing out as much of it as I can. The eager earth soaks it up, and a wisp of shadows escapes from my skin. Tears streak down my face. This will be for the good of all. This will end all the fighting and nonsense we've endured. No matter how much it pains me, I know I'm choosing the right path.

The moment the magic is gone, my mind darkens. I collapse, feeling the earth brace against my fall.

20 years later

"MISS? MISS? COME ON, now. Wake up."

A strong hand gently shakes my shoulder. My head aches to the point that moving seems impossible. I might even be a bit nauseous.

That's a new feeling. I move my head slightly, but it's enough to make me grimace against the pain. I've never felt this weak, this broken, before. Is this what humans feel like all the time? It's awful.

Whoever was speaking noticed my face.

"Hey, there you are. It's okay. You're okay. I got you." He speaks to me like I'm an injured animal. I might be.

I slowly open my eyes. His light brown skin and blue eyes are the only details I notice. My vision is blurry. It takes a moment for me to remember what I set out to do. I wonder how long it took. I smell flowers on the air, notice the warmth of the sun on my skin. I blink my eyes a few more times and the picture of his face clears. He's quite handsome and looks to be the age of a human male in his middle years.

I attempt to sit up and instantly feel the world spin. His hand grasps my sliced one, eliciting a wince from me.

"Whoa, slow down. You're injured."

I look down at the hand he released and see the sticky red of blood on it. Where is my dagger? I glance at my other hand and the ground around me, but it's gone.

"Here, are you looking for this?" He holds the dagger out to me. I swallow and then take it slowly from his hand.

"Did someone attack you? Have you been out here long?"

He's a talker. I swallow and try to answer, but my throat is parched, and my mouth feels swollen.

"Here." He holds out a canteen for me. Why is he being nice?

I take it and sip the cool water. It's a balm to my mouth. I clear my throat and shift to stand before I notice the tree off to my right. My stomach hollows out. If I remember correctly, that tree was very small when I first arrived at the top of this hill. It's massive now, full-grown and spreading its lovely branches over the grassy space. It's been years. It took years for everything to work. *I can't believe it actually worked.*

"My name is Kiran. What's yours?"

I can't tell him my real name. Well, I could. I guess if everything worked properly, he won't know what my name means. Maybe I should test the theory. I clear my throat.

"My name is Arawna Darci. But everyone calls me Darci." I have no idea where the name came from. It simply appeared in my mind.

No reaction. No widening of the eyes. No sudden intake of breath or stiffening of his spine. He...smiles.

"Nice to meet you, Darci. Let me help you up." He takes my hand and guides me the rest of the way up. My stomach churns a moment, and I must look as bad as I feel because he uses his other hand to steady my back.

"Your name is Kiran?"

He nods. "Yes, my mom wanted to name me after light because there's enough darkness in the world."

His name means light. Figures.

"How optimistic of her."

He laughs, and I can't help my smile that comes in response.

"You could say that. She loved to see the good in things. She's been gone for a couple of years, now."

Death. There's always death.

"I'm sorry." What pathetic, pointless words, but they're the only ones I can offer.

He shrugs and steps back from me. "You good?"

"Yes, I think I feel a bit better now. Thank you."

"That cut looks really deep. Let me get you fixed up."

I notice the bow and arrows strapped to his back, and the rabbits hanging from the belt around his tunic.

"I don't want to bother you. I can take care of it now." Before, it could have healed quickly on its own. I guess that's the price I pay for magic disappearing.

"It's no bother. Besides, you look like you could use a good meal. My home is not far from here. Where are you from?"

"I, uh, I can't remember." A lie, but how do you explain *me* to a mortal?

"Well, I'm sure your memories will come back. Do you think you can walk?"

I nod, but he looks doubtful. He takes my hand and moves slowly down the hill. His hand is warm and comforting. Calluses from years of working with them scrape against my skin. I never want to let him go.

"This might sound strange, but where exactly are we?"

His brows furrow in concern, but he answers anyway. "Oria. This is Oria."

I hide my smile. It worked. All of it worked.

Eleven

"When souls leave this world, they pass to a paradise called Arawnia. Unimaginable beauty and wonder await them in this world away from worlds."

—A Study of Life and Death
as revealed by the gods to the priestesses

Marcus

Present Day

A soft hum drifts around me. It feels strangely cold and warm in this place. Where am I? There's something I'm supposed to remember, but I can't. It's just out of reach, floating in the back of my mind. Are my eyes closed? Why didn't I know that my eyes were closed? This is strange. A buzz under my skin feels like millions of needles stabbing me. I reach for my magic, but I feel nothing. Panic grips my chest. Why haven't I opened my eyes?

I force my eyelids to pull apart, but the effort it requires is too great. I take an inventory of my injuries, looking inward to force myself into awareness. Pain radiates from my back to my chest. It's enough to steal my breath for a moment. My mouth opens in a groan, and the sound surprises me. I'm more aware of my surroundings now—-I notice the softness of a bed under me, the stirring of someone or something else in the room with me. My eyelids open to a sliver, but the movement changes nothing about my surroundings. Nothing but darkness greets me.

I need to move. There's a reason I ended up here, but I can't remember. I take a slow, deep breath. Whispers swell around me, but speaking isn't possible. My mouth opens, but my thoughts are jumbled like communication between my brain and my mouth has been severed. I was going after someone, trying to get to someone to rescue them, but who was it? I squeeze my eyes shut and beg my mind to remember.

A name comes out of the depths of my mind. *Adrian.* Adrian! The house! A flood of memories hits me with enough force to give me a headache. The churning in my stomach is not a good sign. Adrenaline pumps through my veins, and I'm able to move enough to realize how badly injured I am. The tearing sensation in my back and sides has me gasping. I must not be dead, or if I am dead, I did something horribly wrong to end up in such a state of suffering as this.

My eyes are open again, and I can distinguish something in the dark. Something is moving in the room with me—shadows. It's familiar, but the pain is enough to pull me under again. I slip into darkness, the weight of my memories dragging me back into the recesses of my mind.

THE FOREST AROUND ME creaks and moans with the wind. I don't recognize this place, at least not at first. If I've been here before, I've forgotten it. It's nighttime, and creatures of the night move about amongst the trees. Owls cooing their soft lullabies to one another. Crickets and other insects are singing to the stars. It's warm out. The full embodiment of a summer night fills my senses. Smells, sounds—-they're all familiar. I breathe in deeply, relishing the scent of moss and earth mingled with the pines and oaks standing watch nearby.

Home. This feels like home. A lightness I haven't felt in years swells in my chest, like every burden I've carried, every sorrow I've felt, is gone.

It's comforting—a relief after the constant strife of my life. I turn around and listen for anyone else sharing this space with me. I look for any clues to indicate a location. Surely, with how this place feels to me, I must be somewhere close to Zaiven.

Shadows shift as the wind slips through the treetops. The moon is full tonight, and the lovely blue tinge it paints the forest gives me enough light to see well. Or well enough. Stepping toward a slight opening in the trees, I hear a murmur on the breeze, a voice or two conversing. Their owners are too far away from me to easily distinguish who they are. I pause long enough to make out the direction they're coming from—off to my right, deeper into the shadows of the forest.

I change course and walk toward the voices. Nothing feels dangerous here. I know these woods even if I don't know when I was here before. Home. That word again. It resonates in my soul like warm water washing away the grime of life. The voices are still faint, but they carry a young, familiar tone. A child. Or two? The farther I walk, the clearer the voices become. They're feminine.

Something about that triggers a memory, or maybe it's a feeling? I should probably be worried about two little girls stuck in the forest by themselves, but I can't seem to feel anything negative here. No worry or pain, no anger or sadness. Just existing here in peace. In quiet. I consider calling out to the voices, but I don't want to scare them—though, how they could be scared in this place is beyond me.

"What are you doing?"

"I want to try. Let me have a turn."

"You're doing it wrong. You always do it wrong."

"I do not. I can do it as good as you and Marcus."

"No one can do it as good as Marcus."

My name. They're saying my name. Their voices. Two girls. Maybe ten and eleven. Why do I think that? My heart pounds with the thoughts. I don't understand. I thought they were dead. Is it possible I was wrong? Dasha? Anaya? That's impossible.

I feel frantic now. Plunging through the murky blue light, breaking branches, and stumbling over logs, I can't stop the desperate feeling growing in my chest. Where are they? I trip again before I remember my magic. Delving into my mind and the depths of myself, I search for the thread that's always waiting there, but I grasp nothing. I can't feel it.

My confusion distracts me enough that I fail to notice the forest ending and a cliff approaching. In the distance, the moonlight reflects off the water. I throw my weight back, skidding in the dirt and leaves, but the next thing I feel is open air and darkness reaching up to swallow me.

Even my screams fall on deaf ears.

I JOLT AWAKE. THE MOVEMENT is incredibly painful, darkening the edges of my vision as a result. A groan reaches my ears. Was that me? I force my eyes open and see the writhing shadows again, all around me. I know what those are now. I remember their name. Cryarsh. I try to swallow, but my throat is parched, and the small amount of saliva I do have hurts instead of helping my discomfort.

There seems to be an awful lot of shadows moving throughout the room. They block my vision enough that I can't distinguish any details about the place. Nothing is harming me, even as my instincts scream this isn't safe. Memories of the house exploding filter in, and I desperately hope it doesn't mean what I think it means—that Adrian is dead. How can I live if he's gone? It's my job to protect him. The flood of images conjures up the pain of my injuries again. They overwhelm me and make it even harder to breathe as I fight back panic.

Trying to focus my thoughts, my mind wanders to the next question. Why is a cryarsh here? I lick my dry lips and try to push myself up to a sitting position. I fail utterly. Something is very wrong with my back, very wrong with my body. It feels disconnected from me, broken and battered.

"Where am I?" The words sound like gravel in my throat.

The cryarsh shifts its position, taking note of my conscious state. The sight is a bit unnerving. The creature has no eyes, no face. Nothing helps me differentiate it from any other cryarsh. I don't think it's Meiora, but I can't forget the cryarsh that attacked me in the forest when I was with Darci. The memory sends chills down my spine.

That dream I had was so real, but it was simply a dream, nothing more. My sisters are dead. It couldn't have been them. Now, Adrian is probably dead, and Darci is a monster, and I'm stuck, injured in a bed being watched by shadows. Hopefully, I still have my magic. Searching for it, I breathe a sigh of relief when I feel the threads of it inside me. A faint blue light appears on my fingertips. It doesn't change the fact that I can't lift my arms very much.

The cryarsh reacts to my magic, though, and divides into multiple entities in the room. Four columns of wispy shadows stand in each of the four corners. Four cryarsh. There are four here. Dread builds in my chest. This is not good.

Their movement gives me a better view of the room I am in. It's mostly bare. The bed is soft with old blankets draped over me. A quilt of red and brown fabrics rests across my feet at the bottom of the bed. There's a small armoire in the corner and nothing else. The window reveals a snowy world outside.

The sight of snow awakens my ears to more sounds nearby. The lively crackle of a fire laughs through the door leading into what must be the rest of this house. The walls creak and moan as a frigid wind attempts to find any sliver of an opening to break into the house unwelcome. I don't hear any voices or footsteps, though. Just me and the cryarsh.

"Could any of you show me where I am? Or are you going to attack me the moment I try to move?"

Nothing. Typical.

I ignore the screaming pain and push myself to a sitting position. I will not black out again. I force myself to stay conscious, to fight the darkness reaching for me. I push the blankets back with my hands and find that I have no boots and no socks. Just trousers and a tunic. No weapons either.

"Where are my things?" I don't know why I expect these creatures to answer. They simply exist and watch me. Somehow. Without eyes. *This is not good.*

I scan the room for my daggers and sword. Maybe they're in the armoire. When I move my leg, the pain intensifies. I'm pouring sweat and gasping for breath. My stomach churns in protest, but I fight to keep my food down. This room feels familiar. There's a smell here that I have encountered. Flour, yeast, and roasted meat.

My hands shake as I reach for the bedpost. I can do this. I can do this.

I definitely can't do this.

A gasp from the doorway draws my eyes. Araina, I'm dizzy. I squint, trying to make out the shape of a person standing there. A woman, maybe? She speaks, and my stomach drops to the floor.

"You're alive. I can't believe you're alive." She breathes the words out and brings a hand to her mouth.

I'd recognize that voice anywhere.

"Darci?" The word comes out slurred.

There is nothing left in me to fight the darkness. A part of me knows that I should be afraid, that I should be fighting to escape her or attempting to detain her, but I'm physically incapable of doing either of those things.

The next thing I see is the floor rushing to greet my face and darkness.

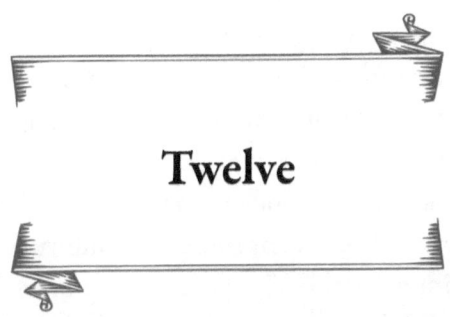

Twelve

"An enemy is a friend waiting for kindness."
—A Myzonian Proverb

Darci

I scream until my throat burns. The avgrunn knows what to do with me. It knows where I want to go. The only place I can go, a home of death and shadows, death always following me everywhere I go. It shouldn't surprise me, but for some reason, I wish it didn't sting this much. I remember a time when I didn't fully know the breadth and depth of loss, when I was immune to the effects of my magic. I saw pain. I saw suffering, but I didn't understand what it meant to lose someone you dearly loved. Not until I lost Kiran. Not until I lost my boys.

I crawl out of the inky black of the clearing—-deep, wet snow soaking into my tunic, my pants, my cloak. My fingers sting with the cold, but I ignore them as I gasp for breath. Adrian's pain is piercing. I imagine it to be the way it feels for one's heart to be cut from their chest. Tears freeze on my cheeks as wind whips through the trees, relentless and unmerciful.

Marcus. Not Marcus. I sent my shadows looking for him. Even for his body, but I didn't sense anything else. It can't be. Denial fights for its place in my head. The connection between Adrian and me is strong, and I know it is not deceiving me. His pain and anguish and the repeated cadence of Marcus's name pound against my defenses. Gone. Life snuffed out. I gag, but nothing comes of it.

77

I rise out of the snow and force myself to move one step at a time. Away from the avgrunn and away from this forest. Instead, I seek the area where the trees thin and the sky clears, up a hill, where a house sits empty and forlorn. Wings beat the air near me. Ryuzio is here. I close my eyes, pausing for a moment to breathe and listen. Calling to the shadows near and far for any source of comfort.

A faint murmur reaches me. My eyes snap open. The pounding of my heart fuels my body as I sprint toward the tree line, down a small ravine, before ascending the hill. The snow hinders my every step, making the muscles in my legs burn as they work overtime to press through the depth of it. But I won't stop. I can't stop. The murmur grows clearer.

It's not long before I burst out of the trees and into the open air. I move as quickly as I can, but my body is wearing down now. The house is there. Its presence is steady and resolute. Ryuzio lands to my right, quiet and light as a bird. Smoke drifts lazily out of the chimney.

I circle toward the front of the house, entering through the worn-out door. Noises and moans are coming from within. A black fire crackles in the hearth, and shadows linger in the corners of the rooms. Cryarsh. They did it. They found him.

When I reach the bedroom door, I freeze, gasping for breath and trying to calm my heart now that I know. The sight of him makes me gasp, which alerts him to my presence.

"You're alive. I can't believe you're alive."

He turns his head slowly toward me, swaying on the bed. His injuries are severe. I sense the brokenness of his body, the death overwhelming the life within him. My magic reaches out to feel him, searching for the signs of decay.

His vision must be impaired because he squints slightly before responding.

"Darci?" My name slides off his tongue with effort. It doesn't sound right, but I don't have time to say more. Marcus tilts suddenly, and only my cryarsh are quick enough to catch him before he hits the floor. A thump sounds on the other side of the bed. Well, it almost caught him. It slowed his descent at least.

The cryarsh sets him down gently on the bed, and I wave it away. The shadows vacate the room, leaving me with silence and Marcus. I step up to the bed and reach a shaking hand out to his head. His color is all wrong. Sickly. Ashen. I didn't see blood, but that doesn't mean there isn't any.

I gently press my left hand to his head and my right hand to his chest. Magic pours out of me into his body, seeking, assessing. The damage is almost catastrophic. His body is wrecked—tiny fractures waiting to snap along his spine, broken ribs, and a head injury to the base of his skull. If no one interferes, I will be guiding his soul into Arawnia soon.

But I can't do that. I can't let go of him, yet. The pain it would cause Adrian—it's not fair. My ability to heal, to create, is weaker than it used to be. Most likely, it occurred when my bargain with the king came into fruition. A sliver of magic siphoned away from me into another.

I have to try, though. Breathing deeply, I grab the tether of magic buried beneath my skin and pull hard to bring it to the surface. This magic doesn't come easily anymore. I haven't truly felt it in a long time. *Please be there. Please exist.*

A spark, a flicker of life as something grows at my fingertips. Soft, green light spreads from me into Marcus. It slides across his chest, into every cavity of his being. If Adrian were here, he might pray to Araina for help. If Adrian were here, he might be able to heal Marcus himself, but Marcus's injuries are similar in severity to Hoku's, and he couldn't save him.

"Please don't die, Marcus. I... I need you here. Even if you hate me now. I can't take you from Adrian. Please."

Nothing changes. His body remains still; his breathing shallow. At least, he still lives. When the light begins to fade, I pull my hands away and walk to the other side of the bed. I have no chair in this room, but I will not leave his side. Not until I know what needs to be done.

I climb into the bed carefully, making sure I don't jostle him or touch him in any way. I sit, cross-legged, and wait. Darkness descends outside as the sun sets and the wind howls louder. I grab a quilt from the bottom of the bed and drape it over his body.

Please don't die, Marcus. It becomes my mantra that I repeat for what feels like hours until I can't keep my eyes open any longer, and sleep comes for me.

I JERK AWAKE, NOT REMEMBERING where I am for a moment. A warm, heavy weight presses against my right arm. Marcus still lies prone on his back, unmoving. I'm not sure how long I was asleep, but his state doesn't seem to have improved. I sit up and climb to my knees on the bed next to him. Placing one hand on his chest and the other on his head, I press my magic throughout his body again. Fighting against the decay that is trying desperately to destroy.

No change is visible. I deflate a bit.

Over three days, I follow the same routine. Pressing magic into Marcus every chance I get. Hoping that each time will be enough to draw him back to me. The cryarsh linger near me, never straying beyond the boundaries of my house. Another winter storm howls outside, dumping snow over the land again.

Worry gnaws at my gut. I drink water only because my shadows won't leave me alone about it, and I nibble on a piece of deer jerky when I think to eat. It all tastes like ash in my mouth anyway.

I'm lying next to him, staring at the ceiling, when I feel him stir next to me. My heart jumps into my throat, but I can't move. I doubt the movement I felt from him is real. I'm certain I imagined it like I did the day before. I close my eyes, letting a single tear slide down my cheek.

He shifts again, enough that I realize I'm not imagining it. I sit up quickly, my head feeling a bit fuzzy from the sudden movement, and stare intensely at his face. He scrunches his brow as if the movement caused him pain. It may have. I reach trembling fingers to his cheek and let them barely graze the skin there. He's warm. Not too warm. Alive warm.

My laugh sounds a lot like a sob escaping my mouth. He's alive, and he's recovering. The sound makes him move his fingers and hands, like a person struggling to wake up on a dark winter morning.

"Marcus, I'm here." I reach for him again, grabbing his hand and squeezing gently.

He squirms, expression pained, and I feel his hand tug slightly away from me. He blinks open his eyes, the light making it hard for them to focus on my face. I release him and get off the bed, walking to the other side to stand next to him.

His vision clears, and when he looks at me, it's nothing like how he used to. Distrust and, worse yet, fear replace the former affection I was seeing there. He knows who I am, the truth of it. Or at least, he thinks he does.

"Marcus, let me explain."

I see him swallow and try to sit up. The movement is labored, but he manages.

"Why should I listen to you? Everything you told us was a lie." His voice sounds like gravel from the lack of use. I want to offer him water, but I'm not sure he would take it.

"It wasn't a lie. I didn't remember. I promise, I didn't."

He scowls. "You expect me to believe that?" He coughs, and I hide my wince.

I can't make him trust me, and I don't blame him. His doubts are completely understandable. To protect my heart, I harden it instead, waiting to see what he thinks he knows because I can guarantee he doesn't know the entire story. My stomach churns slightly, but the mask is on now. I can tell the exact moment that he sees it slide into place.

"What do you believe, Marcus?"

He stares at me, long and hard. "You're working with him, aren't you? You're working with the Dark Lord of Daemons. It's the only explanation."

"It's not the only explanation, and he has an actual name. He's not who you think he is."

He doesn't respond to that. The familiar hate I used to see in his eyes is back. He thinks that everything he ever believed about me is the truth.

Sighing, I murmur, "Marcus, you need to rest now. I was barely able to bring you back from the edge of death. I don't think I'll be able to stop it from coming for you a second time."

His eyes widen momentarily before he whispers. "Your magic is only destructive."

"It used to be different. A long time ago, I used my magic for creation and life, not only death. You can't imagine the things I have done with my magic." A coolness has entered my voice. I'm not sure I recognize myself fully.

It's the same old story. I'm the villain. I'm the one who destroys. I'm the one everyone has to fear. Me. It's always me. No one realizes the beauty I bring to the world. I'm always on the outside looking in.

The way he is looking at me makes my heart harden a sliver more. Monster. I know he sees the glow of magic in my eyes, the shadows dancing across my fingers. I refuse to hide who I am to make him feel safer.

"Get some rest, Marcus. You look terrible."

With that, I storm out of the room, refusing to look back. My rage is building to a crescendo I need to release. I grab my cloak off the hook by the front door and slide my feet into boots.

"Don't let him leave. He needs to rest fully to ensure I don't have to save him a second time." The shadow creatures will stand sentinel for me. I can trust them at least. My creation always stands beside me in battle, throughout eternity.

I leave the house, disappearing into the snow and wind and shadowy woods.

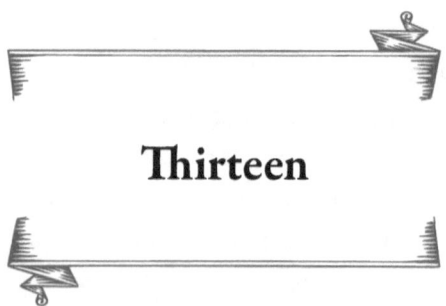

Thirteen

"Araina brings light to creation. The Death God extinguishes it."
—*Scrolls of Myzonia's Origins,*
Passage 48

Darci

Ryuzio greets me in the clearing. His shadowy breaths fill the air around us, and I can't stop the smile forming on my lips. The cold air stings my skin, but I love it. I let the bite of it calm my racing heart, cool the rage burning within my chest. Humans always struggle to see the truth right before their eyes. They prefer to live in denial. I have known this since the dawn of their existence.

Perhaps I should tell Marcus who I am. The truth might shock him. It's the same problem I had with Adrian, though. The history they've learned, the one that's been passed down from generation to generation for hundreds of years, is false. It contains a sliver of truth, and the rest is muddied by lies and half-truths. If I told him I was the Goddess of Death, he would never believe me. Not until he and Adrian confront the strangeness of their histories will they be able to comprehend what I tell them.

Goodness, they think their Dark Lord of Daemons is the God of Death when he's just Khitaen—-the God of War and Peace.

Ryuzio presses his head into my outstretched hand. Our shadows twine around each other; his shadows drawn to me, their creator. The tendrils of smoky shadows drift off every inch of his body, disappearing into the air. I love him. I love all my creations.

"Ryuzio, what are we going to do? Araina will never stop with her lies. Her rule over the worlds is over. The hold she's had on all of them cannot be allowed to persist. I know I promised we were done with war all those years ago. I promised I was finished with all of this." I pause, drawing in a shaky breath. "But I need you and the others to fight with me one more time. We need an army that will ensure our victory, once and for all."

He snorts, and shadows darken my vision momentarily. I listen to the response his mind sends to me and close my eyes. I smile again because he's willing to do what I need him to.

I place both hands on his head now. Black, shadowy magic forms along my palms. Dark light tinged with green spreads quickly across his entire body. He shudders from the impact of my magic swelling inside of him. I don't hold any of it back, instead pouring a surplus into him. He can take it.

My magic rushes into him like a wild river, moving at an alarming rate, to the extent that I almost black out from the speed at which it leaves me. When I'm finished, he glows black and silver, magic sparking off his wings.

"Go. You know what to do."

He growls softly and then takes off into the sky. Shadows and snow blow around me from the wind his wings create.

That's not the only thing he will be creating.

I plow my way through the snow back in the direction of my house. The magic in my veins has cooled to a controlled burn, and my anger simmers rather than boils. The exertion of walking through deep snow makes my lungs and legs burn, but I relish the sensations. I really did grow to love this world. I don't know how I forgot that.

My mind slips away to a time that feels like only yesterday. Kiran, leading me by the hand to his home. Growing fond of each other until that fondness somehow grew into love. Love. What a strange thing! I knew only love between creator and creation, but the gift of love between two humans felt different—-more rapid and heart-wrenching and somehow, subtle. I'm not human, but I experienced it in a way I wasn't anticipating.

Kiran loved me well, and I ruined all of it. I destroyed everything because I wasn't meant to love and be loved in that way. I wasn't meant to belong anywhere, though I am found everywhere. A twinge of grief tugs in my chest, but I suppress it and continue.

Perhaps the time away has calmed Marcus down as well, and he won't be so against me. I can't help the eye roll that escapes me at the thought of willful ignorance. I guess I can't blame him. It's extremely difficult to confront your history when you find out most of it was a lie. Or half-truths. I'm not sure those are any better.

I played a part in this, didn't I? When I created Oria, I erased myself from its history. I think they call that being a hypocrite. I shake my head to clear my thoughts and finally step out of the forest into the open air.

When I reach my house, I take a deep breath and remind myself that Marcus almost died, and I like Marcus. I don't want him to be dead. I don't want him to be injured. I don't want him to make me so angry that I could scream. Okay, this line of thought is not helping.

I stomp my boots on the porch to clean the snow still clinging to me and walk into the house. The fire crackles; a cryarsh greets me at the door. No news from its watch, which is good. I hang my cloak on the hook, removing my boots to keep the snow out of the rest of the house. Here we go, I need to talk to Marcus, or at the very least, I need to make sure he is recovering.

I pause at the doorway and try to peek in as inconspicuously as possible. He lies on his side facing away from the door. By the sound of his deep breaths, he must be asleep. I sigh, but leave him alone for now. After I eat something, I may have more energy to try to heal more of his broken body. It breaks my heart to see him frail when he never shows weakness. He has always been strong and reliable for as long as I have known him. He is a shadow of the warrior he was.

After wasting as much time as possible, I slip into the room and carefully crawl onto the bed at his back. Kneeling there, I place my hands on him gently and press my magic into his body once more. His exhaustion and injuries keep him asleep, even though it wasn't that long ago that I left to go into the woods. The green light pulses over him, painting him an odd shade that conflicts with his warm skin tone.

I feel tired again. This is strange, but it is understandable. I've been expending a lot of energy with my magic the past few days. Giving Ryuzio the amount that I did probably didn't help matters either. I need a good, long sleep.

This is the last thing I think before my vision darkens and my body feels heavy. I curl up behind Marcus, facing his back, unable to force myself to move away.

SOMETHING STIRS ALONG my side. My mind is only semi-conscious. I'm in that strange state between asleep and awake. A pleasant warmth at my back and a heaviness on my side make me want to sleep longer. I want to burrow into the bed and stay cozy here for days. Maybe if I lie here with my eyes closed, I'll slip back into slumber.

The stirring occurs again. It's annoying enough that I can't ignore it. I open my eyes but don't get up. I'm lying in bed facing the door to the room. I don't remember lying down. The last thing I remember is working on Marcus when I came back from the woods. I must have fallen into a deeper sleep than I realized from expending all that magic.

I shift slightly and feel something tighten around my waist. Alarm pulses through my chest. I glance down to find Marcus's arm draped comfortably across my side, his hand resting on my stomach. Oh no. The warmth at my back is him cuddled up to me in his sleep. Because he is definitely asleep if he is cuddled up to my back. *Who knew Marcus was a cuddler?*

A wicked grin pulls at my lips before I force it away. I need to get out of this bed before he wakes up. The moment I move even a little bit, I feel him tighten his arm more, holding me in place. I sigh before lifting his arm away from my body, the movement pulling him out of his slumber.

"What? What's going on?" He sounds groggy, voice rough and unused.

I press his arm away and roll out of the bed.

"I'm sorry. I fell asleep after tending to your injuries." I look to the window. "It's dark outside now. Are you feeling up to some food? It's been a while since you ate."

He rubs his face with one hand, then freezes like the movement startles him. He looks at his hand and wiggles his fingers. A ghost of a smile appears but vanishes quickly. He moves to a sitting position, the look of awe never leaving his face. It must all be happening easier now. The pain, the injuries—-all of it is improving.

"Yes, I..." He clears his throat. "I think I could eat."

I nod. "Okay. I'll be right back." He never fully looks at me. I guess we won't be discussing any truths for the time being.

I go to the kitchen and pull out some root vegetables and place them in a pot of water before setting it on the stone in the fireplace. Nothing fancy, just the bare minimum, but it will be sufficient. I pull some smoked deer meat out of storage and set it on a wooden board. It all feels a bit pitiful, but I don't want to waste magic on creating food now. Besides, old habits are difficult to break.

A thought occurs to me. I need to contact Adrian. He must still believe that Marcus is dead. There has been no evidence to convince him otherwise. Meiora is with him, but I really should tell him in person.

It's not too long before the vegetables are tender enough to slice. I place them on the board with the meat and carry it to a waiting Marcus.

He looks up before casting his eyes away, a warm flush coming to his skin. He looks alive. It makes me smile.

"You need to eat to build up your strength. Then, when you are better, we need to find Adrian. There is a lot you don't know."

He says nothing, only nods.

Yes, there is a lot they need to know before it all comes crashing down again.

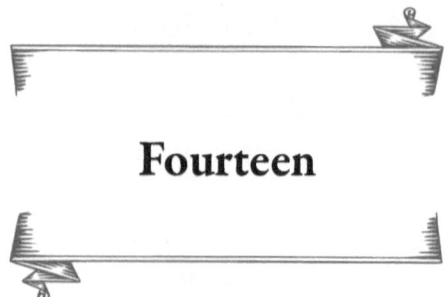

Fourteen

"The God of Death was a power-hungry deity. The gods and goddesses, led by Araina, locked him away to be forgotten by mankind. Now, death cannot come in unbidden into any of the worlds."

—Passage 1334,
The Annals of Leasia

Adrian

Everything feels dead inside me. The joy, the life that once beat within my heart, died. I lie here on the floor, embraced by shadows, seeing nothing and feeling numb. The ache that was present in my chest before has faded, and I am a shadow, a remnant of the man I once was. Meiora swirls and caresses my face, my hands, my body. It is warm and velvety and safe. No wonder Darci found such comfort in this creature.

My best friend is gone, no longer a part of this world. He left me alone. I have no idea how long I have been on this floor. I hear no shuffling of feet, no voices of the others. Did Aella leave? Did the display of my rage and sorrow force everyone to flee from my presence? It's understandable.

It's strange having Meiora here with me, isn't it? Why is the cryarsh not at Darci's side? It's more connected to her than to me, but perhaps the joint connection she and I share has made it possible for the cryarsh to feel me too. A strange thought slips into my head. She sent the cryarsh to me.

It's not exactly a voice I hear, but a presence exists in my mind that I didn't notice before. Something foreign and strange. The thought came from somewhere else, and for some reason, I know it's the truth. The certainty of it settles into my bones. A knowing. Could it be...?

My heart rate picks up as my eyes come into focus more. I reach out a hand to touch Meiora's shadows. Did I *understand* the cryarsh? As my fingers brush over the velvety black, another thought becomes clear in my head. *Yes.* I snatch my hand back reflexively. That's...that's impossible.

I whisper, "I'm okay, Meiora."

The cryarsh slithers away, revealing light that stings my already burning eyes. It positions itself in the corner of the room, almost obscured by the natural shadows of the space, but not quite. I blink a few times and rise to my feet. No one is in the room with me. At least they gave me privacy. I only hope they didn't abandon me entirely.

I stumble a little, bumping into the table next to the armchair in the space. The sound draws the attention of whoever is guarding my room. The door opens, and Anthony steps into the room.

"Your Majesty?" I don't miss the fear in his eyes. Anthony is a tall man with blond hair and pale skin. He's trusted enough to be one of my regular guards here in the capital, but right now, he looks uneasy in my presence. Nervous.

"Yes, Anthony. I'm fine. I'm... sorry for what happened earlier." I feel an apology is the least I should offer.

"It's okay, Your Majesty. Is there anything I can get for you? Do you want me to summon the healer again?"

The healer. There was something about her.

"Actually, yes. I don't think I recognized her when she was here. Is she a new healer in the temple?"

"Oh, she's not from the temple here, Your Majesty. She recently arrived from the Temple of Markyr, I believe."

That's odd. "Do you know what brought her to Rizyrk?"

Anthony scrunches his brow in thought for a moment. "I didn't find out. It does seem a little strange, though. Would you like me to look into it, sir?"

I'm glad I'm not the only one noticing the anomaly, but I need to find out the answers for myself. Her voice reminded me of someone, but I can't figure out who.

"No, I need to go to the temple anyway. I'll see what I can find out about her then."

Anthony nods and steps back into the hallway. I hear the murmur of voices and wonder if Jacob is still standing guard with him.

I decide to change my clothes yet again. The news about Marcus left me feeling stained, like his blood is on my hands. A tightness grabs my chest, but I refuse to let the pain slow me down. The sky is dark outside, but I plan to venture into the temple regardless.

A tray of food rests on the table next to my door. Someone must have brought it to me while I was lost in grief. I feel nothing right now. I need to eat, but my stomach doesn't even hint at its empty state. My mind is preoccupied with the work set before me.

When I'm ready, I slip out the door. I expect to see Marcus out of habit, but Anthony and Jacob are the ones to greet me. A slight tightness takes root in my chest.

"I'm going to the temple. There's no need to follow me. Make sure no one enters my chambers while I'm gone, and I mean no one. Not even Aella."

They share a concerned glance before Anthony responds. "Yes, sir."

"Have a good night. Don't expect me back until..." I pause because I genuinely don't know how long this will take me. "Well, I don't know when, but it may be a while. When the next guards come in, make them aware of all of this."

They nod but say nothing else.

With that, I venture down the halls of the castle and into the streets leading to the temple. The city is caught in the strange in between of slumber and awake. The daytime shops and markets are closing for the day, but the nighttime pubs and food stalls are still in the swing of things. People mingle together, chatting and laughing, living their lives oblivious to the storm raging inside of me.

The sweet and tangy fragrance of meat and vegetables roasting coats every breath I take. The smell alone causes a pang of hunger to pass through my stomach, followed closely by nausea. I don't want to eat. I don't want anything. The casual happiness in the streets is abrasive against the wounds of my shattered soul.

A few people notice me, but they offer only a wave and a smile. No one tries to stop me. Can they sense the sorrow radiating off my skin? Can they see the turmoil in my eyes? I check my hands quickly out of fear that I'll see black light laced with white dancing across it—magic like Darci's coming to life on me once again.

There's nothing there, and I breathe a sigh of relief.

I turn a corner, and the temple of Araina comes into view. It's ostentatious with white marble columns and silver and gold vines of such detail they look real. A library waits inside the walls of this temple for the priestesses and the other acolytes. And me. Being Sovereign has its advantages.

The guards at the large cherry wood doors recognize me and bow slightly before opening them. I simply nod before stepping into the sacred space. My years of education and training required me to read and study scroll after scroll, and even some of the leather-bound books, for hours on end. I'm more intimately acquainted with this library than I ever was with my own father. I hate the memory of him.

I navigate the labyrinthine halls until I come to an ornately decorated door tucked into the end of a darkened hallway. A single torch lights the space to the right of the door. I pause for only a moment before stepping into the ancient library.

The library has two large hearths, one on each end of the room; both are full of a raging fire that heats the space thoroughly. Tables are scattered around the space. The main aisle harbors row after row of shelves and racks filled to overflowing with scrolls and books. It smells of leather and ink, fire and paper. I'm instantly calmed by the scent alone.

A few priestesses look up from their work, whether they are studying a text or cleaning shelves, to see who stepped into the space. They are all dressed in light blue robes. I scan the room for the healer. Why she would be in here, the first place I check, is beyond me, but I can't help the reflex. I remember her light brown skin and a white robe. She isn't here, and I can't help the disappointment I feel.

One of the older priestesses walks over to me with stiff steps before bowing slightly at the waist. I wave off the gesture.

"Your Majesty, is there something I can help you find?"

I smile softly. "So, I'm 'Your Majesty' now? I'd think you know me well enough to refrain from formalities."

She chuckles. "All right, Adrian. I thought that I would maintain appearances, but if you prefer for me to tell them stories of the rotten little boy who almost burned a whole section of Myzonian history texts because he wanted to play swords with a torch, I can." Her eyes sparkle, and for a moment, my heart feels lighter.

"How are you, Saffi?"

"I am well, Adrian. How are you?" She gives me a knowing look, but I can't maintain eye contact. She will see everything in me the way that Gennet does.

"I need your help. I need to find any texts you have, anything, about the God of Death. Who he is. What he does. What he did. What happened to him. Everything. I want the most obscure work that you can find. The texts that people don't frequent often."

Concern etches her face. Before she can ask any questions, I continue.

"I'm also looking for someone. A healer came to the castle earlier today. A woman I didn't recognize," I hold a hand up to silence her. "Though I know I don't know everyone. There was something... different about her."

"What do you mean by different?"

"She wore white robes, and I feel like I recognized her voice, though I didn't recognize her face. When I asked one of my guards about her, he said she had recently come from the temple of Markyr."

Her eyes widen with clarity. She knows exactly who I am speaking of. I wait for her response.

"I believe I can help you with your latter request. As for the former, I will do my best. Is it okay for me to draw help from the other priestesses? Countless texts speak of the Death God. It will not be an easy task."

I think about this for a moment. She is going to need assistance, as much as I wish she didn't need to bring anyone else into this.

I nod slowly. "Yes. But bring in only those you trust with your life. I know you're going to say you trust them all, but I need it to be only those with the utmost discretion. This is important. I'll help too. Point me in the direction of the nearest shelf to start." I attempt a smile, but I'm not sure it does much to ease her uncertainty.

"Okay, I know who to involve in this. As for the healer, I will send one of the acolytes to find her. She was lodging with us the last time I checked."

"Perfect. I don't plan on leaving this library until I find some answers. She can be sent here."

"What answers are you looking for?" She tilts her head slightly, questioning, pushing for the truth.

"I can't tell you that yet. I'm not sure if I know what the questions are myself."

She nods knowingly. "The most trusted texts on the Death God can be found in the general history section. It's the third row on the right, top three shelves at the end. I believe you know the way?"

I do. Saffi calls an acolyte over from her cleaning to tell her to find the newcomer. Before she even gets the words out, the door to the library opens. There she is. The woman in white robes stands there looking at me like I called her to me. She's beautiful, but hauntingly so. Like a ghost of a forgotten land come back to torment me.

Saffi smiles and waves the woman over. As she draws near, I see that her eyes are a striking blue color. The combination of her eyes and her skin reminds me of Marcus. I suck in a painful breath and fight the grief strangling my throat again.

She bows when she reaches us, but never takes her eyes off mine.

Saffi holds out a hand to the woman. "Adrian, this is Sister Cleo from the temple of Markyr. I'm sure she already knows who you are."

I reach out for her hand. "Hello, Sister Cleo. It's nice to meet you. I'm hoping you can help me."

When our hands clasp, she smiles, and the sensation of sparks between our fingers sends chills down my spine. Something is not right about this. It's strange, but I can't figure out what's wrong.

Sister Cleo smiles at me.

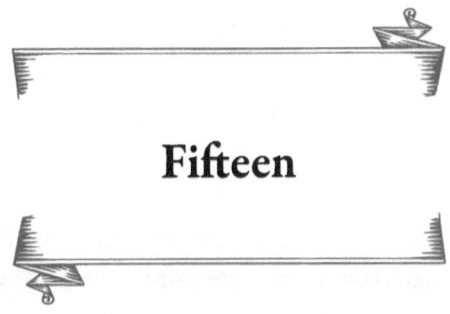

Fifteen

"The truth will always come to light whether you want it to or not."

—Orian Proverb

Adrian

Sister Cleo waits for me to speak. Her eyes sparkle with mischief, which makes me feel odd. It's out of place. Surely, she senses my distress and the loss I have endured. It feels painted on my skin at this point. Yet, she smiles with a twinkle in her eye, a tiny spark of mischief. Another reminder of Marcus to torment me.

"Sister Cleo, it's nice to meet you. Formally, that is. I hope your travels went smoothly?" I need to get her to stop smiling like she holds a secret.

"They were quite uneventful, thankfully. Although I wish I had arrived a few days sooner. I may have been able to get a bit more acquainted with the temple before jumping into work." There's that twinkle. Is she mocking me?

"I wanted to thank you for helping me earlier. I don't know why I felt so much pain. It was...unexpected." I do know why, but I can't say it.

Besides, she had disappeared quickly after Aella arrived with the news, and I didn't notice her leave. Why was she in such a hurry to escape?

Her eyes grow a bit more somber. "Yes, I'm glad I could help you. Though I'm not sure you needed it. I found nothing wrong with you when I checked with my magic."

"Yes, I—-I don't think there was anything physically wrong with me."

She looks sad now, but it's a passing emotion, flitting away as quickly as it appeared. "Is there something I can assist you with, Your Majesty?"

I tilt my head, observing her every movement. She says nothing about Aella or the news about Marcus. She offers no condolences.

"I was curious, actually. I wanted to know what brought you to Rizyrk. I heard you are from the temple of Markyr? That's a long way from here."

Her eyes never leave mine. "I was sent here to assist you. I'm sure you are looking into everything that has happened recently. It was believed you would need an extra set of eyes to see."

She speaks with an odd lilt. Familiar, but where have I heard this accent?

"Who sent you? Mother Jaden?" Mother Jaden is the high priestess of Markyr's temple. Surely, Sister Cleo could not leave without her blessing.

"No, someone else sent me, but they aren't important right now. What's important is helping you."

Her avoidance of answering the question leaves me wary. I don't fully trust her, but there's a reason she is here. I might as well allow her to assist.

"Okay. Saffi will tell you what I'm looking for." I turn to Saffi, who has watched the entire sequence with curiosity and a tinge of concern. I wonder if she finds this entire situation as odd as I do. However, I'm glad she was here because I trust Saffi to interrupt and correct the story if what Cleo told her was different than what she told me. Saffi held her tongue. It looks like I'm going to have to trust Cleo for the time being.

I nod to Saffi before turning and heading for the shelves she was directing me to earlier. I have work to do, and I leave Cleo and Saffi to do their part.

TIME MOVES SLUGGISHLY in the library. It's easy to forget about the outside world and everything happening there. It's a strange feeling, sensing something dangerous coming to us. A war? A confrontation? The Dark Lord of Daemons, who I suspect is the Death God, has been more aggressive in his attacks. I can't waste time searching forever for answers amongst the scrolls. A sense of urgency and a sense of endless time both vie for attention and control of my mind. I could get lost here, but I can't today.

I have searched text after text and scroll after scroll for anything about the Death God and how he works. I'd give anything for a decent lead. Everything repeats itself. The God of Death became power hungry, seeking worlds that were more than he was granted. He wanted to be worshipped and revered by all creation, every world, every human. Instead, he terrified them all.

His power was vast and destructive. Wherever he went, people died painful deaths, and plants and animals fled. Yes, even the trees quivered in fear in his presence. Araina, in her benevolence, realized the destruction he would bring and the ego he carried. She could not allow the worlds to see him and the monster he was; so, she hid his identity, masking the creature from our eyes. People became terrified of death and the unknown aspect of it.

Two thousand years ago, it all came to a climax. The Death God raised an army out of creatures and monsters and marched on the gods and goddesses of old. Araina, the Goddess of Light; Khitaen, the God of War and Peace; Luna, the Goddess of Wind and Sky;

Markyr, the God of Fire and Ice; and Cryirz, the God of Night, joined forces to eradicate the God of Death once and for all.

The next part makes me uncomfortable. My stomach churns slightly at the mention of the war between the gods. The God of Death supposedly destroyed entire segments of armies with a mere flick of his wrist. One moment, they were there; the next, they were gone.

I recognize that power in myself. During the War for the Throne several years ago, my magic allowed me to destroy segments of my father's army, bit by bit. Nowhere near as powerful as the Death God, but strangely similar to him.

I close my eyes, squeezing them tight against the fatigue of the hours-long searching I have done. Many of the other priestesses, the ones Saffi trusted, have gone to bed already. I sent the last straggler out an hour ago, but I can't seem to make myself leave.

Collapsing into the armchair near one of the fireplaces, I drop my head back to stare at the ceiling. Where are the answers that Darci said I would find? Why didn't she just tell me herself? Why am I all alone now? I need Marcus. He's always been my sounding board, and he would know what to do.

Darci said something about history being distorted. That everything we believed was a lie. She mentioned something about questioning the deities, but that's borderline heresy. Who would question the gods and goddesses? I can't figure out who the enemy is or what they want. Is the Death God the enemy or the Dark Lord of Daemons, if they aren't the same person? What did she mean?

I want to scream at the ceiling. Instead, I fold forward and rest my elbows on my knees, burying my face in my hands.

"I take it you haven't found what you are looking for?" The lilting voice is full of humor that I despise. Sister Cleo.

I sit up and find her standing in front of me, backlit by the fire.

"No. I haven't found anything. Not anything useful at least."

Her features are hidden in shadows. I can't get a read on her expression.

"Well, maybe now you will be interested in reading this passage."

She offers me a scroll of crinkly yellow paper, ancient and forgotten, if I could guess by the amount of dust lingering on it.

I take it and turn it over, reading the seal displaying the name and origin of the scroll.

The Scroll of Arawnia, Amenir.

I don't recognize the location, but the name is as familiar as homemade bread and hot soup on a cold day. Arawnia, paradise for those who enter the arms of death. I can't believe I didn't think to check into any scrolls that spoke of the afterlife. We pray for those who pass, and the name Arawnia is a benediction on our tongues. A comfort, a peaceful exchange of hope for the brokenness we encounter too frequently.

My eyes jerk up to meet Sister Cleo's gaze. She smiles knowingly, and then she walks away. I'm a little dumbfounded by the action, but I don't question it further. I need to see what this scroll says.

I carefully break the seal and unroll the parchment. It's long, and realizing I need more space, I move to one of the tables. I conjure light orbs with my magic spreading them out above the table subconsciously while I work to unroll the ancient text.

Skimming the words, I find passage after passage about the afterlife. How death greets those who enter it with welcome arms. How people were not afraid of it. The text at the beginning is dated almost twenty-five hundred years ago. This was before the Thousand Years War.

My heart races as I read. Arawnia is beautiful. It's peaceful. No more death exists there because the final death has already finished, and the soul rests in perfect harmony with the divine. The way the authors speak about death is beautiful, like a rite of passage. A gift given to mankind so they might not endure the troubles of the worlds forever.

It seems odd that as history passed by, fear became the associated emotion with death. Another discrepancy is that I don't see the Death God mentioned anywhere. He isn't spoken of as evil. He's not spoken of much at all. Line after line speaks of what the afterlife might be like. What might await those who enter it, but obviously, it's all conjecture. No one knows what waits for us. There is no mention of other gods or goddesses either. Another odd discovery, but I guess it's not entirely impossible considering this scroll is exclusively about Arawnia. One thing seems apparent—-the other gods and goddesses have nothing to do with this paradise. Neither in its creation nor in its upkeep. It is the sole property of the God of Death.

I'm about to consider this yet another pointless endeavor when I get to the bottom of the scroll. I don't notice it at first. The words blur slightly, and it takes my tired mind a moment or two after I pass over it to question what I saw. Did I read that right? Something doesn't make sense; something stood out as odd.

I pause and move up a few lines and read again.

There it is. The discrepancy. The one place in all the texts and scrolls I have scoured where something is different. A lead weight drops into my stomach—chills running down my spine.

"Arawna welcomes those peacefully into death, relieving the pain and suffering of the frail human body and granting them a place to rest their souls and see the beauty of the unseen world. She cares for them as her own. May those who perish find rest with the deity who authored their home. From Arawnia, they came; to Arawnia, they return."

She.

It's the only time I've ever seen a feminine word used in association with death. She. Arawna. At first, I thought it was a mistake—the *i* simply forgotten. But what if we were wrong? What

if Arawnia isn't just a place? What if it is named after a person? *She.*
It echoes in my head until a whisper replaces the word with a phrase.

Goddess of Death.

We were wrong about all of it.

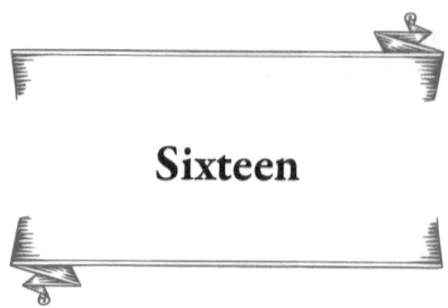

Sixteen

"Healing comes for those willing to face the darkness within themselves."

—High priestess Jaden
from the Temple of Markyr

Marcus

Two days pass while I do everything in my power to regain my strength. I've been able to stand, but a weakness plagues my legs that wasn't there before. My bones ache at the end of the day, and I tire far more quickly than is acceptable for a commander. I'm not certain, but I must have been closer to death than any human ought to be and still live. Somehow, Darci saved me.

It makes my head hurt to think about it. She hasn't said much else to me. We get along well in the silence. I think we always have. Every night, she presses more magic into my body, mending the broken pieces buried inside, but the rest of the time, she watches and waits. Bringing in food and eating together in silence has become as routine for her as it has for me. She hasn't slept in the bed since we woke up together. She stays in the other room at night or leaves the house altogether. I don't know if she realizes that I hear her when she leaves, but I do. I wonder where she escapes to.

Her cryarsh never leave the house. One is always present with me.

She walks into the room where I have collapsed after another strength training session. I'm doing everything in my power to gain strength, and every muscle screams at me as I position myself on the bed. Her bed. My skin heats with embarrassment.

"We leave tomorrow for Rizyrk." Her tone is flat, bored even.

"Tomorrow? I..." I don't know if I have the strength to travel between worlds and then walk to the capital, but I can't decline this chance to get to Adrian.

"Don't worry. You'll be fine. We'll travel my way to get there." She smirks. A hardness in her eyes that wasn't there when I first woke up from my injuries makes her appearance even more ominous.

"What exactly is your way?"

"It's faster, and it won't require that you kill yourself to get there."

Annoyance sparks in my chest. "I'm a lot stronger than I was. I could make it." I'm not strong enough, but I'm stubborn enough to argue.

She rolls her eyes. "Please. If I took you traipsing through the worlds, we'd never get there. You'd be too stubborn to rest, and I'd be too stubborn to wait for you. This way, I can ensure that Adrian will actually set eyes on his beloved friend again."

Caution enters my voice. "What do you want with Adrian? I doubt you care that much about whether he sees me alive or not. Or is this merely another plot to get to him for the Dark Lord?" I need to stay on her good side, but I can't help the anger slipping into my voice.

"Oh, give it up, will you? You don't know anything about the Dark Lord. You obviously don't know anything about me either. I thought—-" She stops and looks away for a moment before forcing herself to make eye contact again. "I thought that some of our time at the temple allowed you to soften toward me. I guess I was wrong." Does she sound hurt?

"Adrian saw you go willingly with him. I saw the room, Darci. It's obvious the Dark Lord is the God of Death we've learned to hate and fear."

A spark of anger flares in her emerald eyes. I hate that I like the challenge I see there.

"The Dark Lord is nothing but a fool who wants what he cannot have."

Every word out of her mouth is slow and venomous. I've never seen her this angry. It scares me a little when I see the shadows forming around her fingers and the glow of her eyes again.

"What does he want?"

Her confused expression makes me repeat myself.

"What does he want? You said the Dark Lord wants what he cannot have. What is it? Tell me the truth."

"Me."

One word. Tension tightens the muscles in my back, making them ache even more than before. Why would he want her? Why can't he have her?

"Is he the Death God?"

"No."

Now, I'm the one who is confused.

"No offense, but what is so special about you? I mean, why would he want you?" I wait in silence for her to answer me. She's thinking. After what feels like forever, she takes a deep breath before speaking.

"He wants my magic. He has coveted it for a long time, and he's coming for me. Or thinks he is. He attacked the house, believing I was still there with Adrian."

My eyes narrow. "You were in the house with Adrian? Before it was destroyed?"

She nods. "Yes, after he left you to come get his things and before he left for Rizyrk. He wasn't in the house, and neither was I by the time your so-called 'Dark Lord' arrived."

Some of the tension leaks out of me. She continues before I have a chance to ask another question.

"You won't have to worry about him for a little while. I think he will be facing some consequences for destroying a mortal's home without just cause." Everything she says sounds backwards.

"What? What are you talking about?"

She lowers her chin slightly but doesn't offer any further explanation. She simply waits for me to think about what she said. A mortal's home. That means he isn't mortal. He is a god? She said he wasn't the Death God, and I don't know why, but I believe her.

"He's a god of some sort. What does he want with you?" The implications are making my head hurt. What magic does she possess that a god would want?

"He's always been greedy. Wanting what he cannot have. He tried to bargain with me, but I refused to give him a foothold here or anywhere, frankly. It's not me who's the monster, Marcus. They're all monsters in some form or another."

I say nothing else but catch myself nodding in agreement. Of what, I'm not sure. I need to sleep.

"Get some rest, Marcus. I'll wake you when it's time." She turns to leave.

"Darci." She pauses but doesn't look back at me. I continue anyway. "I... I really did want to be on your side. I wanted to believe you were good. After all of it. I'm sorry. I can't."

Her shoulders tighten, but I can only see the side of her face. Her eyes are hidden from me. She leaves without saying a word. I lie back on the bed, trying to get comfortable, when I hear the front door open and close.

Sleep comes quickly for me after.

"TIME TO WAKE UP." I'M jostled by Darci's hands briefly. I stifle a moan as I stretch and shift my weight on the bed. I don't remember Darci returning or treating me with her magic last night. Perhaps she didn't, and that's why I feel like I fought a war single-handedly. The ache along my spine stirs worry, but I try to ignore it.

She's already left the room by the time I get out of bed. I push to my feet and give myself a moment to balance before following her. I find her at the door, pulling a cloak on and sliding her feet into boots. I fell asleep in the same clothes I wore yesterday.

After I recovered enough to get up, Darci gave me a fresh tunic, pants, and undershorts to wear. I didn't ask where they came from, though, I could guess. She never brought my tattered clothes back.

She hands me a cloak and, much to my embarrassment, steadies me while I put my boots on. I hate weakness in myself. I can accept it in others, but I have never been able to accept *my* shortcomings.

"You ready?" Her eyes aren't glowing this morning, but I see the cryarsh lingering near her. She is more powerful than we ever expected, and she carries herself in a more self-assured way.

"Yes." I keep my answer short and avert my eyes quickly.

"Come on then." She steps outside, and the biting wind rushes into the house. "Oh, and Marcus, don't panic."

I don't have the chance to ask what I should not be panicking about because she walks quickly into the snowy landscape and around the house toward the woods. I follow her as quickly as I'm able which means I'm lagging and nowhere near her when I turn the corner and see the monster before me.

A massive dragon twice the size of her house stands at attention between us and the woods. I freeze at the sight of it. How did we not hear it arrive? I've never seen one of these up close. The dragons disappeared from our land years ago. We'd hear rumors of them and occasionally the sound of wingbeats, but never encounter them up close. Our legends told us they were fierce, dreadful creatures, but I never heard of them attacking any villages or of people's livestock being slaughtered.

This abomination created by the God of Death stands still and somber as Darci approaches and reaches a hand up to—is she petting it? Araina, she must be connected to the Death God. It's impossible for her not to be.

The dragon's wings are folded to its sides, but there are strange streaks of shadows emanating from its body. Wispy fingers of black drift into the air around it. Its entire being is ethereal and otherworldly. It reminds me of the cryarsh. Are they connected? Are they the same?

"Well, are you going to stand there and stare, or will you be joining us?" Darci smirks at me. This side of her is bolder, unashamed, and confident. I don't know what to think about it.

"I'm coming."

I work my way down the slope in the snow. The beast raises its head and snorts. A plume of smoke escapes him. Or are those shadows? I pause again, trying not to look the monster in the eye.

"Ryuzio, be nice. He's coming with me whether you want him to or not." She pats the leg of the apparently *named* dragon. He snorts again, and more shadows fill the air.

I reach them and watch as the dragon lowers himself to the ground, stretching his leg in front of him. Darci climbs up until she is seated on his back. She looks down at me and raises an eyebrow.

I assess the situation and try to determine the best possible way to climb without making a complete fool of myself. I reach forward and touch the leg to find a velvety warmth there I didn't expect. It's sort of...comforting. I pull myself up slowly, slipping occasionally, trying to figure out what Darci grabbed hold of get up to his back.

After an embarrassingly long amount of time, I'm high enough for Darci to reach out and grab my hand, helping me the rest of the way. I settle myself behind her; our bodies pressed together by necessity. I don't know where to put my hands, but I'm forced to grab her waist when the dragon rises to his feet. She can't see my face, but every part of me feels flushed with embarrassment.

She chuckles but says nothing.

"Ryuzio, we're going to the avgrunn. I'll expand it for all of us to get through. You know where to go once we arrive in Myzonia."

The dragon spreads his wings, and the ground fades away from us frighteningly fast. I wrap my arms instinctively around her, hoping I don't plummet to the earth. Moments later, the avgrunn in her woods appears, but it's larger than any other avgrunn I've ever seen.

A black swirling void has spread out over a massive space on the forest floor, and the dragon doesn't slow his descent as we plunge into the inky black. Absolute darkness consumes us, and only the feel of her body pressed against mine reassures me that we haven't turned into nothing.

It feels like hours pass us by, but the next thing I realize is that the air is less cold and the sun is shining down on us again. The air smells vibrant and fresh. Home. Myzonia.

We're soaring over miles of forest toward only one possible destination. Rizyrk. We're going to Adrian.

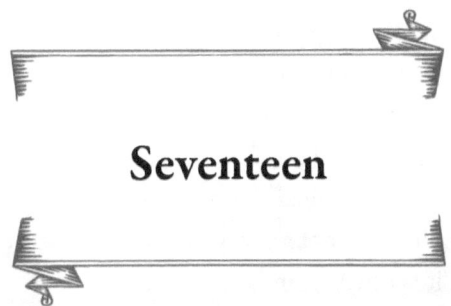

Seventeen

"History has taught us that those in power are not always seeking our best interest."
— *The Fall and Rise of Rizyrk*,
section 901

Adrian

My blood runs cold as I read and re-read the scroll. How, after all this time, did we miss this? Everything in our histories has pointed to a God of Death. Darci knew. She knew the truth, but she didn't tell me. Though I probably wouldn't have believed it if she had told me. Why would I have any reason to doubt what I had been taught? She understood that.

Were the historical records changed, and if so, who changed them? I need to find Sister Cleo. She found this before I did.

I push to my feet abruptly, causing the chair to wobble before I steady it. My skin tingles with anticipation. I scan the room to see if she's still there, but she's gone too. The mystery surrounding her grows more obscure. My instinct tells me there is a reason she is here. I simply don't know what it is yet.

I roll up the scroll and rush out of the library doors. The corridor is dark, lit by only a few torches. I look down both directions. No one lingers in the shadows. Turning to walk toward the end of the hall, leading to the bedchambers, something tugs me in the opposite direction. A strange call saying I should go the other way. I hesitate. I want to search for Cleo, but it is probably best if I don't invade the priestesses' private sleeping area. Besides, I feel the draw of someone or something in the opposite direction. I pivot and follow the invisible line drawing me along the corridor.

Heart pounding now, I call my magic up from its well to be readily available should I need to protect myself. Even my magic feels different than before. I glance at my fingers and see the familiar green light there, but it is once again laced with black.

My footsteps echo in the empty passage, and the pull gets stronger the closer I get to the inner chambers where the throne of Araina is. A heaviness fills the air, pressing down on me. A foreboding grows within me, urging me to stop but forcing me to follow.

When I reach the chamber, I notice a figure standing before Araina's throne dressed in white robes. Cleo. I slow down, certain she will hear my approaching footsteps and turn around, but she remains turned away from me. I stop, not knowing what to say.

The silence stretches taut between us, awkward and strange.

"You found it."

Three bone-chilling words.

"How did you know, Sister Cleo?"

She turns her head slightly, looking over her shoulder at me before turning her face away again.

"She's going to start a war, Adrian. One that the worlds may not survive. And she'll do it believing it is for the good of all the worlds."

I step around her slowly to face her. Blue eyes glow faintly with magic under the hood of her robe.

"It was never a God of Death, was it? It's always been a goddess." She stares expectantly at me, waiting for me to say more. "Who would have changed the histories? It's as if they missed this one document that held her name."

"Who would have the power to corrupt the past? Who would want to?" Her words pierce my soul.

"The gods and goddesses sought to destroy the Death God...I mean, goddess. Is that true?"

"Yes. Arawna created a place so perfect and beautiful that mankind was not afraid of dying. It was a gift. It doesn't suit other powerful beings to have humans unafraid of what awaits beyond after spending time in their worlds."

The implications roll through me like waves battering hard against the pillars of my upbringing.

"They did it. They changed the histories."

Again, she doesn't respond. Only waits.

"Darci is working with her, isn't she? She has to be. She knows, too." I'm rushing my thoughts, my words.

"Sleep on it, Adrian. Take time to get some rest. You need it. Things will be clearer in the morning."

"Who are you? Who sent you here?"

She smiles at me but doesn't answer. In a flash, she vanishes from the temple. I reach for her, but it's futile. She has shifted somewhere and left me with more questions than answers now.

I rub my head with my hand. She's right about one thing—-I need rest.

I leave the temple and head back to the castle. In the morning, I'll search for more answers.

I'M STANDING IN THE shadows of the trees—-alone. The soft creaking of the tallest branches whines in the gentle breeze. Someone is waiting here for me. I sense their presence, the weight of their stare on my back. For some reason, I can't make myself turn around; I can't face whatever is waiting for me in the darkness.

The moon overhead is full, and the air is cool but not cold. It reminds me of harvest time—the sweet season in between the heat of summer and the cold of winter. Leaves crunch softly behind me.

Whoever is there shifts their weight periodically, but it doesn't sound like they are approaching me. Regardless, my stomach tightens with nerves, and my heartbeat increases.

A hum beneath my skin calls to me, pleading for me to let it out—a monster seeking purchase on any tiny ledge I might offer it. Instinct shuns its call. There's another part of me that is curious, that wants to taste the power on my tongue. It's familiar, yet not. It is green eyes and pale skin. It is shadows and light and black fire.

Sweat gathers on my lower back as my skin tingles with anticipation. The watcher continues to wait.

Frustration grows within me. Why are they just standing there? Why am I? I'm going to turn around. I'm going to face the person watching me, and I will get some answers for everything. My feet disregard my mind's protestations with such vehemence I'm not sure they belong to me anymore.

The breeze shifts and increases in strength. A new sound follows the wind into the forest with me. Whispers. Murmuring voices caress my skin, sending goosebumps along my flesh. I close my eyes to focus all my attention on listening, trying desperately to decipher the words being sent over my body.

The sounds are unusual. A different language greeting me—an ancient one. I've heard this before. Whispered and then screamed during nightmares at my home. My home that is destroyed. How did I know the house was gone? Who told me?

Fuzzy images form in my mind, a mystery wanting reconciliation. Am I awake, or is this a dream? I've been here before. I know I have. A headache pulses behind my eyes now. The whispers are becoming more frenetic, bombarding me over and over again.

I press my hands into my temples as the pain grows. Everything builds to a crescendo. I might not be able to survive this.

As quickly as the whispers grew, silence overcame them. An eerie, heavy silence. I hear the breath of another being standing directly behind my back. So close, I imagine if I lean back, I'll encounter their body. The pain lessens, but not quickly enough.

Then a voice—the one I didn't recognize before—brushes against my ear.

"Shhh... your heart is beating too hard."

Instantly, the rhythm of my heart slows. Dramatic enough that I hold my breath momentarily, stunned by the sensation. I want to turn around and face them, this person who controls my heartbeat, but my feet are frozen.

"You're so close. It's almost time to let all of it go."

I find my voice. "What are you talking about? Let what go?"

A breathy chuckle sounds to my left. A shadow appears in the corner of my eye to the right, but I'm frozen in the middle.

I know this laugh. My heartbeat slows more, not because of me but because of someone controlling it. A sliver of panic grows in my mind at the realization.

Thump-thump. Thump-thump.

Slower and slower. Am I about to die? What is this person talking about?

"Soon, Adrian."

Thump-th...

My heart is silent.

I JERK AWAKE, MY CLOTHES sticking to my damp skin. Terror is quickly replaced by relief; however temporary it might be. The racing beats of my heart are a comfort. I'm alive. I force myself to take long, deep breaths. My room is stifling, and I throw the blankets off my body, walking to the window. Sunlight streams in through the seams of fabric, fighting its way into the shadowy space.

I dress quickly, not wanting to waste any more time before I search for more answers. I splash cool water on my face in the washroom before opening the door to my chambers. Anthony and Jacob have replaced the night guards once again. They are somber as they bow quickly at my appearance.

"Is there any news, Anthony? Anything I should know about?"

He doesn't hesitate. "No one has told us anything, Your Majesty. But we just arrived half an hour ago. The night was quiet, sir."

I nod, pleased to know nothing terrible has happened while I slept. Then, I feel it. The tug in my gut that remains with me despite everything. I feel *her*. My skin prickles with anticipation, and I notice a shadow in the corner of my eye.

"Meiora." The cryarsh comes to my side, winding around my legs before draping over my back like a cloak. Its presence is comforting to me, but I don't miss the fear in the eyes of my men. There is nothing normal about any of this, yet I feel that Meiora and I are one, a unit that cannot be separated. A bond has formed between us, a connection I can't explain.

I walk down the hall but stop, holding up my hand to the men. "Don't follow me." They exchange a glance but obediently stand down.

When I'm farther away from them, I whisper, "She's coming, isn't she?"

Like before, I don't hear the cryarsh's response with my ears. A feeling of *yes* fills my head and chest. I'm walking past the throne room when I hear footsteps pounding on stone. Looking to the right, I see Aella running to me.

"Your Majesty, you won't believe it. But someone is here. They're in the courtyard."

"Who is it?" I don't miss the terror in her eyes.

"Marcus." She breathes the word out like she doesn't quite believe it herself.

Every inch of my body goes taut. "What?" I'm unsure if I say the word aloud or not.

She doesn't wait for me before turning and leading the way in the other direction toward the courtyard. Is it possible? He's alive?

He's not alone, though. Meiora confirmed it moments ago. He's with Darci. Is she hurting him? Is he a hostage?

Nothing can prepare me for what I find as we step into the courtyard. Servants are scrambling down hallways, running in the opposite direction. Guards stand with swords drawn, faces fearful but determined to do their duty.

Aella stops, rigid and terrified, and pulls her sword out of its sheath. I stop at the entrance and watch stunned as Darci drops to the ground, reaching up toward a very weak and ashen looking Marcus. He fumbles with his hands seeking purchase on something but not finding much. He loses his balance and slips down onto the leg of a creature I never dreamed of seeing.

A dragon, black with wisps of shadows streaming from it in every direction, kneels slightly and doesn't react with aggression when Marcus lands roughly on its bent knee. Darci grabs his hand and guides him the rest of the way until he stands weak and weary, one arm draped over her shoulders and his body leaning heavily on her smaller frame. She doesn't waver, though. Her body is strong, and shadowy magic ripples around them both, no doubt helping her withstand his weight.

Meiora slips away and rushes to its master. Its absence feels heavy. The tether between us grows more insistent, and I can't stop my feet from approaching them. The dragon turns his great head toward me and stares intensely into my eyes. I should look away, but I can't. His magnetism is too intense. I feel trapped by whatever power runs through his veins.

It isn't until the dragon looks away again that I can snap out of the trance and continue walking toward Darci and Marcus.

The relief I feel at seeing Marcus is overwhelmed by my terror at seeing the dragon and Darci. Anger boils up in my chest.

"What did you do to him?" My voice cuts like a blade, the anger becoming more than I should allow it to be.

Did Marcus subtly shake his head at me?

I ignore him and lock eyes with Darci. The glow of her emerald eyes reveals a truth I didn't want to believe. A voice whispers in my mind—*goddess.*

Darci stops walking toward me and waits until I'm standing only a few feet away. Marcus still leans on her, sweat gathering at his brow. He looks war-ravaged.

"It's you," I speak the words softly, knowing only we three can hear them. "You're the Goddess of Death."

Marcus's eyes widen, and confusion paints his face. He doesn't know. How could he? He was like me, thinking we had a God of Death, not expecting *her.*

Darci says nothing.

"Tell me your name."

We stand there staring at one another. I need to help Marcus, but I can't turn away from this. I need to hear the truth first. Marcus turns his head toward Darci, watching her with fear and anticipation.

"My name is Arawna."

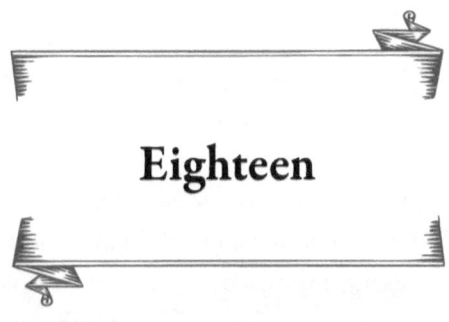

Eighteen

"The gods and goddesses never change. Their very nature inevitably dominates every aspect of their existence and choices."

—Arawna,
Goddess of Death

Darci

Adrian isn't surprised at my admission. He looks strangely relieved. He also looks terrible. Dark circles underline his eyes, and a general weariness weighs heavily on his body. He breathes deeply, and when he exhales, his shoulders sag. Gone is the strong, invincible sovereign, and here stands a shadow of the man I knew. Grief steals from us all.

I didn't miss the way Marcus pulled away slightly at my answer. He was suspicious that I was somehow involved with the Death God. He didn't realize death was closer than he thought. My chest constricts at the stab of pain I feel at his distance. He's too weak to step away from me completely, though, and we're still surrounded by wary-looking guards.

"Ryuzio."

The dragon leans his head down toward my shoulder, bumping me slightly. Adrian's eyes widen, and a few gasps are heard around the courtyard.

"Meet me at the avgrunn." I tilt my head toward him. "Be discreet."

He puffs a breath full of shadows, but I know he will obey. In the blink of an eye, the dragon disappears into shadows, his corporeal form gone to meet me in the forest. Someone screams, and a sword clatters to the stone.

The traveling was too much for Marcus. He sags slightly into my body, growing more cumbersome. Adrian notices his friend and reaches for him, taking my place at his side to hold him up. He doesn't exactly shove me out of the way, but rather wedges his body between mine and Marcus's.

"Somebody, help me!" One of the guards rushes over and positions himself on the other side of Marcus. They rush away from me, and I hesitate only a moment before moving to follow. I'm stopped by a fair-skinned woman dressed in leather armor with a seal on the right shoulder.

"I don't think that's a good idea," she says.

I really don't like it when people tell me what to do.

I tilt my head, eyeing her curiously. She doesn't miss the shift in my demeanor, the predator coming out to play.

"I don't think you can stop me."

She swallows and barely twitches her fingers. Tension and fear seep into the air around us. A few of the other guards step between this woman and the entrance into the castle, hands on their swords.

"The Sovereign didn't summon you with him, and the High Commander obviously needs a healer. It's best if you stay out of the way." Her voice grows stronger with each word, conviction coating her tone.

"I am never summoned but always needed. What is your name?" My eyes run up and down her body before locking onto her eyes. I allow magic to rise to the surface, power growing into a soft green glow. She wants to step back. She wants to run away, but she holds her position.

She resists my question, but I can see her mind fighting her mouth. Her mind loses. "My name is Aella, second commander of the eastern quadrant." Terror replaces any trace of stubbornness she may have had.

"Do you know who I am, Aella?" I draw her name out, savoring the taste of it on my tongue.

Shadows creep along the ground at my feet, spreading outward like an invisible army. The guards move backward, and Aella doesn't answer me.

"Aella, who created the dragons? Who is it that mankind has been told to fear for millennia? Who is it that all come to when time runs out?"

Her skin pales as she watches one of the shadows curling around a small bird that had been flitting about on the ground. The bird turns to ash in the span of one breath. It's my only warning to her.

"Your world, your history, is a lie. Now, move."

This woman trembles before me, but she and the other guards refuse to get out of the way. It looks like I may have to make an example out of them. I'm tired of all this waiting and rejection—this lack of respect.

I'm about to raise my hand to strike when a familiar shadow shrouds me in darkness. Warm, velvety shadows coat my skin, my senses. Meiora. It is the best of me, the best of my creations. Instantly, the anger boiling beneath my skin is reduced to a simmer. I exhale and close my eyes a moment before thinking the word *okay*.

The cryarsh slips away, following the path Adrian took only moments ago. I should follow—I long to follow—but I don't. Adrian needs to deal with the trauma of losing Marcus and finding him alive again. He needs to feel everything and see his friend well. I did what I could to bring Marcus back to health, but healers can take my place now.

There are other things I can focus on that are more important right now.

Meiora's departure exposed me to Aella again, who looks even more terrified than before. I don't want to hurt her; I don't want to hurt any of them.

I lock eyes with her one more time. "Aella, tell Adrian I said goodbye."

She opens her mouth to respond, but I shift to the avgrunn before I hear her. Ryuzio waits near the abyss for me, snorting in irritation at being sent away.

"I know, I know. But you are quite terrifying. I had to send you away." I pat his snout gently. "Now, show me what you have created."

RYUZIO AND I DISAPPEAR into the avgrunn, arriving seamlessly in Oria. The wind howls through the treetops as I turn to face the dragon, who is already kneeling before me, waiting for me to climb on. I move quickly, burying my hands into his velvety warmth to protect them from the cold.

He spreads his great wings, and the ground slowly disappears from under us. I love the feel of flying. The way the land stretches out before me, the sky an open expanse for me to explore. Free. It feels like freedom. For a moment, the memory of another type of freedom crashes into my mind, unwelcome and unannounced.

Kiran pulling me into his arms. Kiran's mouth on mine. Kiran growing a family with me and disappearing into the landscape of a new world without magic. Freedom and belonging rolled up into one.

But Kiran's gone. I'm all that's left, and for two years, I'd been unable to do anything about the attack the gods and goddesses orchestrated against me. A lethal calm settles in my chest again; a warning to any who would get in my way this time.

Ryuzio carries me farther into the land, away from the house and the avgrunn. The forest thins, and the terrain becomes more mountainous. Moments later, the majestic peak of Mount Eirlo stands before me, snowcapped and ominous. The sight of it still takes my breath away.

We descend slowly to the east of the mountain, where the trees have thinned to almost nothing, and a vast snowy plain opens before us. It's not empty, though. A smile curves my lips as I take in the sheer size of them. I absently pat Ryuzio's neck.

"Good work, my friend."

He lands silently as a snowflake on the plain and shakes his head, roaring to the others before us. Thousands of heads turn toward us. Dragons. Thousands of shadowy, black dragons. I imbued Ryuzio with the power to create, and create he did.

An army, vast and indestructible, stands to attention at the sight of its leader. Araina won't be expecting this again. I slide off his back and marvel at the sight. Magic awakens at my fingers, and shadows spread quickly toward every creature standing nearby. Anticipation sends shivers down my spine.

Oh, Araina, look what I've done this time.

As my shadows encounter each dragon, their essence intertwines with the dragon's darkness. Like a dark tapestry, we're connected and threaded together one by one, creating a masterpiece of bones and shadows. I call out to the darkness of other creatures, the cryarsh I'm rather fond of keeping close by.

Across the plain, coming from the tree line in the distance, more shadows emerge. Our collective conscience allowing me to sense and feel them in their entirety. Their thoughts, desires, wills—all of it is mine.

"Ryuzio, I need to pay a visit to one of my favorite gods. He could use a little persuasion, I think."

I return to Ryuzio and climb onto his back. It's time to return to Myzonia.

MYZONIA IS COLD ENOUGH for snow, but not as bitter as Oria. In some ways, it's a softer version of the world I created. Perhaps it was inevitable that a mortal world created by death would be colder and harsher than the others. My talents lie more in immortal creation, perfecting an afterlife for humans to escape to.

Ryuzio left me at the avgrunn not long ago. Honestly, I insisted that he return to the gathering of dragons at the mountain to ensure their readiness for battle. They may be strong and terrifyingly effective at destruction, but they are still susceptible to light magic and the forces Araina might bring to a confrontation.

A tug in my chest reminds me that I'm close to Adrian—present in his world yet again. The call is almost enough to draw me to the castle in Rizyrk. I ignore the pestering summons, mentally shoving that ember a little deeper in the hope it will leave me alone long enough to accomplish this.

Markyr is the God of Fire and Ice, and although his temple would be the obvious place one might search for a god, I know better. On the other side of the mountain, far from the presence of his scarlet and onyx temple, is a mountain more obscure in its appearance. It's smaller, but hidden deep inside it is a river of fire whose banks are shrouded in crystals so vibrant even the sun would cower in their presence.

That is where I will find Markyr.

I shift to the mountain in one thought, hearing the crunch of black rocks under my feet upon my arrival. No trees or vegetation grow near this place. I think the humans call it Eremos, meaning desolate. They're not wrong.

I walk quietly along the base of the mountain, waiting for the cave to present itself. Halfway around, a small opening, barely wide enough for my shoulders to fit, appears. A soft orange glow emanates from the doorway, and I instantly feel the heat escaping into the wintry air out here. I remove my cloak, dropping it to the ground next to the entrance. I won't need it in there.

Entering slowly, I glide my fingers along the smooth surface of the mountain rock, feeling the slight dips and bumps as I move. The passage isn't long. It opens into a great antechamber that is stifling from the heat of the river flowing slowly on the other side of the space. Dazzling crystals spread a strange display of light across the ceiling of the cavern, and I stand in awe of this creative display Markyr has imagined.

"What are you doing here?" His voice awakens me from my reverie.

"I really like what you've done with the place. It's quite beautiful. You should be proud." I chuckle. "Well, of course you're proud. You're a god."

Markyr watches me carefully. He looks older than the rest of us. Not ancient, but not quite as young. His skin is fair but slightly tanned, his eyes a mossy hazel, and his shoulder-length hair a light brown. He stands, stiff and angry at my appearance, with a staff of black wood in one hand.

"Aren't you going to say hello? It's been a while after all." I smile, but I don't hide the ill intent there.

"I'll ask you again. What are you doing here?"

I summon a few shadows to twine around my hands, smirking when I see his body tense slightly. "Well, I have a problem. There's this god I know who created this beautiful world. A world of wonder and filled with lovely little humans who somehow managed to obtain a good sovereign for once. But this god let another run unchecked through the land while he stayed cozy in his fire cave."

My temper grows at the injustice of it all, but I fight to keep it under control.

Markyr's face pales slightly. "What do you care who I allow into my world? You've been absent for years."

"We each get a world. We were ordered to guard those worlds. They were not to be shared or bargained for or stolen from one another. Oh, wait, except for me. I was never supposed to have a world. I was supposed to be feared and then forgotten by all of humanity." The words come out louder now. Shadows trickle off me like water.

"You were supposed to care for those in the afterlife, not seek fame in the present, Arawna!"

"Don't tell me what I was supposed to do! Araina made sure I went from being welcomed and cherished—a peaceful rest after a life well lived—into a dark and foreboding monster who steals in the night and on the battlefield and from their homes. She was jealous."

"She wanted to ensure they didn't seek you, to make you greater than you were supposed to be."

"She only wanted power for herself, Markyr, and you know it."

"When you created a world, Arawna, you broke every imaginable rule to get what you wanted. You bargained with humans, you allowed for the creation of a monstrosity, you isolated a people and wiped their memories. All in the name of something you could never be. Light. Goodness. Life." His words stab my heart, wounding me again and again. Rage blinds me.

"I created life! Without me, none of you would be able to generate these worlds."

"She only wanted to protect the worlds. She didn't want you to lose yourself in the darkness."

"SHE WANTED ME TO BE INVISIBLE!"

Markyr's eyes widen, but he remains silent.

I pant a few breaths, calming my racing heart. He allowed Khitaen to intrude on his world, to terrorize and kill innocents unprovoked. This was never how we were supposed to rule, but Markyr has always been a coward.

"Nothing can kill a god." I watch his knuckles go white as he grips his staff, but I finish anyway. "Nothing but me."

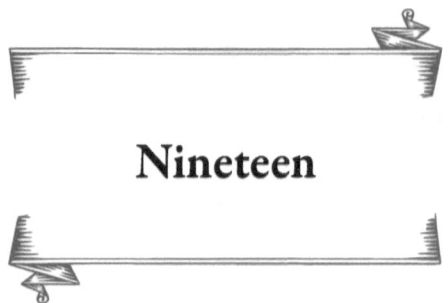

Nineteen

"Here, there is only darkness and shadows and death."

—Unknown

Darci

Three Years Ago

"What are you doing, Shadow?"

I smile at the nickname Kiran has bestowed on me. It reminds me of my heritage, of who I am and who I was. It wasn't as hard as I thought it would be—giving up my magic in exchange for this life. A family, a collection of people who love me. These years with Kiran have been beautiful.

Surrendering my magic didn't make me mortal, though. The reminder that I am still more than him presses the unhealed wound in my heart because all these things in every world die. There are no exceptions. He will start to notice when I have not aged the same way he has.

Time has been gracious to him. He's still as vibrant as the day he found me on the hill. Only the slight crinkling around his eyes when he smiles and the dusting of gray in his dark hair betray the cost of time on his life.

"I'm just finishing up this bread. I figured you and the boys would want something to eat before it got too late. I can't keep up with how much those two consume every day."

He laughs, and I smile some more. My boys with a touch of wildness in them that only nature can give. Raised in the forests and mountains of this world, they are free and vibrant, uncontained and unrestrained, and I love them. Creating life the mortal way, carrying them within me, was beautiful and challenging. I never knew the cost of it on the mortals' bodies until I subjected my own to it. It was well worth it.

"Well, they're growing boys." He wraps his arms around my waist and kisses my neck.

Moments like these, when the world feels too good, too perfect, I feel guilty. Guilty for not revealing my true nature to him, for not telling him everything I've done to get here. That the memories he has of this world are distorted, altered.

Does that make me the same as Araina? Am I guilty of the same lies and deceit? I know the answer, though I don't want to say it. Instead, I bury the guilt again, hiding in the love and grace of a man who cherishes me and was happy to build a family with me.

Even if it was all built on lies.

The air is crisp with the shift in seasons. Harvest time has brought plenty of produce from our garden, and Kiran took the boys hunting with him this year. Together, they caught plenty of deer for our winter, and he showed them how to smoke the meat to preserve it for longer periods.

"Mom! Dad! Cayo isn't letting me have a turn with the bow!"

"You're lying, Luka! I did let you have a turn. You took too long!"

Cayo and Luka are only a year apart in age, but Cayo takes his elder brother status a little too seriously, in my opinion. At eleven and ten, they are at the perfect age to feel like men but still be boys. I love this, every part of it. I worried they would display a propensity for magic, but perhaps the draining of my magic away prevented any exchange of powers between us. I don't know if they will live longer because of me. The consequences could be dire, and I refuse to dwell on them.

"Boys, you're going to have to figure out how to work together to learn and grow. You know that, right?" They both roll their eyes at me. If there's one thing that can unite fighting brothers, it's a mother who doesn't seem to fully grasp the seriousness of their problems. I hide a smile.

"Don't you roll your eyes. Be respectful. Now what's the problem?" Kiran inquires.

Cayo jumps in right away. "I gave Luka a turn, but he took forever to shoot the target. What was I supposed to do? Wait all night?"

"I was trying to get it perfect!"

"Well, maybe you should wait until you're older."

The thought of this is apparently outrageous to Luka. "You're only one year older than me!"

Kiran steps between them, holding up his hands. "Okay, okay. Come with me. We'll work together to learn, and we'll be patient with each other while we do it."

The boys look unimpressed by his suggestion but follow him out the door regardless. Silence fills the room now, and I revel in the quiet. I look out the back window and smile at the sight of the boys listening intently to their father as he demonstrates how to properly shoot the arrow.

This is what I always wanted, but it feels like grains of sand slipping through my fingers. Or shadows I can't quite grasp.

The cost of this life pains me sometimes. I miss the magic, my creatures, but I don't miss the constant threat and turmoil, always feeling like an outsider. Unwanted and feared by so many. At least here, magic doesn't exist, extinguished from the world entirely when I spent myself to create it.

My mind drifts back to the day I made the bargain with the king. He's dead now. This much I know. He was outraged by the outcome, no doubt. His son is nothing like him. I imbued a small piece of my soul into the child as an infant, giving him an unprecedented magic, a power surpassing anything his world has ever seen. With that magic comes a taste of life and death. He destroys, but he also creates.

He took the throne by force and killed his father to gain power. He is good, and he eradicated a great evil tainting the land. There is more light within him, thanks to the others who raised him, than I could have ever hoped to possess. I wonder about him often. He's a man now and full of life. I wonder if he senses the differences in him, the things that are not normal for other humans.

I wonder if he feels me.

Later that night, as Kiran curls his body around me in our bed, I get the sensation that something is wrong. Maybe not wrong, but different. Not the same as it was before. Someone is watching me. The windows are covered by curtains, but I sense a heavy presence in the room with us. The shadows appear more ominous. Something is coming.

I almost ask Kiran if he notices anything out of the ordinary, but his breathing is already deepening, his hand slipping under my shirt to rest gently against the skin of my stomach. Soon, the weight and warmth of him lull me into slumber.

A MAN STANDS, STARING out of a window into the shadows of a forest. I recognize him from somewhere. I observe every detail about his face, his features. His eyes are a dark brown—so dark they're almost black—and there is kindness in his gaze.

The ebony tone of his skin reminds me of a king. The image is fuzzy, but I know I've met him once before.

Someone speaks to him, or at least I think they do. I see his mouth move in response, but I can't hear him. Am I outside the room? Outside in the forest?

Whispers travel along the air around me. A name I should have known at the mere sight of him. Adrian, Sovereign of Myzonia. Well, new Sovereign. He only acquired the position at great cost a couple of years ago. A light green glow of magic surrounds his hands.

I smile because I know.

Suddenly, his gaze sharpens on the spot where I am standing. Am I standing? I can't feel anything. Perhaps I am just a shadow, one with the dark forest surrounding me.

He sees me, but not clearly. His brow furrows as he stares into the dark, into the shadows. He became everything I'd hoped he would become.

When I had gazed upon his infant face years ago, I doubted this would work. I doubted it would be enough. He looked innocent, incapable of evil or death. Yet, his father wanted him to become a god, invincible and destructive, just like the others. He wanted a piece of his soul to be implanted into the child so he might live on in him. Never truly dying. Never truly gone. Connected forever.

I gifted the child a portion of my magic, but instead of giving him a piece of his father's soul, I gave him a piece of mine instead. I am not the monster they think I am. Not entirely. The father didn't know what was coming for him when I established this strange connection between the divine and man. I'm sure he was outraged when he faced death and found no one waiting for him.

The child is a man now. He is beautiful, my greatest creation. I want to watch him forever. A branch creaks behind me. The leaves rustle on the forest floor. Movement, someone shifting their weight. I turn around and see only darkness, but I sense it. The change in the air. The heaviness that wasn't there before.

Something is wrong.

Someone screams.

NOTHING IS AS IT SHOULD be. The sound of trees cracking and thudding to the forest floor startles me awake. Or was it the screaming I heard? Screaming? I sit up straight in bed, feeling Kiran wake beside me.

Something is very wrong.

A humming I haven't heard in years assaults my ears, causing my blood to run cold. Magic. Someone is using magic. All these thoughts rush into my head as I scramble toward my boys' room, Kiran on my heels. Empty. The windows are open, and my children are gone.

"Where are they!?" Kiran shoves past me into the room and leans out the window, searching for them.

Screaming again. It's coming from the woods.

I don't wait for Kiran to follow. My instincts scream that one of the gods or goddesses has found me. My bargain with the mortal king, the creation of a world not sanctioned by the whole, commandeering a life with a human, like I am one myself. I've done many things wrong, and retribution has come.

Nothing stops me from bursting through the door at the back of our house. There they are at the tree line; I see them being carried away. Dark, shadowy creatures haul them roughly over the ground. I recognize them because they are mine or a twisted version of my creations. Death monsters with teeth and claws and shadows enveloping them. My sons are an abomination according to them, a cross between the divine and the worldly. They'll kill them. I know this in my bones.

"NO! NO, DON'T!" I scream; the words scraping my throat on their way out. Unrelenting panic takes hold as I run down the hill barefoot, feeling every nut and stick and stone slice into the soles of my feet. The sounds of wings beating the air overhead distract me for only a moment. Who would dare try to wield my creatures against me!? Rage roars to the surface now, too.

"Darci! Wait!" Kiran races behind. I hear the terror in his words. "What is..." His words end in a swear.

I'll never be able to explain this monstrosity. How did I not sense them coming? How did I not know? I plunge into the trees and forget momentarily that a ravine lies not far into the forest. I stumble down it, feeling my ankle twist awkwardly and pain shoot up my calf, at the same moment my head cracks hard into a branch.

More screaming. More cries from my sweet, sweet sons. Kiran hesitates only a moment before he leaps over me, chasing after our boys.

Darkness blurs my vision, but I fight to stay conscious. Kiran is disappearing into the shadows of the trees. I have to follow them. I have to save them. They'll kill him too if he gets to them.

Pushing myself to stand, I wobble, feeling dizzy and strange. I need magic, but it's not inside of me. I haven't felt a flicker of it since the day I woke up here after creating this magnificent world. As I regain my composure, I look in the direction they ran, trying desperately to see them by the moonlight.

Straight ahead, I see movement. More screams reach my ears, and soon Kiran's words mingle with them. He sounds like he's struggling, fighting against someone. Panic and anger thread together in his voice—a familiar melody I know so well.

Come on, Arawna. Move.

In the corner of my eye, I see a shadow, and a weight forms in the pit of my stomach. I ignore the impulse to look at it and instead force my feet to move, to chase them into the woods. The soles of my feet are sticky with blood, and my ankle feels swollen and stiff. Every hobbling step is painful, but I keep going. I imagine a fire growing inside of me; shadows and black light bleeding into one powerful force.

When I think the image is futile, I feel it. The tiny spark of something, an ember from a blaze extinguished long ago, warms in my chest. I know the sensation. I taste it in my mouth.

The shadow in my periphery swells in size, but I cannot acknowledge it. I have to save them. Flames dance along the trees ahead of me, where a strange clearing has formed among the thickest brambles. A perfect opening of dying grass with an oozing, dark cavity in its center.

No. Fires dance along the edges of the clearing, illuminating the night around me. The monsters have dragged my children and my husband there. They're pressing claws into Luka's back, eliciting more screams from his tiny throat. Near the inky pool stands another as monstrous as I.

He holds his hand up toward me and clenches his fingers into a fist. Instantly, I feel pain slice across my palm as a wound opens and blood seeps out. Kiran notices the stranger and his attention on me and thrashes against the monster holding him back.

"Run! Darci, run away!"

I lock eyes with him, tears pouring down my cheeks. The deal was discovered. My bargain with the king fulfilled, but the gods did not approve. I've been found out—-betrayed when all I wanted was to be free.

As blood slips off the tips of my fingers, I feel it—the magic I once gave entirely to this world awakens and rushes back into me. My dormant magic flares to life alongside it with a vengeance. He created monsters that look like mine but are fraudulent instead. The fire erupting in my veins sparks adrenaline as it rushes ever faster through me. I shouldn't have given it in exchange. My blood mingling with the earth at my feet has reignited the magic, and now a flood is coming, and I won't be able to stop it.

The cloaked god saunters toward me. He'll take my power and use it for wars and conquering. He'll take it and control every realm.

I can't let him have it. The more the magic overwhelms my senses, the harder it is to think clearly, to remember how all of this came to be.

Kiran screams my name, but it's not my name. He breaks free momentarily and stumbles into my body, grabbing my hand. Doesn't he feel my blood? The moment we connect, something changes. A fracture in my mind widens into oblivion.

I yank my hand free. Who is this man? He looks familiar, but I can't remember him. Adrian? No. Khitaen throws the man backward, away from me. I see him reaching for the magic. My punishment should be death, but I'm not sure why I need to be punished.

There are screams. Children. Shadows. It's hot. I'm on fire. Sweat pours down my back, and fire burns me from the inside out. Stop. Leave me. I don't say. I can't open my mouth.

As he reaches me, the only thought that enters my mind is death. If he takes the magic, the power, everyone is dead.

I scream as it floods out of me now, falling to my knees. Black fire explodes from my body in every direction. The God of War and Peace vanishes instantly, escaping unscathed, but everything else is destroyed. Nothing but ash and bones left behind. Darkness embraces me.

I am the shadow.

I collapse, feeling the hard, cool earth beneath me and the remnants of my magic fading to one tiny ember buried deep inside. Echoes of memories float before me, reminding me of what I forgot while blinded by power. Kiran. Cayo. Luka. Shadows.

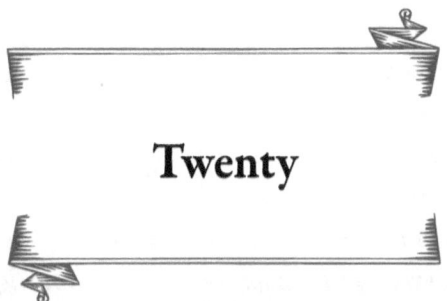

Twenty

"One must always be ready to fight well, even if it's your friends you battle."

—A drunk in a pub somewhere

Marcus

This is humiliating. I'm barely conscious, clinging to light instead of darkness as I lean my body weight on Adrian and some other guard. I should know who it is, but I can't think—I can't process anything. My chest constricts thinking about what Darci told Adrian. What they both revealed to me.

Impossible. It must be impossible because if it's not...

I don't finish the thought.

"Come on, Marcus. Don't you give up now. Get me a healer!" Adrian's voice grates on my ears. Everything hurts.

There's a flurry of activity as people run back and forth through the halls. Adrian mumbles something about finding someone named Sister Cleo. Isn't that the name of the woman from the temple? It sounds familiar. A strange yearning for Darci grows in my chest. I want her here. I need her here. The thought startles me.

We stumble into a room, and I'm about to say something when everything goes black. The last thing I hear is Adrian yelling for help.

THE WOODS AROUND ME are warm and welcoming. I recognize this place. It's peaceful here. The smell of dying leaves and earth mingle

together in the air, and I glance up at the sky to see only stars. It must be a new moon. The darkness doesn't scare me though. It feels like a friend I knew a long time ago.

I sit down in the dirt and press my fingers into the soil. The cool silk of the earth beneath the leaves grounds me. Home. It's cool but not cold. The perfect season to spend in the forest among the creatures that rest here. I close my eyes and focus on the sounds of the night around me. Crickets chirping, an occasional hooting of an owl, the rustling of leaves as some creature scurries around in the dark or scampers up trees.

Perfect rest. Perfect peace. I love it here.

Then, voices carry on the wind toward me. The sound is familiar enough to cause pain at the memory.

"What are you doing? You know Marcus won't like this. We should do my idea."

"I don't want to do your idea. He will like it just fine. You wait and see."

The voices turn to bickering—two young girls fussing at one another. A tear slips down my cheek, but I keep my eyes closed and I don't wipe it away. Is this real? Because if they are here, then I must be...

"I thought you would like it here."

Her voice. The truth dripping off every word. I knew it, but I didn't want to believe.

Without opening my eyes, I answer. "It feels like home."

"They're not far now. You could choose to stay. If you wanted to." She whispers the last part. I open my eyes, sensing her presence before seeing her.

Darci. No. Arawna. The Goddess of Death is sitting cross-legged in the leaves, too.

"If I stay, does that mean?"

She sighs. "If you stay..." Her smile is sad. "I did all I could at the house. You were very near death then. You shouldn't have survived. It took a lot to bring you back long enough to make the trip."

"What did it cost you?" I genuinely want to know. Because knowing this truth about her, it has wrecked me.

She looks down at her hands but doesn't answer me.

"You knew I might not survive?"

"I didn't know you were alive to begin with. My cryarsh found you and brought you to my home. I could take you the rest of the way. Your sisters are safe and happy. You could join them."

I feel sad, but only briefly. I could see them. This goddess has kept them safe for all this time. There is no fear mixed with the sadness.

I'm untouchable. The opportunity for rest is tempting. No more conflict or struggle. I could give in, let go of all I cannot hold onto anyway in the world. I... I like it here.

"What do you mean I could join them?" I lift my hands in the air, gesturing around me. "Isn't this evidence that I'm already dead?"

"But you're not dead, Marcus. Not yet. I've done all I can do. Adrian will do whatever he can do, and there is another, I'm sure, he will attempt to summon. But ultimately, it's up to you at this point."

I sit with this revelation for a moment. I'm not dead. I can still return to Adrian and my kingdom. But I could be with my sisters again. I feel a slight pain in my chest at the idea. It sounds too good to be true, but I can't abandon Adrian. I can't leave him to face whatever is coming. Whatever Darci is bringing. No, Arawna. Her name is Arawna.

"I don't know what I should do. How do I trust you?"

She looks down at her hands again. Thinking.

"I can't make you trust me. But you see this? This world? I created it for all mankind. A place of rest for the weary souls. Each person feels a sense of home, of rightness, when here. Each person sees something a bit different when they arrive."

"That makes sense. Why am I not afraid of you here?"

Her eyes narrow slightly, a hardness filling them that I've never seen before. I still can't feel fear in her presence, though. Something about her fills me with a calm I didn't expect. Home. She makes the feeling of home deepen in every portion of my body.

"Why are you afraid of me there?"

"I... I never really was afraid of you. I didn't like you, but I wasn't afraid of you." I offer a small smile. I'm reminded again of feelings I shouldn't be feeling toward someone as dangerous as the Goddess of Death. She's a goddess! I shouldn't be feeling anything!

"Weren't you, though? Aren't all people afraid of death?"

I open my mouth but decide against responding because she's right. Most of us are afraid of death. It's ingrained in our very existence at this point. The more I ponder this, the more questions I have about everything.

"Don't." Her voice is gentle but strong.

I lock eyes with her. A soft green glow emanates from them now. She sees the questions in my eyes. The confusion surrounding who the Death God was. How we didn't know the Death God was a goddess.

"You can't have all the answers, Marcus. It's not the way things are supposed to work. You know more than you did before, and that is all that matters. I can't linger any longer." She looks around the forest before bringing her eyes back to me.

Only then do I notice the subtle changes occurring. The lightening of the dark around us. The silence dominating the space instead of the usual night sounds. The cool air.

"What's happening?" I stand up, spinning in a circle. It feels different now. Strange, yet familiar. The sense of home is fading.

"You choose, Marcus. It's up to you now."

I turn back to face her, but she's gone. With her went the sense of calm and home that I felt deeply in this place. I choose? Does that mean I choose whether I live or die in this moment? I breathe hard, feeling my heart speed up. I already know what I'll choose. I'm not finished yet.

GASPING, MY EYES FLY open, and white light blinds me briefly. My body aches with the memory of old injuries, but the muscle soreness I had felt is fading. The weakness coursing through my veins earlier fades as well. I blink several times, and my ears finally open, allowing a rush of sounds and noises to assault my senses.

"Marcus! Thank Araina, you're alive!" My vision clears, and Adrian's panicked face becomes clearer. "I thought I'd lost you, brother." His friend's eyes are glassy as if he were on the verge of tears.

I turn my head to the right and see another face I recognize. My eyes widen at her presence. Sister Cleo from Markyr's temple is here. She's the one who greeted Darci and me when we arrived weeks ago. What is she doing here?

My face betrays my confusion because Adrian glances at Sister Cleo before turning back to me.

"It's okay, this is Sister Cleo. She's a healer. She helped bring you back."

A healer? I don't remember her saying she was a healer at the temple. I open my mouth, but my throat is parched. My mouth tastes like ashes, like death. I can't help the thought that flashes into my head. We shouldn't be thanking Araina. It was Arawna who greeted me in whatever that place was.

Arawna, Darci. A twinge of pain at not seeing her face here surprises me. When did I start to feel less hate toward her?

Adrian helps me sit up and offers me a glass of water. I sip at first, licking my lips, but soon I gulp down mouthfuls of it. It's been a long time since I felt this thirsty. When I'm finished, I close my eyes again, leaning into the rest that my body finally feels.

"How are you feeling now?" A cool hand presses to my forehead. Sister Cleo.

I keep my eyes closed, but answer anyway. "Better. Tired, but better."

"You were very close to her. I'm surprised you came back."

I open my eyes, furrowing my brow in confusion as I gaze into the blue eyes of the healer.

"I couldn't very well ignore my responsibility to my world, to Adrian." Did she think I wanted to stay in Oria with Darci? Could she hear the traitorous thoughts that ran through my head moments ago? "What do you mean by close to her? I was injured, and Darci helped me."

Adrian stands and paces in the room before deciding to order everyone out. Everyone except Sister Cleo.

She continues to gaze at me curiously.

"I wasn't referring to Oria, High Commander." My heart skips a beat.

"Sister Cleo, you knew who she was, didn't you?" There's a note of accusation in Adrian's voice I don't understand. I've missed a lot, apparently.

The healer stands and faces my friend, but she remains silent.

Frustration creeps into Adrian's eyes. "You knew she was the Goddess of Death. That everything we had ever been told was a lie. You handed me the scroll. You knew what I would find." His words are angry, icy even. Most would shrink away from him, but Sister Cleo doesn't change her stance at all. She almost looks nonchalant, unbothered by the accusations.

"I'm afraid I cannot tell you more."

My mind races through the encounters I had with this woman. The familiarity she had with me. How she knew my name and Darci's... Wait. She greeted us by our names, but Darci didn't have a surname. Sister Cleo somehow knew that. I narrow my eyes at her.

"You knew even then, at the temple, didn't you?" Her eyes shift to mine, and Adrian's body tenses.

"I'm sorry?" Like she didn't hear me.

"You knew Darci wasn't Darci when we arrived at the temple. You always seemed to know where you were needed and what was required before anyone spoke. I thought it had to do with the magic of the temple and the fact that you were a priestess. But it was just you who always showed up. You who spoke my name and hers. None of the other priestesses acted similarly." The effort of speaking still leaves me feeling more tired than it should.

Adrian's eyes widen at the revelation. "Who are you? And why do you know so much?"

She ignores him and looks at me. "Marcus, you had the choice to leave, and you didn't. You could have gone with her. But you stayed. She may not be entirely evil, but her intentions are dangerous. You both must stop her before it is too late."

"Too late for what?!" Adrian yells.

She smiles sadly and then vanishes. She's gone like a shadow blending into the night around it. I turn to look at Adrian and notice a green glow in his eyes, and shadows twined around his hands and feet. He reminds me of Darci, and my skin chills at the sight.

"Adrian." My voice snaps him out of whatever trance he was succumbing to.

He strides toward the bed. "Marcus," he pauses and closes his eyes, composing himself for a moment. "You almost died. I tried to heal you as much as I could, but I needed Sister Cleo. She brought you back. Her healing magic is very powerful, but it was barely enough."

"I know." The words come out a little stronger this time. Perhaps I am recovering.

"You don't seem incredibly surprised by all of this..." he waves his arms around momentarily. "Madness."

I swallow, feeling unsure how to explain to him all I have seen over the past several days.

"Adrian, when I was... close to death... I..." I swallow, trying to gather my thoughts, but I don't know where to begin.

"You can tell me. Listen, I thought you were dead days ago. Aella came in and announced my house had been incinerated, and you were last known to be going to it. They found no trace of your body, and I felt it. I felt when you died. Or didn't die. I don't know. But I knew something terrible had happened to you."

I don't know what to say for a moment, but I settle for the truth.

"I saw her, Adrian. I saw her in my mind, or wherever it is that we go when we are faced with eternity. It was peaceful—the place she gave me. I know Darci isn't her name. I understand she is the Goddess of Death, but I think we were wrong to be taught to be afraid of her. Being in her presence there—it felt like home."

Sorrow fills Adrian's face. I want to reassure him, reassure myself, that it's okay. That death was not scary, but I'm uncertain if that's why he looks devastated.

"I heard my sisters," I whisper, and I hear Adrian draw in a quick breath.

"Did you see them?" His voice shakes.

"No. But I could have. She said she had done all she could to save me. She spent a lot of magic to bring me back to life the first time. I don't think I was supposed to survive the attack on your house. But she saved me. Well, her cryarsh saved me first and brought me to Oria, to her house. But when she found me, she worked for days, pouring magic into me, creating life where there was only death. She brought life, too, Adrian. She didn't only bring death. What does that mean?"

"I don't know. All I know is that every text, every scroll, every piece of history I could find spoke of a horrible, monstrous, power-hungry god that sought only his gain. Until I read a scroll given to me by Sister Cleo. It was as if someone missed it while erasing pieces of our history. One scroll that should have said something different." He pauses, looking thoughtful. "Arawna," he murmurs. "We've known all along. We call it Arawnia, but we didn't know it was named for her." He smiles now, a strange smile that speaks volumes about the turmoil beneath the surface.

"Why do you think everything was changed?"

It's the one question that continues to bother me. Why the lies? Why distort the past? And who doesn't want us to know about her?

"That's what's bothering me. That and not knowing what Darci is up to. Sorry, I can't quite stop thinking of her in terms of that name." Adrian shrugs.

"I can't either," I confess.

"We need to get you well. For what it's worth, I'm glad you didn't die."

He knows. He saw the longing in my eyes about the place hidden from mortal view. The place my sisters rest.

"I couldn't leave you to clean up this mess now, could I?" There's a strange ache staying with me. Lingering in the back of my mind. Death might be coming for all the worlds. I'm not sure if that's a good thing or not.

"We need to figure out what Darci is up to and why the histories were changed. What she plans. How I'm connected to her." His tone on the last part bears remnants of anger.

"Your magic is changing, isn't it?"

He jerks his head up, reading my eyes and the knowing there.

"Not changing entirely. But there's more to it than before. It's expanding."

"It looks like hers."

"I know."

Two words bearing such weight. I fear the answers we might find.

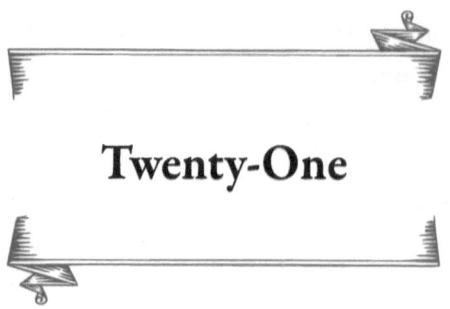

Twenty-One

"We battle for what is good and true in the world. Evil battles for only Death."

—*History of Myzonia,*
passage 305

Darci

S hadows swarm the cavern, filling in every crack and corner. Fire erupts around us, raging against the dark I have unleashed. The shadows quickly smother the flames, but it isn't permanent. Markyr launches his ice magic on me as shards of knife-like glass fly toward my face.

A cryarsh whips out from behind me and absorbs the ice effortlessly. Markyr grips his staff tightly before launching himself toward me. Wielding my shadows, I swing their power into the brunt of his weapon, hearing a resounding crack as darkness meets wood. He grunts in frustration but isn't slowed down much.

Only anger greets me from his eyes. No fear.

Good.

I smile and lunge into another attack, this time pulling my daggers from their sheaths. If he wants to use a mortal weapon, I will too.

We clash together, dodging each other's blows but never slowing. A blade of ice slashes at my back, but my shadows shield me, allowing me to focus only on Markyr. I need to get the staff out of his hands. He has greater reach than I do with my daggers. I imbue my blades with shadow magic, strengthening them as I block another swing of the wood toward my face. The increase in strength works because a large portion of his staff is cut clean.

Markyr stumbles at the give that comes with the loss of the wood but recovers quickly. He's being smarter now. He calls fire forth, surrounding us in an inferno he is immune to. Perks of being the God of Fire and Ice, I suppose. Sweat pours down my brow, my neck, my back. It's distracting, to say the least. The shortening of his staff has given me an opening I otherwise wouldn't have, and I use it to my advantage.

I go on the offense, lunging into his space, slicing sideways, and then plunging upward toward his chest in a quick move he doesn't expect. While he blocks my dagger that slices near his throat, the movement forces his arms upward and in front of him, exposing his belly. I plunge the blade into his flesh easily, feeling him draw in a painful breath.

His arms drop to his sides, one hand grasping my hand that still holds the blade steady. A slow trickle of shadows creeps along the blade into his body. I don't let go. He looks dumbly down at our hands. The thud of his staff hitting the stone floor of the cavern echoes briefly before being absorbed by the sounds of the river of fire behind Markyr.

"You cannot kill me with a blade." He speaks but sounds confused, and he's right, of course. I cannot kill him with a blade, but he knows this doesn't feel the same; something is wrong. He feels the strangeness moving about him—the magic that is not his own slipping through his veins, casting shadows behind his eyes. His brow furrows.

"I don't ever need to kill with a blade because I am the great balancer. The one who holds the strings of power and doesn't let them go unchecked for too long." I still grip the dagger's hilt. I feel the warmth of his blood on my skin now.

His legs grow weak and bend. I follow him down, never letting go until he kneels, and we are eye to eye.

"You're exactly the monster she said you would be. What have you done to this world? Without me?" Speaking is a struggle now. He's still confused, not understanding why the life in him seeps away.

A flare of anger threatens to consume me at his words, though. "Do you think this world needs you? You were the one who let the monster in, and it wasn't me. Innocents have died because you preferred your solitude to your duty. You sacrificed mankind on the altar of your ego when we agreed to rule them with benevolence."

I lean close and whisper the next words into his ear. "I am nothing but what I was made to be. You broke the covenant we all agreed to. You pay the price for your arrogance and indifference."

Pulling back, I wait a few more moments, allowing the rest of the shadows I'm unleashing to flood his body. Then, staring into his eyes, I pull the blade free. He gasps, but it's weak. I rise to stand before the kneeling God of Fire and Ice.

"It will never work." He chokes out. "Your plan to rule everything."

"I am your retribution, Markyr. You know nothing of my plans." And he doesn't. He doesn't know the full extent of the judgment I am bringing.

His eyes grow vacant, shadows filling them while a pained smile graces his lips. "Death...comes for us all." He collapses to the ground. The river of fire behind him swells with white light before cooling to black stone.

No one can kill a god.

No one except for me.

I WALK OUT OF THE CAVERN into the dark of night. Breathing the fresh, cold air of winter in this world. Not bitter but refreshing. Pleasant even. The earth beneath my feet rumbles, restless, wondering who is to rule it now. This world needs good magic. Magic that will hold it together and imbue it with life and power, fed by a ruler that cares for it deeply.

Markyr lost the privilege of his position when he chose to turn a blind eye to Khitaen's acts of aggression.

The world already feels the absence of its god. I squat down and press a hand gently into the dirt. The ground is cold and wet from the snow, but I close my eyes and press my palm flat against it.

It quivers beneath me, uncertain and lost.

"Shhhh..." I breathe out the calming sound. A faint green light glows behind my eyelids. I coax the magic into the earth, feeling the tremors lessen at my touch.

"Everything will be alright." I mouth the words, thinking them more than speaking them. The ground calms, and I rise to standing again. Ryuzio lands softly before me.

"Okay, let's go home."

He spreads his massive wings, and I opt to shift upon his back instead of climbing. I'm weary and ready for some rest before we begin the next stage.

We're airborne quickly, and I bury my hands in the velvety shadows in front of me, reveling in the beauty of this moment. The perfect peace I feel at having rid this world of Markyr. Araina will be furious, but it is for the good of all the worlds. She'll see that. She'll understand when this is all finished. She can't deny the truth forever.

Ryuzio glides across the forest, heading for where the avgrunn is hidden amongst the trees. As we draw closer to it, I stretch out my magic toward the darkness calling it upward and outward. The shadows grow until the opening is wide enough for Ryuzio to dive through saving us the need to stop and go in separately.

He doesn't hesitate as he flies directly into the shadows. I am momentarily blinded by the darkness before we burst out into a bitter cold wind, and snow turns our vision white before us. A blizzard. We've flown straight into one of Oria's constant annoyances. He roars his displeasure, but I reach my hand forward to pat his neck.

"I know. Get us to the house." My words are lost on the wind, but he hears me through our connection. I intended to go to the army, but this weather is too much. I'll have to wait to check in on them.

Ryuzio delivers me safely to my home on the hill. I shudder at the realization there isn't a fire waiting for me inside. I'll have to start one from scratch which will take longer, but I need to rest. I need to wait this storm out.

I command the dragon to leave, and he is gone in the blink of an eye, turning into wispy shadows that venture somewhere safer than this.

As I step into the house, knocking snow from my boots, I sense the presence of another. My eyes dart to the corner, and I can't stop the foolish grin spreading across my face.

"Meiora, you're back now."

The shadow forms a man's silhouette and reaches a shadowy finger toward me.

"Yes, I know. I need to rest." I pull my cloak off, hanging it on the hook.

"Is Marcus alive?"

The feeling of yes resonates in my mind.

"Good. That's what I wanted. I need him to live. I need Adrian to have a reason to fight." Meiora morphs again and slips around my legs like a cat.

"I know you miss him. I miss him too, but we can't go back." I laugh softly. "Well, I can't go back. You can."

The cryarsh glides across the floor, inky and strange, exactly how I made it to be, but it doesn't leave. It takes up residence in the corner and waits.

I move about the room, gathering wood and preparing a fire. Perhaps some rest and time to refill my magic will do me some good. It's not until I'm setting the logs in the hearth that I notice the blood still on my hand. Sighing, I grab a cloth and step outside to plunge my fingers into the snow, using the cloth to wipe away the rest of the blood.

Returning to my efforts, I soon have a roaring fire in the hearth and time to do nothing for a moment. I'll need to mobilize soon, and I need to confront Araina. I'm not sure how she'll react to the news about Markyr, but I'm certain it won't be good. I need to be ready for anything.

"Meiora, wake me if you get news, okay? It's all for their good, you know? I never intended for anything to go wrong."

The cryarsh settles itself across me as I lie down on the sofa next to the fire. A confirmation of understanding, of believing that what I say is true. The gesture comforts me. I only wanted family. I wanted to belong. But if I can't belong anywhere, then I'll have to change the rules of the realms.

Meiora's warmth floods me, and I sigh contentedly.

"I missed you. It was good you were with Adrian, but I'm glad to have you back now." The shadows stretch a bit more across me.

"He'll be okay. When this is all over, you'll be there to keep him safe. To lead him. Always."

That feeling of yes resounds in my mind again, seeping into my chest, my fingers, my feet. Perfect contentment. Meiora has been faithful from the beginning. It will be faithful to another in the end. This thought is a comfort, not a burden. I smile as I close my eyes, soaking in the warmth of the fire and the cryarsh in this moment.

Sleep draws me into its arms not long after.

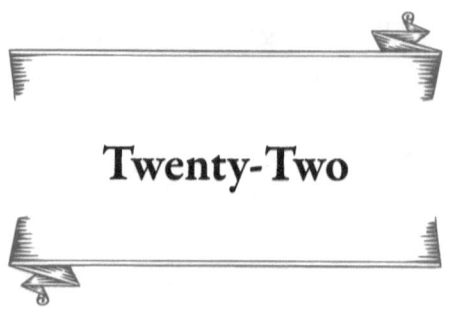

Twenty-Two

"Dragons and shadows collided with the armies formed by
Araina and Khitaen in their bid to defeat the God of Death."
—*History of Myzonia,*
Passage 265

Adrian

Magic hums beneath my skin, a constant buzz that makes me itchy. I wish I could ignore it, but it's getting harder to press it down. I need to use some of this power, expel some from my body before it becomes too much. Marcus knows I'm changing. It's not the same as before, and I feel it morphing gradually every moment.

With aching feet, I collapse in bed, trying to keep my mind off everything. I don't want this. I don't want a power that controls me or upends my world. For all the answers we have discovered, I feel more have entered the mix, and constantly questioning everything going on has left me exhausted, mentally and physically.

I lie here, staring at the ceiling, feeling the constant whir of my mind. I want to shut it off—to silence the noise, the never relenting hum. I poured massive amounts of magic into Marcus when it looked like he was going to die. Why isn't that enough? Why do I have a connection to the Goddess of Death, and how am I going to live with myself if I possess her power? Who am I if I'm not the person I grew up thinking I was?

"Stop!" I press the heel of my hands into my eyes until I see stars behind my eyelids. When I release the pressure, I keep my eyes closed and imagine I'm sinking deep into the mattress. Every muscle in my body begrudgingly releases its tension. Rest. I need to rest, even if it's temporary.

Marcus is stable, though tired. He's not going to die today. My friend, my brother, who I thought was dead, has come back to me. I relax my fingers and let a smidgeon of magic surface. Peace. I want peace. Is that too much to ask?

Before I realize it, I'm slipping into a dreamless sleep, lost to this world.

I JOLT AWAKE TO THE sound of rumbling. The wardrobe shakes, and the water cup on the stand next to my bed topples to the floor, shattering upon impact. I sit up quickly, feeling the movement of the ground beneath me. Screams and shouts of alarm echo through the hall outside.

The shaking stills as quickly as it came; the ground settles once more. My heart pounds in my chest, and I wait, fully expecting the rumbling to return. When it doesn't, I draw in a long, deep breath.

The doors to my room fly open as Anthony and Jacob stride in.

"Are you okay, Your Majesty?" Anthony addresses me while Jacob checks the windows and the washroom for any damage or intruders taking advantage of the chaos.

"Yes, I'm fine. What on earth was that?" I rub my face and swing my legs over the side of the bed. I'm not sure I slept much at all.

"There was an earthquake, Your Majesty. There doesn't seem to be any damage from what we've seen. I haven't heard anything about those on the outside of the castle walls."

I nod before standing. "Is Marcus okay?"

"We checked you first, sir. I can go check..."

"No, no, I'll go. I'm fine as you can see."

Jacob joins Anthony again, and they step out of the room into the hall. I'm about to follow them when I hear a strong voice and the rhythmic click of boots on stone.

"Adrian! Are you okay?" Marcus steps into view, and I can barely believe my eyes. He looks completely healed. Strong and confident yet again, as if the entire ordeal he went through hadn't happened.

"Marcus, you're okay."

He looks down at himself before returning his gaze to mine and shrugging. "I guess I am. The shaking woke me up, but I felt completely normal when I did." He flexes his fingers, and blue magic flicks across his fingertips. "I feel strong again."

I smile because it's the first piece of good news I've heard. "I'm glad you're not dead."

"It'll take more than an attack by strange shadow creatures to kill me."

I laugh. "I always knew you were too stubborn to die."

He chuckles, then grows quiet. "I have this feeling, Adrian, that something is coming."

I nod. I've felt the same way for the past couple of days. "We need to go to Oria."

To see her. To find the Goddess of Death and pray we don't die when we encounter her. She is familiar, but dangerous; this I am certain of. A forgotten god seeking vengeance may not take kindly to our involvement, but I need to know how I ended up connected to her. I need to know how we are the same.

Because that's what I feel. Oneness with her. Like I belong to her or she belongs to me. The cryarsh communicating with me also points to something dark and strange. If I'm being honest, I'm terrified.

"Before we return to Oria, I want to see my house."

Marcus gives me a concerned look before he speaks. "You know it's completely gone? I've never seen magic like it. It was absolute.

But whoever destroyed the house, it wasn't Darci, and if she's the Goddess of Death, then who is the Dark Lord of Daemons? Why is he causing all of this trouble in Myzonia?"

"I'm not sure, but I need to figure it out. I feel like I'm on the cusp of understanding all of it. If I push a little more, everything will be clear." I turn my eyes away for a moment, not wanting to betray the vulnerability I feel.

"Okay, let's go then."

Marcus leaves to get a rucksack to carry some supplies. I gather a change of clothes and a water pouch, filling it in the washroom. When he returns, I stuff my few items into the rucksack too.

"Wait, I need to grab the scroll." I can't believe I forgot about it. I opt to shift to the library, not wanting to take the time to walk. It's probably a mistake with how much traveling we'll have to do. I should conserve my magic, but the well of power I sense is deep. Deeper than I remember it being.

Appearing in the library, a few priestesses shriek at my sudden appearance. I raise my hands in apology and hurry to the table I'd been at the night before.

There's nothing on it. No evidence I had been sitting here, reading a scroll that could change history. I scan the other tables, hoping I've confused them. A few priestesses are sitting in various locations, reading other scrolls, but none of them look as old and frail as the one I had held. Where did it go?

"Where is Saffi?" I ask the nearest priestess.

"She's in the temple throne room."

I don't wait for her to go on and immediately shift to the throne room in the temple. Saffi is standing near the altar, speaking softly with another priestess. My presence draws her attention, and the look on my face makes it clear I need her now.

"Your Highness, how can I help you?"

"There was a scroll Sister Cleo gave me last night. I left it in the library, but I can't find it now. I need it right away. Do you know where she is?"

Her brow crinkles in thought, "Sister Cleo left shortly after she finished with Marcus. I'm not entirely sure where she was going. What was the scroll called?"

"It was a scroll about Arawnia. Ancient. I had never read it before."

A part of me silences the thoughts about to spill out. I don't want to tell her what I found.

"I can try to find it for you, but it may take some time."

I shake my head. "I can't wait. If you find it, send word to me right away. Marcus and I are returning to Zaiven so I can see the damage done and to speak with Gennet." And to speak with Risa, but I won't risk the young seer's life by speaking her name in a public place.

She nods and looks like she wants to ask me more questions, but I don't linger. Without much effort, I shift back to the castle, arriving in the foyer next to Marcus. I don't know how I sensed his presence, but a part of me knew exactly where he was and how to find him. It unsettles me, but I don't dwell on it.

Marcus jumps slightly at my appearance. "That was quick. Find what you need?"

"No." I pause, glancing around to ensure no one is close enough to listen to my next words. "It's gone, and so is Sister Cleo." I keep my voice low, trying to hide my worry.

Marcus eyes me, and there is something there I don't recognize. Something dark and maybe even a little scared. It passes quickly, and I wonder if I truly saw it.

"You shifted an awful lot. You sure you can make the trip?"

"Yes." I don't hesitate. He quirks an eyebrow in question, but I don't offer an explanation.

"Let's go."

WE ARRIVE IN ZAIVEN, where my house once stood. Nothing fills the space anymore other than ashes and snow combined into a gritty gray slush. It looks like more snow has fallen since I was last here. The sight leaves me breathless. The only evidence that a house once stood here is the amount of black ash left behind. Trees several feet into the forest are gone as well. A power capable of this level of destruction is incomprehensible.

Marcus breathes hard next to me. Traveling from the capital to Zaiven is long and taxing. He's obviously not back to full strength since the attack, whereas I feel as fresh as I did before we traveled, which doesn't make sense. Another strange thing I don't have time to dwell on at the moment. I step forward, the slush beneath my feet offering the only sound. My stomach aches at the level of loss. All my best memories lie buried in the aftermath. Of all the places I have lived, this was the only place that was truly home.

Marcus places a hand on my shoulder, standing silently with me. I scan the tree line for any evidence of the monster that attacked. There is nothing but shadows and branches swaying in the breeze. I draw in a deep breath, composing myself.

"Did you see what attacked?" I ask, wondering how this came about.

"I saw monsters. Creatures of shadow and teeth. One moment they were there, the next moment they morphed into a massive dark force that obliterated everything. The last thing I remember is flying backward and feeling my spine crack upon impact. Everything went dark then."

I stare at Marcus, realizing how close I came to losing my friend.

"I don't know how you survived, but I guess I am thankful to Darci for that."

Marcus nods but doesn't say anything else.

"Did you inform Aella we would be returning here?"

"Yes, she wasn't happy to hear that you wanted to head back into danger, but I told her she couldn't keep you locked away somewhere."

I turn away for a moment, listening to the quiet of the space—the silence that should be broken by life and laughter and bustling activity. Instead, it's all gone. I swallow the lump in my throat and head to the road.

"I want to go into the village to see how things are. Perhaps Ginger and Gwenyth have heard some news. We need to ensure the people are safe before we venture anywhere, and I need to find Gennet." I flex my hands at my side and walk to the dirt road, leading into the village center.

"Lead the way." Marcus follows me away from the wreckage of our home.

I hope we find Gennet. I hope we can secure this tiny haven in my kingdom before we go to Oria. Finding Darci is important—a priority even, but I can't forsake my people here. Besides, I suspect Gennet might be able to shed more light on our situation.

As we get closer to the village, the evidence of my army's presence becomes more apparent. Tents are erected along the road and toward the tree lines. The houses are shuttered, and the life of the village has grown quiet. Another sight that is out of place, breaking my heart. My people suffered through one war already, and before that, the ruthless rule of my deranged father. I had hoped my time on the throne would be a reign of peace, but it looks like more death is coming for us.

Soldiers notice my presence quickly and stand to attention. I don't miss the shocked expressions on their faces at the sight of Marcus. As far as any of them knew, he was killed when my house was destroyed. The return of their commander has several scrambling to fix their tunics and strap daggers and swords onto their bodies.

"I'm gone for a few days, and they've fallen into laziness and disarray." Marcus's famous scowl forms on his face, and I try to keep my expression somber. It feels good to see his reaction, though—the old Marcus, coming back to life again.

"I'm sure they're not a complete loss. Aella should be returning soon, too. I wonder who she left in charge."

"Probably some fledgling who doesn't know his right boot from his left." Marcus's scowl deepens, and I'm not sorry to say that it makes me happy. He's acting more like himself.

"Aella knows what she's doing. I'm sure she left someone capable in charge."

Marcus isn't listening at this point. He's too busy glaring at every soldier we pass. The gaping mouths of a few young fighters are enough to awaken the beast inside my friend.

"What are you staring at!? You, there! Who is in charge here?"

A young warrior stumbles as he stiffens his back and stands to attention in front of Marcus. "I... I... uh... Coty is in charge, Commander. I... mean, sir... Commander, sir." The poor boy doesn't even realize I'm standing there with Marcus. Marcus has a presence of control and power about him that frightens even the bravest recruits.

"Captain Coty is a good man." Marcus mumbles. I'm almost certain he says something about him being the one he'd put in charge, but I'm not certain. He turns his attention back to the soldier.

"Did you not realize your Sovereign stands before you?! Be alert, man!"

The soldier's eyes widen, and he fumbles through a bow and other unnecessary salutations. I wave him off.

"At ease. You may return to your post." I chuckle as relief paints his face before he scurries away.

"You're too nice to them."

"And you're too hard on them."

"War has a way of requiring much of you, or did you forget about the last conflict we endured?"

"Marcus, you know I haven't." My mood sours at the memories.

We continue along the road, passing more houses until we arrive in the circular market at the center of the little village. A few vendors are still open, but many have closed their stalls. The pub on the other side is a little quieter than usual.

"Mister Sovereign! Mister Sovereign! You're back!" A little girl's high-pitched squeals echo across the space, drawing all eyes toward the commotion and the cause of it. Risa bounds toward us with her arms out wide and launches herself into the air, fully trusting I will catch her. My heart aches at the absence of Hoku from her life now. His death was a tragedy, but I will make sure she is cared for and protected.

Aster hurries after her daughter, followed by Gennet, bringing up the rear of their little group.

"I'm so sorry, Your Majesty. Risa, what did I say about running off from me?" Her brow is furrowed and frustrated at her daughter's inability to mind well.

"It's okay, Momma. I saw him coming. I knew he'd be back with Mister M." Risa responds from the safety of my arms.

Neither Marcus nor I can stifle our laughs. Gennet walks up slowly and smiles in approval.

"Oh, child, I wondered if you had seen something. Remember, you must not speak of it so boldly."

Risa's seer magic must be growing stronger and more precise. For her to see that Marcus lived and was coming with me is a great feat for such a young seer.

"Risa, I'm glad you are safe and sound. We were on our way to find Gennet, and you brought her straight to us."

She smiles proudly before a strange look fills her eyes. A pulse of magic spreads outward from her body, passing through my arms as I hold her.

Gennet and Aster both frown, realizing that Risa is having another vision. Before we can move into the safety of a private space, Risa leans into my body, whispering one phrase over and over.

My skin feels clammy, and my heart speeds up at the phrase. She's looking at nothing but seeing everything.

"Death is coming."

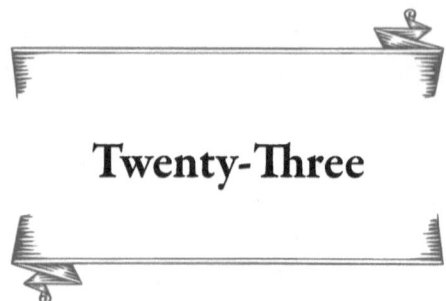

Twenty-Three

"The mark of heroism is bravery in the face of great fear."
—Polarium,
Scholar of ancient texts
and histories

Marcus

My skin grows clammy at Risa's vision. No sooner does she snap out of the trance than screams reach us from the far side of the village. Adrian hands Risa to Aster and casts a worried look my way. I don't wait for him before I run toward the sounds. The screaming is coming from the side of the village near the forest, and all I can think about are the creatures I last saw destroying everything in their path.

Gennet yells something, but I can't hear her over the commotion. I slide my sword out of its sheath; my stride never breaking or slowing as I navigate the panicked stragglers still out and about. Well-trained warriors all dash to the forest, urging civilians to run to the center. Adrian matches me stride for stride, but I can't think about him right now. Everything in me screams that we can't be too late.

We can't let what happened to the house happen to the entire village.

As the tree line comes into view, my heart drops into my stomach at the sight. Soldiers dressed in black and deep purple march toward the village, but even more disturbing is the appearance of bizarre creatures with bladelike teeth prowling ahead of the line of troops. A few of the strange creatures have captured unsuspecting villagers, making quick work of killing them. Others scramble away, screaming and desperate to escape whatever monstrosity this is coming for us.

"What, in the name of Araina, are those things?" Fear laces Adrian's voice, but his resolve is strong.

"I don't know, but let's find out if they die as easily as we do."

The creatures notice our arrival, and the troops behind them withdraw their swords, preparing to attack. More and more of my men and women fall in line next to us. Several others grab children and elders and lead them to safety. The only consolation is that I don't see any sign of those strange shadow monsters that obliterated the house.

There's no time to hesitate. No time to give orders or form a plan. I need to trust that my soldiers are well-trained enough to face these adversaries.

What takes only seconds feels like hours as we sprint to form the front line and then collide with these horrid creatures. Their hands have claws, and their feet are bare but deformed-looking. Other than their natural weapons of claws and teeth, the creatures carry nothing else.

I waste no time before I swing my blade parallel to the ground, and the creature's head is parted from its body. Black blood sprays from the monster, and the sounds of battle resound through the air. Out of the corner of my eye, I notice Adrian bearing no weapon, but green and black light emanates from his hands as he uses magic to destroy creature after creature. Soldiers fall on both sides, and soon we encounter the army marching behind the monsters.

"Don't let them get to the village!" I scream the order, knowing my people will do everything in their power to protect the village no matter the cost.

"Marcus!"

I swivel toward Adrian's shout while an enemy's sword comes swinging for my head. I meet his attack with my blade, feeling the sting from the clash of metal against metal. I shove with all my strength, knocking the soldier back a couple of steps and freeing my sword to attack. He meets my every strike, though, and then I notice the silvery glow of magic on his hands.

I need to react fast. We parry for a few more strides, and I force him farther into the forest. I steal the briefest moment to release my sword with one hand and send a stream of striking blue magic toward him. His response is fast, creating a silver shield against my power. The rebound drives me back a step and slightly off balance.

It's enough time for him to recover and swing his sword at my abdomen. I stumble backward, but it's not enough—the blade slices across my stomach, tearing through my tunic. I grunt but refuse to dwell on the pain. It doesn't feel deep, and I can't get distracted. Sweat pours down my back and face, and I bring my sword up to block another swipe.

Suddenly, the soldier is lifted into the air and simply dies suspended above me. I don't see anything protruding from him, no weapons, no apparent injuries. The body drops to the ground in a heap, and I pivot, searching for the source of his demise. Adrian stands a short distance behind me, hand outstretched with green light and black shadows twining around his fingers. A shadow slithers across the ground and returns to him.

The sight makes me a little nauseous. He just killed someone with magic in a way I've never seen. Invisible and quick. He was lethal on the battlefield before, but you could see his power striking out like lightning, quick and destructive.

This magic is different. I shake the discomfort from my mind; I need to focus. I run my hand across my lower abdomen where the sword cut me. It stings, and blood comes back on my hand, but it's not deep. I can still fight.

I run back out of the forest toward the fighting. Too many bodies lie across the ground. Too many that are mine. Where did they all come from? Why did they come here? My answer comes when I see movement across the way. A figure stands in the shadows of the trees, watching, not engaging in the battle—a figure with strangely white eyes and a cruel face.

The Dark Lord of Daemons, or whoever he is. I used to wonder if he was the Death God, but now I know that's not true. I launch into a run, heading straight for him. The confrontation that's been waiting to happen for years is finally here. But why at this village, and why now?

The Dark Lord senses me coming because his eyes turn slowly toward me, and he smiles. I feel cold power pulsing off him—a magic strong enough to make me stumble at the weight of it. What is he? He feels more powerful than anyone I've ever encountered.

"Marcus, wait!" Adrian crosses my path and shoves me back toward the battle.

"Adrian, it's him! It's now or never."

"He feels wrong! There's something not right here. We need to protect the village. I don't... I don't know what he is." Adrian pants next to me, and I turn my gaze back toward the Dark Lord. He's not where I last saw him. I quickly scan the trees searching for any sign of movement, any evidence that he is lurking somewhere closer.

There! He's moving toward the village square. Adrian follows my gaze and swears. We both take off running to head him off. Maybe the two of us will be able to take him on. Whatever he is.

He must sense us coming because he stops and faces our approach, lifting one hand and using magic to raise us both into the air. Power winds around my throat, and it takes everything in me to fight the instinct to drop my sword and claw at the invisible hands holding me off the ground.

Adrian struggles, and I see traces of magic shooting out from him as he fights with all he can to get free. It's not working. My lungs are starting to burn as they scream for oxygen. My vision gets blurry. Araina, I'm going to die, and Adrian's going to die. Then the village is going to fall. Risa, Gennet, Aster, Gwenyth, Ginger—they're all going to die because we failed. I try to call magic to my fingers, but nothing happens.

There's so much I wanted to say and do. Not enough time.

A plume of darkness erupts around me, and I imagine this is the moment I embrace the shadows and leave this world. But it isn't. The opposite happens. Creatures shriek and humans cry out, and something roars as I'm dropped to the ground. My vision is too blurry, but I see someone standing between us and the Dark Lord. Someone, shrouded in darkness and smoky shadows and green light, holds the line now.

I blink my eyes and take gasping breaths, desperately seeking relief from the stranglehold he had had on me. I see Adrian on the ground to my right, doing the same thing but looking a bit worse than I do, if that's possible. Though I can't see myself.

As my vision clears, the person standing before me becomes more apparent. Every hair on my body stands on end at the sight of pure power. Deep brown hair swirls around her, moved by an invisible breeze, while shadows spread from every part of her body toward the Dark Lord. His face pales, and the fear there is unmistakable.

Shadows strike out from her toward him, and he is the one on the defensive now. I press myself up to my hands and knees and quickly look around us at the chaos that arrived with her presence. A dragon makes quick work of the enemy, breathing out plumes of shadows that burn or suck the life out of any who stand in his way. I'm not sure which it is from this far. All I know is that he is leaving behind piles of corpses, both the monsters and the men who attacked us.

A cryarsh sweeps out and chases down every creature and enemy soldier running back into the trees. Screams and cries of anguish and pain are quickly silenced. My skin aches at the memory of one of those monsters attacking me in the woods when I was with Darci.

Darci, who now stands as the most powerful being I've ever seen, sends blast after blast of magic at the Dark Lord.

I crawl toward Adrian, still feeling too weak to stand. Adrian stares ahead at Darci, a mixture of awe and terror on his face. The sight of her stripped down, revealing herself, is stunning. The squeeze in my chest at what I thought we might have had is painful but makes me feel ridiculous. To think I had been falling for the Goddess of Death! A goddess for Araina's sake!

"Are you—-" I swallow, but I'm not sure it will help my voice much. "Are you injured?"

Adrian turns his gaze to me. "I'm not dead." His voice sounds as scratchy as mine.

I chuckle but wince. It hurts to laugh. "Well, I guess that's a good thing."

We both turn our heads back to the pandemonium of the battle—or what was a battle. The dragon is standing at the tree line with shadows twining around it. I wonder if the cryarsh here is Meiora. The Dark Lord vanished, and Darci (I still can't get my mind to think of her as Arawna) shakes her hands out before turning on her heels and heading toward the dragon.

It must be the same dragon I rode on with her. The beast stares at me with a look of knowing as if he remembers me, too, and he isn't sure he likes the memory. I cast my eyes away from him, only peeking briefly to see what Darci does.

She speaks to the creature, and soon he spreads his wings and takes flight. Every wingbeat sends shadows outward from his body.

The cryarsh remains, and one twist of Darci's wrist has the creature draping her like a cloak once again. It has to be Meiora. The familiarity is uncanny.

"Here," I press to my feet slowly and reach a hand down to Adrian. His hand is damp with sweat and blood but feels strong, not shaky. The relief I feel is an unexpected emotion.

Standing to my full height brings pain to my abdomen. The adrenaline is wearing off, and now my body feels the fatigue of battle and the injuries I incurred during it. Adrian wipes his brow before looking around us, taking in the tragic scene.

Too many bodies. The enemy and our men and women. Even a few civilians who didn't escape the onslaught in time. My stomach churns at the sight. In death, we are all the same. Companions on a journey ending with the grave and our return to the earth. How tragic that throughout this short life, we fight and look down on our fellow humans, selfishly wanting what isn't ours or demanding more than we ought to have when we could be sharing the bounty of these worlds. Grief is not a strong enough word for the emotions I'm feeling at the sight before me.

Adrian stands as solemn as I for a moment before walking to greet the Death Goddess. I follow because I can't not approach her. She draws me to herself like a moth to the flame.

"Are you both okay?" Her eyes betray a coldness inside her despite the warmth of her concern.

"As okay as we can be," Adrian responds. "I guess I should say thank you. If you hadn't come..." He doesn't finish the thought. Doesn't dwell on the implications of her absence.

"You couldn't have defeated him. He is too powerful for humans to destroy." Something dark passes across her face.

"What do you mean?" Answers. I need answers about who this enemy is.

She looks off toward the forest before scanning the area and absorbing the sight of death and injured beings around us. Several of our own are injured, and other people have come from the village to assist them.

"He is not a human. Why should he be defeated by humans?"

Cold dread builds in my chest.

"What is he, Darci? Come out and say it." There would be more bite in my voice if I had more energy.

"He is Khitaen."

Whatever I thought she was going to say, it wasn't that. Adrian and I attempted to take on the God of War and Peace. I'm not the only one shaken by the news.

"What... Why would he attack us?" Adrian rubs a hand under his chin before dragging it across his head. He winces, encountering an injury he forgot about.

"There's a lot you don't know about the gods and goddesses, Adrian."

Anger flares in my chest. Yeah, there's a lot we didn't know about her, and she's one of them.

"What does that mean about you, then, Darci? Or should I call you Arawna? Which name do you prefer to go by?"

She doesn't flinch, doesn't look offended. Her green eyes simply lock onto mine, and I feel my anger slip for a beat.

"The truth is hard to swallow, isn't it? When everything you thought about someone changes, it paints everything differently. It wasn't me who lied in the beginning. It wasn't me who was your enemy."

I turn away because I'm too angry to face what she's saying. Before I know it, I'm walking across the grass toward the town, coming upon a young captain, her cloak bearing the insignia in the top right corner of her rank.

"You." She looks up at me inquiringly. "We need to get the dead burned."

"What do you want us to do with the... with the others?"

The enemy. The ones who cost us lives—the ones who brought terror to our town, our world.

"Burn them, too. Burn them all." Her eyes widen in shock.

"Let us give them the dignity they didn't extend to us."

Resolve settles in her eyes, and she nods. I walk away toward the pub, toward anywhere Darci isn't. I don't care if I have to walk into the shadows to escape her.

But you can never escape death, can you?

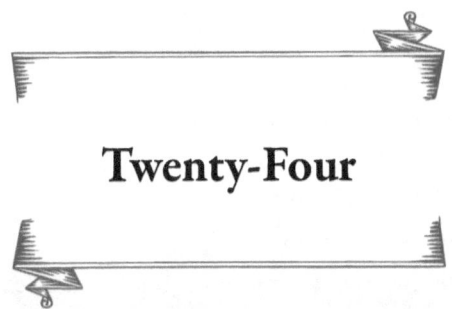

Twenty-Four

"The great uniter of man is the time limit we all face in the end."
—Milos the Wise,
Myzonian Scholar

Darci

Marcus doesn't look back. He continues with purpose, though a bit stiffly, toward the town's village center. I watch him for too long before I catch myself and draw my eyes back to Adrian. His eyes are darker than usual, but a rim of green still surrounds each iris. Concern and caution stare back at me.

"Why are the histories wrong? Who changed them?" He wants clarity. It may be time I give it to him. Now that he knows the truth about me, he might be more willing to listen to all of it.

"The gods and goddesses changed the histories, deceiving man into writing things that were not true. Most of the deceptions were subtle. Things you wouldn't notice changed unless you knew where to look. But over time, the longer a lie is passed down, the easier it is to believe it's the truth."

I rub my hands on my tunic and then reach up to feel the comfort of Meiora on my shoulders. The cryarsh slides down my arm and spreads across the space between Adrian and me. He extends his hand and welcomes the presence of the shadows.

"Hello, Meiora. Thank you for your help." A sad smile forms on his face. Too many people lost their lives today. He looks up at me.

"Why would they lie? Why change it in the first place?"

"I'm not sure you can understand the answer to that. It's... complicated."

He says nothing for a moment. He surveys the scene before us, his shoulders growing heavier as if the weight of the worlds rests there.

"Let me attend to your injured."

Surprise fills his eyes at my offer, but it's the least I can do to assist. He nods, and I move to the nearest soldier writhing on the ground.

Kneeling next to the young man, I send my magic into his body, assessing his injuries. They're not fatal, but they could become life-threatening if left unattended.

His breaths are ragged, and his hands grip his stomach as blood seeps from the wounds. I'm not one hundred percent certain that he's not holding his guts inside.

"Shhhh... It's okay. You're going to be okay."

His eyes open and lock onto mine. Pain etches his pale face. I press my hands onto his body, one hand on his chest, the other over top of his hands that clutch his stomach. Magic pours out of me, spreading throughout his battered body. Peace fills his eyes and rest. Within moments, he settles and removes his hands. I stand up and offer him a hand up before moving to the next one.

I continue like this, person after person. Some are already gone. Some are close to death. I give each of them the option of staying or going. Most choose to stay. A few decide to leave. The death monsters are gone. Every one of them was destroyed either by Marcus and his men or by Ryuzio and Meiora. A pang of sorrow twists my stomach at their loss. They abandoned me—their creator—in favor of following Khitaen and whatever plans he may have led them to believe were good.

Their death is their choice, but it is no less tragic.

"Darci?" The familiar voice sends shivers down my spine. Gennet, who I suspect was more aware of my identity than even I in the beginning, stands behind me now, waiting for a response.

I face her, masking the sorrow I feel with the face of a ruthless goddess. I cannot allow them to see such mercy from me for the monsters I created that attacked them.

"Child, there is another who is close to death. She is a villager who was attacked before help came." The tears in Gennet's eyes fill me with dread. Who is the one who has fallen?

I nod but remain silent, following close behind her toward the market center. We walk straight to a small house built next to the pub. I send shadows ahead of me to seek answers. Their response sends grief crashing over me.

I push past Gennet and step into the crowded house, wasting no time going to the back bedroom where I know I'll find her. Adrian and Marcus stand in the doorway, whispering. At my appearance, Marcus scowls but doesn't stop me from entering. Adrian offers a cautious smile.

Weeping fills the room. Gwenyth sits hunched over, holding her sister's hand and resting her forehead on the bed. Bloody bandages dot the floor like a bizarre form of art—a macabre painting of life and death fighting each other. Ginger's pale skin looks almost translucent. It's strange seeing the twins like this. One version is alive and well; the other version is hanging on to the tiniest thread of life. Her breathing is shallow and growing slower. Her injuries are extensive. It looks like one of the monsters found her first and feasted on her abdomen. She must have been searching for new ingredients for her experimental meals when they arrived.

I hurry to her side and press my hands onto her broken body. There isn't much life left in her. I rest one hand on her chest and my other hand on her bloody stomach. The blood is warm and sticky, but I don't mind. She winces at the pain and opens her eyes. Gwenyth looks up, red rimmed eyes puffy and worn.

"Darci?" Her voice is raspy, but I ignore her questioning eyes. Adrian comes up behind her and places a hand on her shoulder.

Ginger's eyes search the air above her, confused before she finds me. A sigh escapes her lips, more life-breath leaving her body. I smile reassuringly and send magic searching and mending throughout her body.

Her lips move, but no sound comes out. Gwenyth notices and leans forward desperately.

"What is it, Gin?"

But Ginger doesn't look for Gwenyth. She looks at me, communicating with me alone.

I lean forward to catch her words when she moves her lips again. Her voice is a little stronger this time, fighting to speak what her soul knows.

"It's... you..." Peace dawns in her eyes at the sight of me. A green glow spreads from my hands throughout her body. Her eyes are unafraid. We're old friends, meeting again.

"Shhh... you're okay." Through my magic, I know she hears the silent question I ask in her mind. The question of whether she wants to stay longer or go home.

Her eyes flicker in sorrow briefly. The peace there blinks out of them for a moment before seeping back in. She must sense her sister's grip on her hand on the other side of the bed. She shifts her head slightly toward Gwenyth. The movement isn't missed by her twin.

"Gin, I'm here. I'm here, and it's okay. You're going to be okay. You and me, right?" Tears stream down her cheeks. Pleading for life when her sister can so easily choose death.

I feel the turmoil inside of her—the longing to go home and find rest, but the other part sees her sister and wants to stay. They don't always get to choose, but I'm willing to give her the option this time around.

Ginger's eyes shift back to mine, and her breaths become more ragged.

"Gin! Please stay with me. Please don't leave me." Gwenyth turns her begging to me. "Please save her! Can you save her? Is that why you're here? There's something special about you, isn't there?" I want to spare her this sudden loss, but violence has stolen what should not have been taken this soon.

"I... want..." Ginger tries to speak. I call to Meiora, and instantly the cryarsh appears, draping itself over her body.

Her answer is clear. I nod and close my eyes as magic pours from me to her—life, not death.

Her breathing becomes more rhythmic and steadier. Her skin flushes pink with new life, and the wound on her stomach stitches itself back together. Most importantly, I pull back the death that was at her doorstep and draw it back into myself.

Life. She chooses the mortal world for now.

When I finish, I remove my hands and brush the hair back from Ginger's face. Her eyes are warm and awestruck. Gwenyth gasps at the transformation and throws herself sobbing onto her sister's body. Tears of joy. Tears of not being left alone. Adrian jerks his eyes up to me, stunned. I lay a hand on Gwenyth's shoulder and walk from the room.

Footsteps follow me out of the house. I know it's Marcus and Adrian, but I don't have the energy to fight with them right now. Fortunately for me, Risa bounds toward me with Aster trailing behind.

"Miss Arawna! Miss Arawna! You're here!" She doesn't hesitate as she launches herself into my arms. "Why do you have two names, Miss Arawna? Why did you say your name was Darci? Hmmm?"

I laugh, "Well, I didn't remember my other name. But I can see your magic is getting stronger if you know my real name."

She smiles, proud of her accomplishment. "I am! I'm getting really powerful. Almost as strong as you."

There is no such thing as too much joy when one encounters the innocence of children.

"Well, that's good. We need powerful little girls in all of the worlds."

"You should say you're sorry, Miss Arawna." The scolding expression on this small human's face makes me laugh again.

"Why? What did I do this time?" Aster and Adrian stand side by side—one of them more nervous than he should be that I am holding the child.

"I had to say sorry for calling you the dead woman, but that's what you are! I wasn't lying!"

"Risa!" Aster looks shocked. She looks at me, a tinge of fear in her eyes. "I am so sorry."

I shake my head. "Risa, you're right. You weren't lying. I'm not exactly dead, though, but..." I lean forward and whisper the next part. "I am the Goddess of Death after all."

Risa beams at me, and I set her down gently. Adrian and Aster share a brief look before Marcus's hand grabs my arm firmly and pulls me away from the market center.

"We need to talk."

Twenty-Five

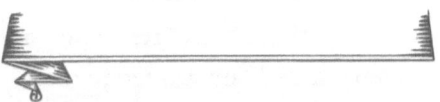

"Wonder is the natural state of the human."

—**Unknown**

Darci

Once upon a time, a spark of goodness came to life deep inside the heart of the cruel and relentless Goddess of Death. The spark grew and grew until her actions inspired her to create a world of goodness beyond the realms of these mortal lands. Then someone came along and smashed the little spark, and now it was dying a long, slow death, never to be revived.

At least that's what I tell myself as Marcus rudely drags me away from the market square. A few frightened faces avert their eyes quickly at the cold rage simmering under the high commander's skin and the lethal glare growing on my pale face. Adrian's quick footsteps trail behind us, and I can tell he is trying not to draw more attention, but it's inevitable. The Sovereign of their land is following their rather angry High Commander, and I have no doubt word has already spread about what I did in this place.

Curse the day I decided to be kind and gracious to these petulant humans.

When we've moved far enough down the path to where Adrian's beautiful house used to stand, I decide Marcus has had enough fun and send a striking shadow across my arm, stinging his hand. He hisses and releases me, staring at his palm. I roll my eyes. It didn't sting that bad.

He glares at me and shifts his weight forward, but Adrian grabs his shoulder and stops him. "Marcus, enough."

There is power in his voice—authority and confidence. He is unafraid of his commander and ultimately knows his friend will obey him. Marcus crosses his arms but never takes his eyes off me.

I brush my hands together like I'm removing the dirt from them, even though they aren't dirty. "You wanted to talk?"

If he wants to be mad, he can be, but I have done nothing to warrant this fiery rage he keeps sending my way.

"I want the truth. The complete truth. No more riddles or speaking in strange ways." He seethes, keeping his arms crossed.

"You don't want to understand the truth at all. Besides, you're not supposed to comprehend everything. You are mortal and will always be limited by your human mind."

"That's not an excuse!" Marcus shouts as Adrian places a calming hand on his friend's shoulder.

"Darci or Arawna..." Adrian scrunches his brow with indecision.

I hold my hand up to interrupt. "I am both of those names, but I prefer Darci. Don't feel like you must play a guessing game to figure out what to call me."

"Perhaps you would prefer if we just called you death?" The words bite, coming from Marcus.

I freeze, and Adrian's eyes widen.

"Marcus, step away," Adrian commands.

Marcus opens his mouth to protest, but Adrian's eyes leave no room for argument.

"Take a walk." Marcus spins on his heel and heads farther down the road away from town. Adrian watches him leave for a few moments before he faces me again.

"He forgets who you are." Is that fear in Adrian's eyes? Now that he knows the truth, is he afraid of the power I have?

"It's okay. I don't make it a habit to smite people for rudeness."

"I don't... I don't know how to be around you." He looks around but won't make eye contact.

"I'm still me, Adrian. There were forces you can't understand that stole my memories away. It's not for you to know these things."

Finally, he makes eye contact. "Can you answer one thing for me then?"

I raise my eyebrows but wait for him to continue.

"Why are we connected? Why do I have magic that looks like yours?"

I guess we are having this conversation today. I thought he might avoid it and ask about Khitaen and the reason for his attack on Zaiven. But the turmoil I see in Adrian's eyes, the uncertainty about himself and his identity, sparks the tiny ember of compassion into a more vibrant flame.

"Many years ago, your father sought me out."

His eyes widen in surprise, his mouth opening slightly. I continue before he starts asking more questions than he can have answers to.

"He sought me because he wanted power and life everlasting. He was dying, and you were only a baby. He didn't ask for himself to be healed, but rather for you to be given power and might beyond anything the mortals of this world are granted. He wanted to train you up to be as ruthless and vile as him. He longed to rule all the worlds and not only Myzonia. He believed the only way to make that possible was to imbue you with power from the most powerful of the divine."

Adrian's jaw tightens. His father was ruthless, a cruel man, and Adrian was right to overthrow him. It doesn't make the truth of hearing it confirmed any easier to swallow.

"We made a bargain. I would give some of my power to the infant son still on his mother's breast and a portion of the king's soul. He would be granted years of life to live and train you in the ways he desired, and you would become the most powerful sovereign any of the realms had seen."

"What did you get out of the deal? Why would you help him?" Anger flares in his eyes.

"I had lived through a war with my fellow divine and had seen the destruction they brought. They had made me out to be a monster. When my sister, Araina, saw how the mortals reacted to me—how they treated me with respect and adoration instead of the fear she believed they should—she became jealous. That is what spurred the Thousand Years War. I was tired of not belonging. I was tired of people being afraid of me because of lies woven by others."

I pause and turn to face the forest, taking a moment to listen to the sounds of life around me.

"The problem is, they painted me as a god of death, when in fact, I am the god of life too. Without me, they would not rule. I grant safe passage to the souls of men that they might find rest. I don't let all of them in. Some are too cruel, too broken by lies to find rest. But I wish I could give it to them, nonetheless." I pause.

"This still doesn't explain what you got out of the deal with my father." He crosses his arms and turns to stand shoulder to shoulder with me, both of us facing the forest known for its darkness and monsters.

"Your father reminded me far too much of the corrupt nature of my sister. He thought only darkness resided in me. He didn't realize there was also good. Instead of giving you a piece of his soul, I gave you a part of mine. I gave you the best part of me. Your gift of creation comes from me. Your kindness and gentleness also come from me, fostered by Gennet."

He drops his arms to his sides, and I can feel his gaze on me.

"I was never granted a world of my own to rule and live in. Never fully belonging. Always wandering and unwanted thanks to Araina."

Footsteps crunch on the dirt and snow mixed on the road. I don't have to look to know it is Marcus.

"In exchange for my gift, I took the northern portion of your kingdom and created a new and separate world out of it. It took everything in me to create Oria. Years went by as every drop of magic was drained from my body and into the earth. He was more than happy to let go of it. He thought he was going to be able to live on through you. He didn't realize that you would be good and betray him in the end. That your magic would grow, and you would destroy him and his beliefs. He died surprised and angry, and I could no longer grant him rest."

"Why did you forget who you were?"

"I found love, Adrian. I found one who cherished me, and we built a beautiful home together. But the gods and goddesses found out what I had done. They invaded Oria. They stole my children and my husband, and in my pursuit of them, I bled. My blood mingled with the earth of my created world. Khitaen's arrival brought magic into the world I made.

"The magic within me awoke, and I knew then what Khitaen wanted. He wanted my magic—my power. If he took it, he would be invincible, and he would become a destroyer of worlds. A ruthless tyrant seeking only what benefited him. He would make your father look like he was the epitome of goodness. I did the only thing I could."

I stop, the words a painful memory I don't want to release. Adrian waits, but I see him shift his weight—his body betraying him.

"I released all my magic outward. Khitaen escaped unscathed, of course, but everything else was turned to bone and ash. The result of my actions caused a rift in my mind. One I couldn't mend without magic. I knew I had a husband and sons, but I had forgotten their names. Losing them destroyed that part of me. My magic was spent, and I was left alone again."

"You killed them."

I turn to face Marcus, losing myself for a moment in his deep blue eyes. They are hard, jaded by all he's learned—a return to how he used to look at me.

"Yes." One word. One confirmation, and I have slipped back into the role of monster permanently.

"What am I?"

I drag my eyes away from Marcus to face Adrian.

"Am I a monster? Am I becoming the shadows we have feared?"

"You could never be a monster, Adrian. But I may have use for your gifts yet."

"What's that supposed to mean? You aren't going to do anything to him. He's not yours to use." Marcus's hands are fists, but they don't hide the magic building on them.

"I don't intend for anything bad to happen to him, Marcus." I focus on Adrian. "War is coming. I will not stand by and let Araina continue to deceive. Khitaen wants to rule all the worlds, and my sister has failed to check him. He can't be allowed to destroy everything good. I will not allow her to lock me away anymore."

"You plan to go to war?" Marcus crosses his arms.

"Yes. Do you want unexpected attacks by him whenever he pleases?"

Adrian speaks up, "Why did you do it? Why did you give me magic and do all of this?"

I cross my arms and turn back toward the forest. Shadows slither around the trees and through the branches. Cryarsh are waiting for me—waiting for my command.

"It is not for you to know the secrets of the gods. I cannot tell you anything other than to prepare."

Marcus glowers at me. "Prepare for a war we want no part in."

"Prepare to defend your world, Marcus. Wars are bloody affairs, as I'm sure you are aware."

I face Adrian again. "Don't be afraid of who you are. Don't be afraid of the magic coursing through your veins. It is a gift, and you will need it one day soon."

I can't tell him more. I can't reveal everything, or he may not understand enough to agree. It's the only way to end this once and for all. To end the rule of the ruthless and open the door to all the possibilities of a new world.

I walk toward the forest, toward the shadows and my army.

"Where are you going?" Marcus yells.

I keep going. "Ready your army, Marcus. I have a feeling Araina is going to bring the war to Myzonia."

As I slip into the shadows, a smile graces my mouth. It'll all be over soon. A flick of my wrist and I've shifted to the avgrunn. Time to return to Oria.

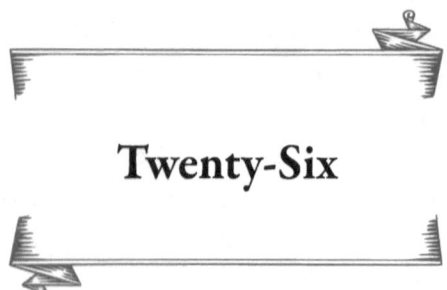

Twenty-Six

"In the final battle for the worlds, the gods and goddesses vanquished the Death God into obscurity. No longer allowed to roam freely. No longer allowed to be recognized by the mortals."
— *The Gods and Goddesses of Old,*
Tract 698

Marcus

"That's it? That's all? She shows up and saves us, only to leave moments later." I pace like a trapped animal, back and forth.

"She gave us answers. We're more prepared than we were before," Adrian reasons.

"We don't know what she plans, though. Something tells me we aren't going to come out on top by the end of all of this. A war with the gods and goddesses? How is that supposed to end other than in tragedy?"

I can't take this. These half answers are going to be the death of me. I heard plenty of what Darci told Adrian, and none of it sounded good.

"We will do what we must do. I... I can fight too. I feel stronger, more powerful than I ever have. I don't understand it, but I think that the magic she gave me is affecting me more now."

I stop and face my friend. My friend who has a piece of the soul of the Goddess of Death. My friend whose magic is changing to be more like hers. How is this going to work?

"Do you feel like you have control of it?" Memories of our discoveries at the temple of Markyr haunt me.

Adrian thinks for a moment before answering. "Yes. I didn't at first, but I stopped being afraid of it." He looks at his hands before speaking again. "She told me not to be afraid of it after all."

Something about his gaze bothers me—something he hasn't told me yet. I clench my fists and feel a spark of magic dance across my hands.

"Before the house was destroyed, when I returned to get a few things before traveling to Rizyrk, she was there. Everyone was gone, and I walked in the front door to find her standing in the foyer, waiting for me."

Anger flares in my chest. "Why didn't you tell me?"

"Why would I? I'm not afraid of her, and she didn't pose any threat to me."

I throw my arms up. "Oh yes, let's trust the Goddess of Death to be the safest deity to be around."

"Marcus, I'm connected to her. In a far more intimate way than I could have imagined. I still don't understand her purpose, her intention behind all of this, but it's true, nonetheless." He pauses and stares at me thoughtfully for a moment. "You saw the goodness in her once."

"The goodness in a lie? She deceived us." Why can't I make him understand this? How has she buried her talons into him so deeply?

"I don't think you really believe that. She says she doesn't remember, and I am inclined to trust her. A part of me calls out to her. We need to listen to what she said."

"If what she says is true, how can we hope to battle an army raised by the God of War and Peace? How can we survive a war brought to us by Araina!? It's hopeless, Adrian. Who can stand against them?"

I face the forest and try my best to forget every moment I spent with Darci in it. The journey to the temple, hiding in the cave, her presence around me felt like home.

Home. She felt like home and safety, and goodness all rolled into one body. I want to deny what Adrian is saying—that we don't have to be afraid of her, but he's right. I've been cautious around her, worried she was a great enemy we didn't understand. Instead, she has been the peace in the worlds I didn't know we needed. We didn't need to fear her—to fear death—because she was making a way for goodness to shine through amid great evil. Death was like an old friend, not an enemy. Not a monster.

Adrian remains quiet, waiting for my heart and mind to agree for once. He's always been better at trusting the unknown between the two of us.

"Alright." I feel his gaze on my face, but I keep my eyes on the trees.

Nodding, Adrian whispers, "We're going to need to assemble our army."

"The problem is we don't know where Khitaen will attack next. He could hit any number of small villages, and we wouldn't know it happened until it was too late."

Adrian's jaw tightens, and I know he's reliving the losses we endured today, the lives that were extinguished too early. I'm pondering our dilemma when I remember something Darci had said.

"She told us that Khitaen wants her power. He might be after yours, too. I don't think he'll take out tiny villages. It would serve no purpose other than inciting terror. Which might be exactly what he's going for. But..."

Adrian interrupts. "But it would be a waste of resources. He's going to know Darci intends to come to our aid. If that's the case, he'll need a vast army to stand against her power."

"And a vast army needs space to fight."

We stare at each other, thinking the same thing. The Plain of Okira stands between Zaiven and Rizyrk. It's the perfect location for an army to stage a battle. Myzonia has always been full of magic and power. If this world were to fall, the power Khitaen could possess would be more than enough to empower him for domination of all other worlds.

"He's going to make his stand on the Okira," Adrian whispers.

Small huts and farms are spread throughout the Plain, providing food and resources to the capital and Zaiven. Homes with people in them who will be caught in the crossfire.

"We have to evacuate the Plain." Blue magic sparks at my fingers again.

"We may not have enough time." Adrian protests.

"We'll do it anyway. I'll gather the armies together. We're going to need every able-bodied soldier and anyone else willing to carry a sword. You need to spread the word to the farms. You said your magic is feeling more powerful. You can shift faster than any of us."

Determination fills the Sovereign's eyes. "Okay. I'll begin evacuations. I'll send as many to the capital as possible, but some of the farms and homes closer to Zaiven should come here. Prepare the armies, friend. Let's finish what was started long ago."

"For all worlds," I speak.

"For all worlds," Adrian confirms.

IN THE BLINK OF AN eye, Adrian vanishes. I only pray we will have enough time to clear the way for the battle. I jog down the road toward the village, preferring to conserve my magic until I have no choice but to use it.

As I near the market, I spot Aella stepping out of the pub. Perfect timing. She sees me coming and quickens her pace to meet me in the center.

"Commander, I'm sorry I wasn't here to assist in the battle."

I hold up a hand to stop her. "No apologies. No one could have known that was coming. We have more important things to worry about now."

She quirks an eyebrow but waits for me to continue.

"We have reason to believe a war is coming to Myzonia. Specifically, to the Plain of Okira." Her eyes widen, but I press on. We don't have time for questions. "The Sovereign is working to evacuate the homes and farms in the Plain. Send your fastest shifters to assist him. We also need to assemble the entirety of our army. Gather the other captains and send word that anyone strong enough and willing enough to fight should report for duty. We'll gather two-thirds of the army at Rizryk and the rest here."

"Sir, who are we fighting? Who would require the entirety of our forces?"

I debate telling her, but I can't keep this a secret. The men and women willing to fight should know what they will be standing against.

"A god, Aella. We go to face a god."

Her pale skin somehow gets paler as the blood drains from her face. I understand the feeling.

She nods and spins away to fulfill my orders. I march into the pub in search of Gennet. She sits in the back corner with Aster and Risa, smiling though it's more somber than usual. Her eyes dart up to my face as I approach, and concern etches into her features.

"Gennet, I need to speak with you."

She nods and slowly rises, whispering something to Risa before following me to the other side of the pub, void of any customers.

"What is it, faolàn? What has happened?"

"Adrian and I have it on good authority that a god is about to wage war in Myzonia."

Her eyebrows shoot up toward her hairline. "On whose authority do you know this?"

"I think you already know the answer to that. You know who she is." I keep my voice low, desperate not to frighten anyone with news of death.

"Why does she believe he is coming to start a war? Why would Araina allow it?"

I didn't think to ask that. To question why Araina would allow him to destroy these mortal lives in a bid for all-consuming power. Surely, she would not want to see innocent people destroyed.

"I don't know, but he is the one who attacked us here. I think he'll come back, and he'll come with far more soldiers this time around."

She nods and glances over my shoulder toward the table where Risa and Aster sit.

"What do you need us to do, faolàn?"

"Do you think Risa has seen anything?"

She purses her lips, thinking. "I'm not sure. It would be hard for one so small to grasp the severity of war."

"Okay, if she does see anything, I need you to get word to me as soon as possible. And I need you to take them and leave. Go to the temple of Markyr. Anywhere but here."

Her eyes darken, but I interrupt her. "Please, Gennet. Keep them safe. If you're at the temple, ask for Sister Cleo. I'd love to ask her a few more questions."

"Faolàn, she will come with retribution, and many will fall because of her. The worlds might even fall, but it is not for us to understand the minds of gods."

I say nothing to this because I fear she's telling the truth. Death is coming for Myzonia. We'll either stand to face it, or we will all fall together in the name of all that is good.

Twenty-Seven

"In the face of great adversity, one discovers the depths of their devotion."

—From the Annals of Markyr

Adrian

I wasted no time shifting to the Plain. I probably should have rested or even waited for other shifters to join me, but I couldn't stand the idea of failing to evacuate everyone. It isn't an option. If Marcus's thoughts on the coming battle are true, then we don't have time to waste.

My mind scatters in the direction of every little village around my kingdom. Villages like Zaiven dot the land around the capital. All I can envision is Khitaen attacking them the same way. There is no room for error now.

The Plain of Okira stretches out in every direction as far as the eye can see. To the south of it is Zaiven. To the north is Rizyrk. Two tiny villages are nestled near the heart of the Plain, but mostly it is farmland and the occasional house. Usually, those who prefer a very quiet existence, living completely off the land, occupy the space.

The challenge is they are all spread far apart, making it difficult to spread news from person to person—farm to farm. Soft rolling hills spread before me, covered in a light coating of snow. The growth of the previous summer pops up throughout the area. In the summer, this Plain is covered in flowers and produce. Wild fruit sprouts wherever it pleases, the earth giving much of itself for the benefit of man. Very few trees grow, offering little protection against the elements and enemies.

My skin grows cold at the thought of war, but more so at the thought of what Darci revealed. The truth of where my magic came from, of how I'm connected to her, still has my mind reeling. How is it possible she has known me since I was born? How will this impact me long-term to carry a piece of the Goddess of Death in my body?

I pause to take a breath and a sip of water from my pouch. I need to focus. I can't let my mind run away with me—not when a god is coming for us. As I sip one more mouthful of water, the ground beneath my feet begins to shake. *What the...?*

The earth rolls enough to make me feel unsteady for a moment. Pheasants cry as they take to the air, and a general sense of unsettledness disturbs me. Khitaen can't be coming now, can he? Panic grows in my chest, but as quickly as the earthquake started, it stops.

It's time to get moving.

I see a home in the distance. With the house in sight, I shift to arrive there quickly.

Banging on the door, I call out. "Hello! I mean you no harm."

Shuffling reaches my ears, and I step back to give the door some space. Whoever approaches sounds tentative, unsure of the stranger at their door. It creaks open, and a dark pair of eyes set in a weathered pale face peek out.

"Hello, I am not sure you know who I am."

The eyes scan my face for a moment before widening. Suddenly, the door swings open, and an old man bows.

"I'm sorry, Your Majesty. I didn't expect...uh...you."

I smile. "No apologies necessary. I'm sure you don't wish to be bothered, but I need you to take what you need and flee the Plain."

He frowns and looks behind him to an old woman I didn't know was standing there. "We have always worked this land. My family has owned this house for three generations. I have tried to bring in the correct portions for tax every year."

Araina, he thinks I'm evicting him for no reason. "No, sir, this isn't about that. We have reason to believe war is coming, and the enemy is planning to attack on the Plain."

Shock splashes across his face. "War." He breathes the word like it's a curse.

I nod, "Yes, war. Zaiven was attacked most recently. I know it's the closest village to you here, and I believe it will be safe since we have defended it once already."

"O—okay. I—I suppose—we must—-" The poor man is going into shock.

"Dear, what is it?" The woman's frail hand rests on her husband's shoulder. The touch alone seems to bring him back to himself.

"It's the Sovereign, love."

She gasps and bows awkwardly, her old bones not quite cooperating. How will this old couple manage the walk to one of the villages? There's no evidence of a horse or oxen. They'll never make it in time.

"Ma'am, I was telling your husband you need to flee to Zaiven. War is coming." The woman's eyes harden with determination. She doesn't doubt me. Instead, she seems to be the rock on which this couple stands.

"Alright, dear, you heard the Sovereign. Let's gather our things." She tugs him gently inside.

"Please hurry. Do not carry more than you absolutely need." I dread this task I'm giving them. This impossible task of traveling before a god comes for blood.

"If you encounter anyone on your travels, tell them too. I'm going to travel as quickly as I can to each settlement. Can you point me in the direction of your nearest neighbor?"

The old man blinks before pointing to the east. His wife speaks up, "They are about a half day's journey in that direction."

"Thank you." It's the perfect amount of information. I turn and shift to the next house.

This pattern continues. House after house, farm after farm. I arrive, knock, and warn people to leave. I encountered an old hermit who slammed the door in my face and ignored my warnings, but I couldn't waste time begging him to flee. Several places were individual homes, but a few were family groups. People who had settled near each other and grew their families on the same land. Not enough to be a village, but safer than true isolation.

When I arrived at the last location, two shifters arrived, sent by Aella. Thank goodness, because I was growing weary traveling so much. My magic may have felt boundless, but it wasn't.

I hope I will have enough to stand in battle.

I press on anyway and shift to the next home. I sent the other shifters to the two villages. News is spreading, though we've only made it halfway across the Plain.

My stomach protests its neglect, and I finished my water a few hours ago. I sway on my feet as I take in my surroundings. I lift my foot to step toward the tiny cabin with warm lights glowing, and smoke drifting from the chimney. My skin is damp with sweat despite the cold from all the magic I've been using.

I stumble when I plant my foot and collapse to the ground, grunting when I land hard on my shoulder. I'm spent. All the determination in all the worlds will not fill me with enough energy to crawl, let alone walk. The sun vanishes below the horizon, and as darkness descends, the shadows dotting my vision threaten to drag me into oblivion.

I blink, trying to clear my eyes, but my head is getting fuzzy. When I open my eyes again, a figure walks quickly toward me, light on her feet. Her white cloak blows behind her in the cold breeze. I think I recognize her, but as she steps into view, my mind fogs over, and only shadows greet me.

THE FOREST IS DARK and quiet. A quiet that comes only from death. I'm standing here staring into the shadows, expecting to see someone, but no one is there. At least no one is there I can see. I feel them, though. The presence of a being both powerful and dangerous.

Whispers scatter across the tree tops and descend around me in languages I don't understand, but familiar nonetheless. I know this place. I've been here before. A piece of me calls out to the darkness around me.

No moon paints the landscape in blue. I'm not even sure how I can see at all, but the darkness isn't normal.

Something is wrong with this place.

A crack from a broken stick resonates through the air around me. I whirl around to face whoever stepped on it, but when I turn, the forest is gone. The trees have vanished, as if they never were. Mountains stand in the distance and the night has turned into day. Something is writhing along the ground in the distance. A black body moving forward and side to side, like shadows given form. Like cryarsh.

But it's not cryarsh. It's something darker. I move toward the shadows, and I must be dreaming because I'm moving fast. The ground flies beneath my feet. The shadows are dragons. Thousands upon thousands of dragons disrupt the land. Snow falls heavily, turning the world white; the dragons create a dramatic contrast in this blindingly bright landscape.

Someone touches my shoulder, and I turn my head to face them, only to find myself on an expanse of rolling hills lightly painted in snow. The Plain of Okira—it must be. Only the Plain is now covered in monsters. Abominations created by someone who wants to destroy all that is good. The monsters reach for me. Claws slash across my back.

Screams and cries of death and agony fill the air. Blood taints the purity of the snow.

I collapse into the slush and blood, crying out in pain. The thread of my life mingling with the thousands of others who have fallen. A figure, dark and ominous, stands near me. It looks like someone I know. It looks like Darci. Terror grips my heart, but the life seeps from my body.

She stands there in full armor, covered in shadows and blood, holding a black sword to the side. She attacked me. I... I think she killed me. My mind grows confused. The screams never stop, though they get muffled. Am I underwater? I force my eyes open to see her. To see Death standing over me with a sword in her hand. She raises the sword with both hands, gripping it, the point aiming for my heart.

I can't stop it. I can't stop Death. It's come for me after all.

She plunges the sword downward.

MY EYES FLY OPEN, AND I gasp, sitting straight up in bed. Wait. How did I end up in bed? I glance around, seeking answers for how I ended up here when I remember I had seen someone approach me before I passed out. A woman dressed in white. The same figure stands with her back to me, staring out the window as fresh snow falls on the ground.

I swing my legs over the side of the bed and move to stand, unsure if I can. My body is still drained.

"I wouldn't do that if I were you, Your Majesty."

I know that voice. I push to my feet and immediately regret it, feeling my legs shake with the effort. I fall back to sitting on the bed with a grunt.

"I told you not to do that." She faces me, and I find the blue of her eyes to be as haunting as they were when I first met her. *Sister Cleo.*

"What are you doing out here?"

"I live out here. For now, at least." She tilts her head and stares at me for a moment before she steps to the fire and uses a cloth to pull a pot off the coals. The smell of something savory cooking wafts in my direction, and my mouth waters.

"Why aren't you at the temple?" I don't understand it, but her presence here, on the Plain of Okira, feels wrong, misplaced even.

"The temple is not the same as it used to be. Nothing is the same anymore. It is...changing."

What in all of Myzonia is she talking about? She ladles out what looks to be soup into a bowl and carries it carefully toward me along with a cup of water. I want to question her further, but my baser needs are demanding attention. I accept the food and can't restrain myself any longer. The first bite of soup tips me over the edge, and my hunger consumes me.

I can't think about anything other than refreshing my energy stores. When I finish the first bowl of soup, Cleo takes it to refill. It's not until I finish three cups of water and two bowls of soup that I can think clearly. I feel refreshed. Magic thrums awake under my skin.

"I'm surprised you didn't wear out sooner than you did with how much you shifted today."

I look at her, surprised at what she knows, though I probably shouldn't be. She always seems to know a lot more than she lets on.

"Yeah, well, I didn't have a lot of time to waste."

She smiles softly, a sadness about her that feels odd. She opens her mouth to speak, but instead, she remains quiet as she walks toward the fire again. I take another sip of water before asking her the same question again.

"Why aren't you at the temple?" She stiffens for a moment but forces her shoulders to loosen. "Don't tell me the same lie you did before. Or at least don't speak in riddles again. I can't handle much more of this constant confusion."

She faces me, and I think, for once, maybe someone will be forthright immediately. She draws in a slow, deep breath like she's preparing to give me bad news. Maybe she is.

"I'm not really a priestess in the temple of Markyr."

I furrow my brow. "What do you mean? Marcus said he and Darci saw you there when they traveled weeks ago."

"I was there, but I am not normally a priestess in that temple. I serve another, one who is very interested in the things of this world. In the happenings that are occurring in all the worlds."

Her icy blue eyes pierce my very core.

"Who? Who do you work for?" Frustration bubbles beneath my calm façade.

"I serve Luna, Goddess of Wind and Sky."

Luna. Another goddess dipping her fingers into the water of our worlds and the conflicts we are facing. My face must betray me.

"Yes, another goddess. This one does not have ill intentions toward your world, though."

"What does she want then?"

"She wants only to ensure Arawna does not destroy the order of everything."

That seems intense. The Darci I have seen multiple times doesn't seem set on destruction.

"You knew who she was at the temple." Cleo nods. I close my eyes and rub my forehead with my hand, willing the headache forming there to go away.

"You said she wants to destroy the order of everything. What exactly does that mean?"

Cleo picks up a whistling kettle off the stones next to the fire and prepares two small cups of what looks like tea. She speaks as she brings me one of them.

"The order of the worlds. The way they were created and upheld. Her role in them as the Goddess of Death was disrupted when she decided to bargain with a mortal king in exchange for land to create her own world."

I blow on the hot tea before trying a sip. Still too hot.

"You're referring to the bargain she made with my father for Oria. What was disrupted?"

"Every world needs a god or goddess to guard it and keep the balance of magic in place. Without one, the worlds start to crumble. The magic is broken from its source, and chaos resumes. Arawna was never supposed to rule one world. She was given all the worlds to shepherd. Her magic works to create peace and comfort for the mortals within. She lost sight of that. Unfortunately, so did the other deities."

"She told me all she wanted was to belong somewhere. To love. Was that all a lie?"

"No, she *did* want those things. Luna regretted her actions and her part in the deception that came with Araina's efforts to distort the truth about Arawna. I think Arawna wanted only to be known and remembered. Her name whispered with adoration and reverence instead of fear and sorrow."

"But it is."

Cleo tilts her head at me. "What makes you say that?"

"We whisper words to our dying and dead, prayers for them to go to Arawnia. Never once have we feared that place. It has always been viewed as beautiful, as a paradise."

She nods her head slowly. "Yes, but she was replaced in the histories and called a god. It broke something in her to be rejected by time. To be rejected by those who were her kin."

The wind howls outside the little house. I've never heard of a storm this fierce hitting my kingdom. The sense of wrongness grows in my chest. I feel strong enough to rise now and make my way to the tiny window by the door. Snow smothers the world in white outside. It's piling up quickly next to the house as far as I can tell.

"This isn't normal, Your Majesty." I jerk my head toward her. Her unwavering gaze sends chills up my spine.

"What is wrong? Why is it like this?"

"The world is losing its connection to magic."

"What? That's not possible."

She crosses her arms. "Why isn't it? I told you every world needs a god or goddess to shepherd it."

A heavy weight settles in my stomach. "Who? Who is Myzonia's god?"

"You should be asking who *was* Myzonia's god."

"The divine cannot die. Who could possibly kill one?" I'm feeling panicky now. Frantic even. Everything is more dire than I could have imagined.

"You're right to a degree. No one can kill one of the divine. Except for one other. A fail-safe was put in at the beginning of time. A protection in case any god or goddess became too proud. Too power hungry."

I don't know why, but a clarity comes over me that I didn't have before. Arawna with all her plans. Arawna, with all her desires for vengeance. Arawna—the Goddess of Death itself. Death and life.

"Darci."

Cleo might nod, or I may have imagined it. My skin feels too tight, the room too small.

"Darci can kill one of the divine."

"Yes."

"She killed Myzonia's god."

"Yes." Her eyes bore into me, willing me to understand who.

Then, I realize who the god of Myzonia is. She mentioned that the temple of Markyr wasn't the same.

"Oh gods, she killed Markyr." *She killed Markyr!* The God of Fire and Ice. That's why this storm feels wrong. That's why the earth has been shaking. If there is no god to protect the world, the world can't continue to exist.

True terror suffocates me now.

"Yes, she did. The world is already feeling the consequences of it."

The war with Khitaen is the least of our problems. "What do we need to do? What is Darci planning?" I still struggle to call her by her real name.

"She cannot be allowed to kill Khitaen. If she does and there is no one to take his place, his world will fall too. And she cannot be allowed to die; for the world she created, Oria, will cease to exist if she is gone as well."

"She can't die, though. No one else could kill her." I'm pleading now. Begging for something to go right.

"She cannot be allowed to destroy herself."

I cover my face with my hands, my mind reeling and searching for a solution. A problem to solve. A political ally to make. But this isn't a war between men. This is a war between the divine.

"I had a vision. A dream."

"I know."

I narrow my eyes at her, but I don't want to know. "Will it happen?"

She sighs and sips her tea. Mine sits forgotten. "I don't know. It might. It might not. Only you can choose your fate."

I face the window again and the broken world out there. How will I fix this? I don't know, but I need to make sure the rest of the Plain is evacuated.

Destruction is coming sooner than I thought.

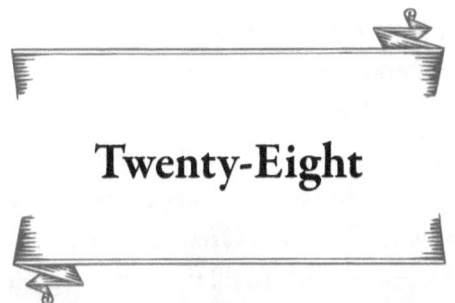

Twenty-Eight

"When faced with life or death, the mortal must always choose for himself."

—Unknown

Darci

The vastness of my army fills me with excitement. I shouldn't be thrilled about flying into battle with a fellow god, but I can't deny that I am. Ryuzio pushes his big head into my hand.

"I know. It's almost time. Myzonia is trembling because of Markyr's absence. Khitaen will make his move soon."

A plume of shadows escapes his great nostrils. Meiora twines around my legs, a constant contact, keeping me grounded in the here and now. I stroll through the rows and rows of other black dragons. My magic is pulled thin because of their existence, but they will be far more effective in their attack than I alone. There aren't as many cryarsh as dragons. I could create more, but I don't want to risk weakening myself unnecessarily.

I love these creatures, and I sustain all of them with my magic and my lifeforce. They need nothing to drink, nothing to eat. They are powerful beyond mortal capabilities and are fiercely loyal to me. Unlike the monsters I created millennia ago. The ones that betrayed me and followed Khitaen's false promises.

I pass dragon after dragon, marveling at the beauty of the creatures, but I also feel a tinge of sadness at what they will lose. If

Araina joins Khitaen on the battlefield, many of these will perish. Her light magic is powerful, and it is not easily stopped by darkness.

When I reach the base of the mountain, I pause and scan the area before moving again. This valley is shielded from most eyes, but the sovereign of Novundo has been getting bolder in his movements. It is my one regret when I created Oria—allowing the void to remain where leadership was needed. To fill the vacuum, a wicked man came to power by force and bloodshed. He doesn't care about the world he rules. He seeks only to obtain more power, more prestige.

I failed them by allowing him to rule, but I wasn't thinking about anyone but myself. A selfish act to begin a world. A selfish one to end it, too.

There is no sign of soldiers. None of my dragons or cryarsh have noticed any disturbances either. To be safe, I twist my wrist toward the nearest dragon, watching as it takes flight amidst shadows. I wait a few minutes and feel the answer through our bond. No one is there. No one is coming.

I face the mountain again and follow the base eastward until a narrow crevice appears in the rock—an opening easily missed if you aren't sliding your fingers across the surface of the mountain. I touch the crack, and a pulse of green magic spreads outward from my hand. A deep rumbling echoes through the snowy valley as the mountain opens before me. Wasting no more time, I step into the darkness of its belly and follow the narrow path into the heart of the shadows. The darkness is not dark to me.

When I reach the core of the mountain, my heart beats louder—my breaths coming faster. A pool of swirling shadows with onyx stones around its mouth rests in the center of the cavern. I walk straight to the edge of the pool, squatting to bring my fingers skimming across the top of the strange mixture. Velvety darkness reaches up toward me in response.

Tears stain my face. A sorrow deep and wide and all-consuming swells within my chest, threatening to overcome me. I press against it, but I don't resist entirely. I let the pain wash over my senses until it withdraws.

I have sustained this world for years, allowing my magic to be buried within its very soil, deep within the bowels of the earth. Now, the magic is awake and pulsing throughout the land, stirring in the hearts and souls of mortals throughout the world. Dangerous and beautiful all at once.

"I'm sorry for the mess this has become." I choke the words out. Pausing to clear my throat, I continue.

"There was so much I thought I would be. So much I thought I would do. The worlds are falling, but justice requires it. I cannot allow them to remain the way they are. I should have let go of the anger before it became all that I am. I can't remember what it's like not to be so angry. I should have held tightly to love, to peace, to goodness."

I stop, swallowing past the lump in my throat. The emotions of the moment threaten to silence me further. I refuse to bow to them.

"You were made for more than what you became. I'm changing it all."

I whisper more words, but I can't raise my voice louder than the sound of my breath slipping past my lips. It's okay. They know.

The ache in my chest will be with me until the end, but if I am not the keeper of endings, who is? Closing my eyes, I brush my fingers across the pool of shadows once more, feeling the tendrils of darkness reaching up to meet me.

Traveling through the darkness, the call to return to my house beckons. Araina has come.

I SMELL HER BEFORE I see her. The house is filled with the perfume of flowers. It's lovely and a little bit nauseating.

"I see you still have a fondness for lilacs, sister." I hang my cloak on the hook by the door and slip my feet out of my wet boots.

"I see you still have a fondness for isolation and dramatic effects." Her snide tone tells me she's in a fighting mood. I smile. It's my favorite mood to find her in. I glide into the main room with a fire roaring in the hearth and my sister lounging like a queen on my ratty old sofa.

"What can I do for you, Araina?" She picks at a nail for a moment before raising her eyes to meet mine.

"What do you have planned that you aren't telling me about?"

I cross my arms, defiant to the end. "You should be asking why Khitaen attacked an innocent village full of women and children." She opens her mouth to respond, but I hold a finger up to silence her. "And—this was the second attack he orchestrated. He destroyed the home of the sovereign of Myzonia there as well."

She rises to her feet, elegant and regal as always.

"I did not sanction his attack, nor did I approve of it."

"You weren't there to stop it either." I stride to the fire, holding my hands out to the flames to warm them. "I thought after I brought him to you the first time, you would put an end to his outrageous plans, but I guess you are not as powerful as you think you are."

"Perhaps he is not the only one who has outrageous plans, Arawna." I cringe inwardly at the name from my sister's lips, but I maintain outward composure.

"Sister, I have no plans. I am merely doing my job. The task I was given to do."

"You are too involved in the worlds of man." She chides.

"And you are too negligent!" I snap. "You who can sit in your temple and hide away while the world worships at your feet. Every day, mortals die, and I am the one who gathers them in. I was always meant to be involved in their worlds!"

"You were given a purpose, but you were not permitted to be with them. To take on their form. To love them in a way meant only for them." Every word, a knife stabbed into my chest.

A shadow slides across the window outside. A serpentine movement I recognize but want to deny seeing. My blood runs cold, and my stomach cramps at the sight of it. She wouldn't.

I rush to the window and push back the blanket blocking the view. Nothing is there, but I know I saw it.

"I loved them only because they needed love. I am not perfect, sister, but I cared for the mortals better than you ever did. You hated me for it, too. You despised that they grew to cherish me instead of remaining afraid of my existence."

"You gave one a piece of your soul, Arawna! This cannot be allowed. It is too dangerous. It is no better than what Khitaen wishes to do."

My brow furrows in confusion. "What are you talking about? It's nothing like Khitaen's plans."

"You're telling me Khitaen doesn't wish to become more powerful, spreading his magic around like seed on fallow ground? He is the only one strong enough to stand against you, and that is why the others and I allow it."

The serpent shadow passes the window again, and I am certain I saw it.

I turn an accusing finger at Araina. "You dare bring them into my world? Into my home?"

Araina's face remains neutral, but I see the slight tension building under her skin. The stiffness of her posture. The flash of fear in her eyes.

A screech like a sea monster shakes the house. My sister brought myrukim with her, a myrukim that destroys darkness with light magic. A direct threat to my dragons and cryarsh. To my true family. She created them after the Thousand Years War when she saw the power my shadow creatures brought. She was never one to be outdone by me. Of course, she created the opposite of my creatures—dragons with serpentine bodies and light magic capable of vanquishing any shadow.

"There is just one. It will not harm any of your creatures unless attacked first."

I scowl at her, feeling anger bubble under my skin.

"Why do you allow Khitaen to do whatever he wishes?"

"Why did you kill Markyr?"

The question silences my thoughts. The hum of bees resonates in my head for a moment. I had almost forgotten I had killed him.

"He allowed Khitaen free rein in his world," I say, though I lack the conviction I want to feel.

"So, you destroyed the god who shepherded the world, leaving it vulnerable to takeover or destruction? You opened the door for Khitaen to walk in and steal it for his own, Arawna!" Her arms flail in frustration. I know the feeling.

"I did not leave the world abandoned. It will not fall."

"It is already shaken! The earth groans. A snowstorm like Myzonia has never seen before is raging on the eve of the battle set to take place between a god and a goddess. Do you think you are doing anyone any good here? Do you not care for the mortals whose lives you've endangered?"

No. No, this is going to work. I have a plan.

Araina shakes her head at me before walking toward the front door. "Sister, I hope you realize the truth about yourself before it is too late."

"And what truth is that, Araina?" I don't want her to say, but I know she will.

"You are the bringer of destruction and desolation. You are no better than the one you claim to fight against. The worlds would be better off if they had continued to forget your name."

The last sentence is a fatal blow to my heart. Forgotten. Always forgotten. Never remembered. The worlds would not truly be better forgetting me, would they?

I say nothing to her. Her eyes are sad, but she knows there is nothing left between us. She moves toward the door, raising her hood over her beautiful, dark hair.

"Arawna, for what it's worth... I'm sorry."

With that, my sister leaves the house, pulling the door closed behind her. Alone again. Always alone. Always forgotten. A name whispered in terror, but soon to leave the lips of the mortals forever.

Twenty-Nine

"In the shadows, there is still life. It is harder to see, but it
persists, nonetheless."
—Luna, Goddess of Wind and Sky
as recorded in the temple of Amenir

Marcus

Aella stands stiff and somber next to me. Zaiven is as protected
as we can make it. I intend to leave some of our soldiers here to
guard the perimeter, but the rest will march to the Plain and make
camp along the border. I turn slightly toward Aella, trying to think
of something that may ease the burden, but I cannot say anything to
reassure her when war is the topic of discussion. There is no comfort
when lives will be lost, no matter what, on both sides.

I've always hated it.

Maybe that means I've always hated death, too. The world is
cruel, and mankind makes it so. Death comes whether we want it to
or not, visiting all of us. Good and bad. Kind and hateful. In the end,
the earth takes us back to itself, and Arawnia welcomes us home.

I'm conflicted now because I know what Death is and who
guards it, and I have stood face to face with it in more ways than one.

It was beautiful and full of so much peace. Even in the chaos of
the act and the tragedy of the moment, for me, there was only peace
and rest and beauty. I cannot reconcile this picture with the histories
I have known. I cannot reconcile the image of Darci as the kind and

gracious goddess she appears to be with the fear I once associated with the Death God. Everything is blurred together.

"We're going to die, aren't we?"

Aella's tight voice breaks my contemplation. I look to her, but she keeps her eyes forward. Her chin is slightly lifted. An attempt to look bold and brave when on the inside she is wavering.

"I don't know." I turn my eyes back to the soldiers, watching as each one gathers belongings and sharpens swords. Daggers are sheathed; some archers in the ranks fill quivers with arrows. The Plain of Okira is not an ideal place for arrows, but at this point, we may need everything we can take.

"I... I lost my best friend. Today."

My eyes snap back to her, but I'm still greeted by only her profile.

"Who?"

She swallows, and her bottom lip quivers, barely noticeable. The hard exterior of a captain is pulled back for a moment.

"Jaxis. They fell. In the battle."

I place a firm hand on her shoulder.

"Then we honor them, as we walk into war. We will not shy away from the blade. We will not back down until there is nothing left."

Her watery eyes shift to me. "Until there is nothing left," She whispers.

I remove my hand and check that my swords are secure, crossed at my back. She and I both know this is a war to end all wars. We face not our fellow man, though I do not doubt that mortals will be among the ones we battle. We face a god on a vengeful path of destruction and domination.

Can mere mortals walk away from that?

"I'm going to Rizyrk. I know we sent word, but most of the army is there. I want to ensure everyone is mobilized accordingly."

"The snow will make traveling difficult."

I hum in agreement. She's right. The snow falls thicker and heavier by the minute. It's unusual weather for Myzonia. It reminds me of Oria from the short amount of time I was at Darci's house.

"I don't have a choice. I need to get there. When they are ready, you must move out right away. I want you to set up quickly. Get fires started. There's no use trying to hide when we have no idea where he'll come from. No point freezing to death in this mess before we go to battle."

Her resolve returns, and she nods firmly this time. "Be careful, sir."

"See you on the field, Commander."

I wrap my cloak tighter around me before I begin my travels to the capital.

RIZYRK IS IN CHAOS. News has arrived about the attacks in Zaiven and the impending battle coming to the world. Several servants rush past me when I step out of my rooms in the castle, not even looking back at who they bumped into in their hurry. Faint shouts and orders echo down the long corridors. I move quickly, passing tapestries and safe rooms along the way.

Fear is tangible in the air, thick and heavy. I exit the hall into the foyer and don't stop until I see another commander giving orders outside the castle doors. Anthony and Jacob, Adrian's regular personal guards, stand at attention while James gives them directions. They both stiffen when they see me approaching, causing James to look over his shoulder to see what distracted them.

"Marcus, I didn't expect you to make it here in this weather."

The snow has piled up along the paths, making everything slick and the air feel even colder.

"I wanted to make sure everything was going smoothly. We need to move out soon."

"The civilians have been warned. Most are seeking cover in the safe rooms within the castle, but others are fleeing to the northern portions of the city. Do we have any reason to believe war is coming here?"

I shake my head. "No, I—it's hard to explain. There could be minor skirmishes, but my instinct says the armies will meet on the Plain."

"Whatever you say. I've been in enough battles with you to trust your leadership here."

I grasp his shoulder and smile. "Let's pray this isn't our last stand."

James' face betrays concern before he guards his expression again. He turns to Anthony and Jacob to wave them off. They turn without question, moving quickly through the other bustling bodies.

When he faces me, I see the question in his eyes before he asks, "Is it really that dire? Are our chances that bad for survival?"

I hesitate. These men and women need to be encouraged, but I can't lie to them either. I can't make false promises and give false hope. The consequences of this battle may in fact be the most severe we've ever faced.

"How much do you know about our enemy, James?"

His brow furrows. "Honestly, not much. We received word that a formidable enemy had attacked and killed many in Zaiven. We even heard the Sovereign's house was destroyed."

"Well, you're not wrong. It is not a man we face, but a god, and the army he brings is—-honestly? Terrifying."

James draws in a deep breath, absorbing the information.

"Then we will make a stand that our ancestors would be proud of."

A smile slips on, then off, my face. "Yes, we will."

We begin walking toward the gathering of soldiers near the gates when I remember something I wanted to ask. I stop him with a hand to his forearm.

"Have you heard word from the Sovereign? He and others were working to evacuate the Plain."

"I'm sorry, Marcus. I haven't heard of or seen him. He must still be on the Plain. Maybe the weather has delayed him?"

My brow scrunches. He should be done by now, but it is an unusual snowstorm. He did have to shift a lot. Perhaps he spent his magic. Concern climbs up my back like icy fingers, but I need to press on. I don't have time to search for him, and I wouldn't even know where to begin.

"Let's get moving to the Plain. We need to set up camp near the flat stretch before the villages. I want a secure wall of our people between whatever army is coming and the capital's outer defenses."

"Sounds good."

Together, we rally the warriors of this great army, leading them by divisions into the snowy night. I linger behind to ensure proper protection remains for the city.

It takes longer than I would like, but we make good progress. We might have a chance of establishing camp before the battle begins when a young soldier runs to me panting.

"What's wrong?" I can't help it. My first thought is Adrian.

"High Commander..." She gulps another deep breath. I notice her hands trembling. She must be a shifter and be worn out.

"Breathe, take your time."

She bends over, hands on her knees, for a moment. When she looks up at me, tears stream down her cheeks.

"What is it? What has happened? News from the Sovereign?"

She shakes her head and lifts a hand to her mouth before swallowing.

"I bring news. News from Yeeri." Yeeri is a tiny village on the western side of the Plain of Okira. It's the size of Zaiven.

A weight sinks in my stomach. She speaks again before I can say a word.

"It's gone, sir. Yeeri is gone."

"What?" I breathe the word, then harden my face, refusing to reveal my emotions to the others. "What happened?"

"News says a small contingent attacked. Monsters and a man with white eyes. He was...he was too powerful. I was on the Plain helping evacuate the farms and villages when I heard a man screaming. He clutched his head like he was in immense pain, and the pulses of magic I felt off him were almost incapacitating."

A seer.

The shifter continues. "He had a vision of the town of Yeeri falling to monsters. He kept screaming about blood and death. I wasn't far from there. I shifted to the edge of the village, hoping he was wrong."

"You took the chance the enemy might find you? That was foolish!"

The young woman looks sick. "I know, sir. I'm sorry. But it was true. There were so many bodies. No sign of the enemy, but everything was destroyed. No building was left standing. I checked..." She swallows. "I checked for survivors. Both with my magic and my hands. There were none."

"You checked the entire village? How long did it take you? Any idea how long they had been dead?"

"It hadn't been long. Yes, I couldn't risk leaving any of them behind. There were so many..." A tear escapes down her cheek. I know what she saw. She saw children and the elderly. She saw all of them, taken from this world too soon.

"How could an army disappear that quickly? Why would they destroy innocents in an obscure village?"

"I'm not sure. He may be using it to incite fear and panic." It did work. She is terrified. "We can't falter, now. Get some rest. Refuel your body and magic. Remain here at the castle to join the guards protecting the wall."

She nods slowly before dipping her head and stumbling toward the doors.

A whole village gone. It makes no sense to attack Yeeri. There was no purpose for it. The village is tiny and not along any major trade routes. Is it just a game? Is the God of War and Peace playing with us because he can?

I only hope we can protect what's left of this world. If he leaves any of it at all. Will Darci come to help like before? She is planning something. I feel it.

A great moaning sound reaches my ears over the wind and snow. No, not a moan. A rumbling groan makes the ground beneath my feet quiver. Large slabs of snow slide off the roofs around me and onto the ground. A lantern swings from a pole before crashing to the stones. A few servants scream; others shout for people to move away from the walls. I kneel and press a hand through the snow until I find the frozen stones beneath. The earth quivers. Why is the earth shaking?

Magic sparks to life on my fingers, spreading downward into the soil. The trembling subsides, but I wait a few more moments to be certain. Nothing else happens.

The feeling that someone is watching me makes the hair on the back of my neck stand up. A chill creeps up my spine as I slowly rise from the ground. When I turn around, no one is paying attention to me. No eyes are drawn in my direction. No one is wondering what I was doing. People move quickly and purposefully around, and I am but a speck amid the chaos.

But the sensation doesn't go away.

Whispers reach me—strange voices in a language I don't recognize. They crescendo, growing in intensity to the point I almost cover my ears. I force myself to be still, to wait.

"High Commander?"

I spin around to face the voice. It's a young man—a servant from the castle. He's holding out a pouch of water and something wrapped in a cloth.

"I'm sorry. What did you say?"

"I brought something to eat for you. She said you needed food."

I pull the cloth back to reveal a stygo and a piece of bread. The sight of the native fruit stirs a memory in my mind. A moment shared between Darci and me in the forest on our journey to the temple of Markyr.

"Who gave these to you?"

The servant looks a little flustered at the question. "I don't know her name, sir. She was right over there." He points in the direction of the castle doors.

"What did she look like?"

"She was pale and had dark hair, green eyes. I promise she was there, sir. Should I take this back?"

"No. Go get somewhere safe."

The whispers are gone, but the eerie sense that I'm not alone in my own head lingers.

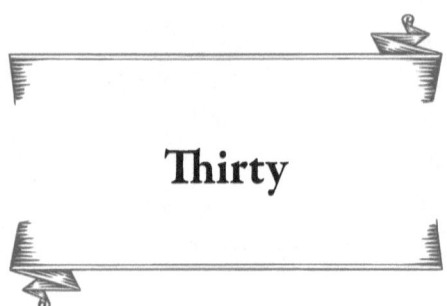

Thirty

"When faced with hate, mortals either stand against it or hide in silence."

—Khitaen
God of War and Peace

Adrian

The night stretches on for what feels like longer than usual. The storm finally blows itself out as the first evidence of dawn breaches the horizon. A soft, bluish glow comes through the window. I slept restlessly, tossing and turning most of the night after Cleo revealed the dangers of what was coming.

When I woke up, she was gone. No warning, no messages left behind. She simply vanished into the storm. If she is someone who works for Luna, perhaps Luna gifted her with powerful magic. Speaking of magic, mine feels stronger, my body refreshed, even with the lack of sleep.

I hold my hand out, palm up, and watch as green light glows along my skin. It has changed more. More shadows are twining themselves around the magic. More than half of the green light is darkened now. More of the Death Goddess's magic infiltrates my body.

A few more tremors happened through the night, the earth shifting and moving, distraught at the loss of its god. I still can't wrap my mind around that. Darci killed Markyr. Why would she do that?

What could she gain from his loss unless she wanted this world for herself? But that doesn't feel right.

I walk to the dying fire and use a poker to break up the remaining logs. The ashes plume outward, and the last embers fade. A stale piece of bread rests on the table, and another cup of what was once hot tea. I suppose I should eat, though my body doesn't feel hungry.

When I finish, I grab my cloak and daggers, slip my feet into my boots, and step out into a transformed world. The sky is gray, and the landscape is covered in a thick blanket of snow. It's deep in places, coming up to my knees at times. A battle in this is going to be challenging.

I close my eyes briefly, letting the cold air heighten my senses.

When I open them, a shadow flickers in the corner of my eye. I smile and turn toward it. Meiora's inky black spreads over the snow, pooling around my feet.

"Hello, there. I can honestly say, I missed you. Which is strange."

The shadow's tendrils wrap around my legs, moving up my body until they pull away and form the silhouette of a man.

"Have you been with Darci?"

An affirmative feeling swells in my chest.

"Is she going to help us?"

Silence.

"Will you help us?"

A shadowy hand extends toward me. I reach forward with mine until the velvety warmth presses into my palm, and the silhouette melts into the form that I usually see the shadow in. The shadow wraps strands of darkness around my forearm before releasing and spreading out along the ground again. A deep sense of peace and affirmation spreads throughout my whole body from my head to my toes.

At least, we will walk into battle with one cryarsh on our side.

"Thank you. Now, I need to get to camp near Rizyrk. Will you come?"

The shadow gathers itself around my feet before spreading upward and draping over my shoulders like an additional cloak. I'm sure the sight is quite terrifying, a man clothed in moving shadows.

A flick of my wrist takes me from this place, leaving the house behind. I hope the other shifters evacuated as many as possible, and I pray they escaped the Plain before the storm became too fierce.

THE CAMP IS CALM AND productive. A steady rhythm of work creates a hum of activity, but it's not rushed. It's not even urgent. They've been here for a while. More and more fighters recognize me as I walk through the rows of tents. A few bow, most nod before continuing their work. I scan the area for any sign of Marcus. I hear him before I see him.

"What do you mean you can't remember? Did you bring anything with you?" Frustration laces his words. I follow the sound of a whimpering reply to find Marcus towering over a small male soldier. He must be new.

"Find Commander James. Please."

The soldier scurries off in the opposite direction from Marcus, and I chuckle at the sight. Marcus hears me and turns around.

Relief fills his eyes. "You're safe. I was beginning to wonder if I was going to have to go looking for you." His eyes dart to the cryarsh draped across my shoulders.

"You know I wouldn't leave you to do all the heavy work." I pull him into a hug, and Marcus remains stiff and awkward as usual.

Releasing him, I say, "You could be instilling confidence and boosting morale, you know. Not terrifying the young ones."

He scowls. "The young ones are going to get themselves killed. That one was supposed to stay at the wall, at least giving him a chance to live to see his next birthday."

I frown. "He came against orders?"

Marcus sighs. "A lot of confusion occurred when they set out. Multiple earthquakes occurred. People were scared and running around like chickens. I think he ended up with the wrong group. It's too late to send him back. I don't want to risk him being alone, trying to walk back to the capital."

Marcus is right. The capital is a few hours' march from here. If Khitaen attacks from a different position or sends scouts, they could easily capture or kill him.

"What do you think Commander James will do with him?"

"He'll probably yell at him. Then he'll position him in a strong group and make sure they go out last." He shrugs. "At least, that's what I would do."

I smile. "It's good to be back with you, brother."

"Likewise. Where did you find Meiora?"

"That's a long story. But I have news for you. We need to discuss it somewhere private."

He sobers and nods, leading me through the throngs of men and women preparing for war.

We enter a tent on the edge of camp with a single cot in it and a small table. Not a war room in the slightest, but probably the best we could manage.

"What's going on, Adrian?"

"You're not going to believe who I ran into on the Plain."

"At this point, I'll believe anything."

I stare at him for a few moments, letting the silence stretch between us.

"Cleo."

"Sister Cleo? What in the name of Araina was she doing out there?" He clenches his hands at his side.

"I used a lot of magic, and I managed to stumble across a cabin. She was there. Not at the temple, and I don't think we need to call her sister. She's not a priestess if my instincts are correct."

"Who is she? Who is she working for?" Marcus paces in the tiny tent. His energy is building up. He's always been this way. Always moving. Always expressing outwardly what he feels deep inside.

"She said she works for Luna." He freezes and faces me. "Yes, I said Luna. The Goddess of Wind and Sky."

"Another goddess. Another deity getting mixed up in all of this?"

"She seemed to be concerned about something Darci did. She claimed Luna was concerned about what Darci might do."

A flash of concern passes over his face.

"What did Darci do? Did she tell you?"

I rub my fingers together, remembering the magic that was dancing there not long ago. "You said you noticed trembling? The earth shaking, or things feeling out of place or wrong?"

His eyes widen. "Yes. We had several quakes. Nothing major. This snowstorm is strange, too."

"Everything feels wrong. Cleo claimed each world has a god or goddess who cares for it. I think she used the term shepherd. A world without its deity loses access to its magic. It cannot sustain itself. Not for long."

"Okay? I guess that makes sense. Six gods exist. That means there are six worlds. Right?"

"There were only five until Arawna created Oria. She broke some rule that said she wasn't supposed to have a world all to herself. She was supposed to care for the mortals, the dying, in each of the other worlds. But that's beside the point. The point is... Myzonia doesn't have a god anymore."

"That's impossible." Blue light flickers along Marcus's hands.

"Cleo said Darci killed Markyr, the god over Myzonia. We are feeling the effects of his loss. The world needs magic. The storm. The quakes. Everything points to the world dying."

"How could she kill a god!? How can a god even die?!" He's pacing again.

"She's the only one who can kill a deity. Cleo wasn't sure why she did it. But she said if any other worlds lose their gods, it could be detrimental."

Realization dawns on his face. "If Darci or Khitaen dies in this battle, their worlds lose their access to magic." He mumbles something else I don't catch.

"What was that?"

He shakes his head before looking at me. "I said it makes sense. During one of the quakes, I pressed my hand into the earth, and my magic sort of seeped out of me into the soil. I didn't will it. It just left. When it was absorbed, the earth stilled."

Magic. If we give the earth magic, will it be enough?

"Adrian, how could Darci die? If she is the only one who can kill a deity, then she should be safe."

"Cleo included her. She may have sensed something she wasn't willing to tell me."

Marcus blows his cheeks out with a long exhale. "You're telling me we are going to war against a god who wants to destroy us. But we can't do anything to kill him...not that we could... because if he dies, another world could die too. Oh, and our world is already dying because we don't have a god anymore. And Darci is on some vengeance kick and might try to kill Khitaen. And we can't let her. But she's the Goddess of Death. We can't kill any of them. We can only hope we die fast, or they are merciful?"

I want to laugh, or I want to despair. He's not wrong.

"That about sums it up. Any other news I should know about?"

Marcus cast his eyes downward. A heaviness fills the air. I'm about to push when his eyes meet mine again.

"Did you hear about Yeeri?"

"Yeeri? I haven't heard anything."

"Yeeri was destroyed. A shifter heard a vision from a seer in one of the towns. He became frantic when he saw the news. She went to check it out. Everything was gone. The buildings, the people. It is nothing but rubble and death."

A churning in my stomach makes the air in the tent feel too warm. I turn my back to Marcus for a moment, trying to get a grip on my emotions. The feel of his hand on my shoulder steadies my heartbeat.

"Do we know if it was Khitaen?" I still can't face him.

He speaks to my back. "From what it sounds like, yes. The seer explained the vision to the shifter. It sounded exactly like what happened in Zaiven, but no one was there to fight against him."

I pivot to face him. "Are we sure they're all dead? What about the children?"

Marcus shakes his head. "The shifter spent time checking all the bodies. She used her magic as well. No one survived, Adrian."

"He intends to traumatize us before he destroys us." I used to worry death was a monster, but I didn't realize the living were more likely to be one. I shouldn't have been surprised. My father was a monster, and I am plagued with a magic I didn't want, and a piece of death itself embedded in my soul.

Marcus nods his head toward the tent opening. "I've already counseled with the other commanders. A contingent remains back with the castle, and one remains near Zaiven. We have eighty thousand to our number here on the Plain."

Eighty thousand. It won't be enough. How many bodies will paint the snow red?

He continues. "I have a tent set up next to this one for you. You should rest. We're going to need every drop of magic possible. Everyone has been commanded to conserve energy and magic stores. Not all are powerful, but they all have something in addition to sword skills. There is a rotation of scouts on the south side and the north side. News will come quickly when he arrives."

"Okay. Meiora, join the scouts, please. You can get back to me faster than anyone else."

The shadow slips off my shoulders and slithers out of the tent. An understanding remains steadfast between us.

"Does Meiora being here mean Darci intends to help us?" Marcus sounds hopeful.

"It wouldn't tell me. I sensed its agreement to help us, but when I asked about Darci, there was nothing. I can only hope she will. She did once."

"Some good dwells in her. I sensed it the longer I was with her. I saw it when I was dying at her house. I felt it when I could have chosen to leave this realm for the next. Surely, the goodness within her will compel her to come."

I say nothing, but I hope he's right. We go our separate ways. I need to rest.

The tent next door is a replica of this. I leave my cloak and boots on and lie on the uncomfortable cot. Willing myself to sleep, I close my eyes and envision a world without war. Without death. With only peace.

A hum buzzes along my skin, in my ears, in my mind. Darkness follows quickly.

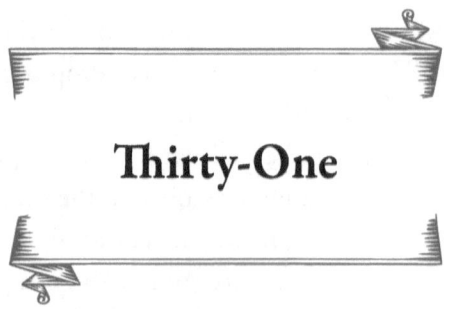

Thirty-One

"The God of War and Peace has always given himself more to his violent side than his gentle one. He stirs up strife where there is none because he is entertained by the bloodshed of many."

—*A Study of the Divine*,
tract 59 paragraph 2

Adrian

A warm, velvety caress awakens me from a dreamless sleep. I can't remember the last time I slept as soundly. The touch is familiar. I sit up, finding Meiora gliding over my body on the cot.

"What is it? Has he come?"

The sensation of danger and terror washes over me, overwhelming my senses. I imagine it's what it would feel like to be swept away by a massive wave.

I jump to my feet, noticing the change in the colors of the sky. It looks like the night before the dawn, an eerie glow of deep blue on the horizon. I slept for longer than I thought.

I push through the fabric of Marcus's tent and find him sitting up, grabbing a sword.

"Adrian, I could have run you through! Why are you barging in here?"

He stands and sheaths his sword, swinging the scabbard into place on his back and buckling the straps.

"Meiora returned. He's here."

A mask of determination locks into place on his face. He wastes no time jogging to the next tent and barking commands at whoever is there. Before I realize it, several soldiers are running through the camp, drawing the attention of the entire army. A single shifter appears at my side, forcing me over a step.

"Sorry, Your Majesty," she gasps. Marcus hears her and turns to address her.

"What is it?"

"They're on the southern front. An entire army just appeared. It was like they crawled out of the darkness."

My eyes shoot to the horizon again. What time of day is it?

"Spread the news. Send a shifter to Zaiven and one to the capital. The soldiers there need to be aware of what's going on. How many were there?"

"I couldn't count them, sir. They were beyond number. They were not all men."

Monsters, exactly as we feared.

"What time of day is it?" The question is bothering me. I had arrived here in the camp in the morning. It wasn't even midday when I went to sleep. Surely, I didn't sleep all afternoon and through the night.

Marcus looks to the east and furrows his brow in confusion. "I went to sleep after midday. I know I didn't sleep that long." He looks at the shifter.

"What are you talking about, sir? It's evening. Maybe an hour before dark?"

"Why is it dark already?" I demand.

She flinches. "I don't understand, Your Majesty. It's not all the way dark. The sun is still above the horizon."

She points to the west, but all I see are shadows. Marcus must see the same thing. He looks as confused as me.

"Go. Do what I asked. Conserve as much energy as you can. Be safe."

All around us, the army rises. No one else shouts in alarm or asks questions about the sky. No one seems to notice the darkness. No one except Marcus and me.

Marcus steps close to me, whispering near my ear. "Do you see how dark it is already?"

"Yes, I thought it was close to morning. What's the glow on the eastern horizon?" I murmur in response.

Marcus looks east, shaking his head. "I see no glow, but it is as dark as the middle of the night."

Everything is wrong about this.

"Is it the world? Do we notice the change because of the lack of magic?" In response to his question, the earth shakes under our feet. A stronger quake than I had felt before. Several men stumble; a couple of tents fall where the pegs holding them in place slip from the ground.

We look at each other and then at the ground.

"What if we..."

"No, we need all the magic available to fight this war."

"Marcus, if we don't do something, give it something, the world might kill us first."

He looks conflicted. A terrible choice—to spend magic on the ground on which we stand or to conserve it to fight a god in a war we cannot win.

"I'll do it." My decision is made.

"Adrian, you're the strongest of us all."

"Which is exactly why I can afford to give some away."

I don't wait for his response. I kneel quickly to one knee and press my hand flat against the snow. Nothing happens.

"I think you need to touch underneath the snow. That's how it worked for me."

I scrape with my fingers until I reach the frozen earth underneath and press my hand again to the cold dirt. A stream of shadowy green light seeps out of my pores and into the ground, quickly being absorbed. I can feel the magic leaving me, but it's not too much yet. My reserve of power is deep.

"That's enough, Adrian. Stop."

"I can give more."

His hands jerk me roughly to my feet. "You have given enough. No more." The icy glare he gives me is enough to make me agree.

"Okay. Let's go fight a god."

The strange glow on the eastern horizon remains. The shadows do not lift. We go to battle in the darkness against an enemy with monsters.

I follow Marcus to the front line, shifting alongside him. The army behind us stands still and firm. No nervous rustling, not even the crunch of snow, can be heard. In front of us, an army full of monsters can be heard, but not well seen. It's too dark.

As if in answer, the darkness stretches out even more, allowing only the torches to light the camp on all sides.

"Marcus," I warn.

He grabs a captain who stands off to our left. "Put out the torches. We're lighting ourselves up for target practice."

The word spreads quickly, and soon everything is in shadow. The thumping of war drums in the distance and the marching of thousands of feet through snow echo across the Plain.

They sound a good distance away, but every step brings them closer.

"Our world is threatened by a god who wants only to destroy! Today, we choose to stand and fight. If we are to die, we will face it bravely, knowing our reward, our peace, waits for us on the other side. We will not back down. We will not shy away when the war cry sounds."

Marcus's voice is magically enhanced, spreading down the line into row after row of fighters. A roar of defiance rises from the army at my back.

Swords are drawn. No one needs to be told what to do next. No one needs to be reminded they will die. The reality that all of us might fall weighs heavily on everyone's shoulders.

A mercy comes as the sky parts, and a full moon shines down on the field. None of this makes sense, and none of it is natural. I can't help but wonder if Luna, the Goddess of Wind and Sky, is aiding us this night.

The light of the moon bathes the Plain in pale blue while the snow reflects and amplifies the glow. My heart pounds at the sight. The enemy is massive. There must be twice as many of them as us, and they bring monsters. Meiora appears again at my side. A couple of gasps escape from those nearest me at the sight of the cryarsh.

I will the creature to understand my gratitude.

Marcus looks at me and pulls both swords from their sheaths at his back. He tosses one to me, which I catch and swipe the air a couple of times to get the feel for the weight of it.

I understand what he means. Swords first, magic last. Every drop matters.

I look at my friend, my brother, and think of all the times we have stood on a battlefield together. At one time, we fought to overthrow my father and his accomplices. Once, we fought only against a man and his wicked schemes. Today, we fight for our world and all the living in it now, and all the dead slain too soon.

"Until Arawnia, brother?"

Marcus nods slowly, his eyes hardening. A faint emerald glow shines on his face, and I know my eyes must be glowing.

"Until Arawnia," he replies.

Together, we face the army that has finally stopped marching. The man with white eyes stands at the front. Khitaen. His creatures snap and snarl, his men stamping their feet in the snow. Both sides wait for the call to charge. The vastness of his army sends a temporary chill down my spine. Flashes and memories of previous battles threaten to overwhelm my senses. The dream, the nightmare, I had of Darci and her killing blade coming straight for me, flashes before my eyes.

The part she will play in this war is still unknown. I wish she would come and bring her dragon. But she could come and destroy Khitaen as well, and what else might fall in the path of such destructive power? No, I don't think we need her. If my nightmare was a vision, maybe I should pray to Araina Darci doesn't come.

The cryarsh must sense my thoughts, my distress. It spreads around my feet, and if I'm not mistaken, I imagine that Khitaen's eyes are drawn toward the sentient shadow. He's too far away for me to see that, but I sense it, nonetheless. He knows who it belongs to. I hope that means he is afraid.

The pregnant pause, the stillness of anticipation, builds. Then, Khitaen raises his arm and shouts something in a language I recognize but can't understand. His army roars, shaking the earth with their battle cry, and surges forward.

Our line holds, waiting for Marcus to give the command. I should be afraid. I should feel terror. But I am not afraid of death, not anymore. Death is like an old friend I've known all my life. A smile passes over my mouth as I tighten my grip on the sword.

They're drawing closer. Marcus raises his sword and roars, "For Myzonia!"

My army and I cry together and charge to meet our enemy.

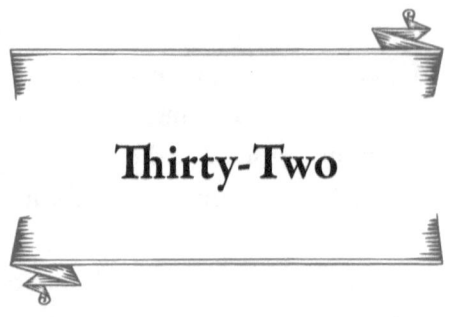

Thirty-Two

"In war, there are no victors. We all lose when our fellow man dies."

—Queen Ahira of Amenir

Marcus

The clash of metal and bodies creates a constant cacophony vibrating the air around us. Every movement is automatic. Training and years of previous battles take over amid shadows and enemies. The snow makes every step feel precarious. Men, women, and monsters all slip and slide in the slushy mess. The blood from both sides has marred the beauty of the frozen landscape.

I lost track of Adrian moments after the armies collided. I can only hope he remains standing, and our numbers can hold against the brutality of this giant. One of those strange creatures I battled at Zaiven launches itself at me. Its only weapons are claws and teeth, but it moves with preternatural speed, and I find myself pivoting in the slush to keep the creature off my back. I'm not fast enough, but the sound of an arrow hitting flesh gives me time to face the creature who now stands with a shaft in its chest before it collapses. There isn't time to see who shot the arrow before the next man is upon me.

Khitaen's army is comprised of men and monsters. I can only assume he brought them from another world. Perhaps the world he is supposed to care for. They are skilled fighters and move with agility even in the snowy setting. Their deep purple tunics and black leather armor make them even more difficult to see in the eerie light of our battle. Our swords clash as we parry back and forth for a few moments before I'm able to knock him off balance and run my sword through his center.

More and more of our people fall. We take as many as they do, but their ranks never diminish. For every creature I take down, every man I kill, three more take their place. We cannot win this battle by numbers alone.

Screams of agony join the chorus of war now. I stumble over a body I could barely decipher as I push forward into the fray. Flashes of magic light up the sky, illuminating everything in a strange and jolting rhythm. Not all our people have magic useful for fighting. Those who do are commanders and captains who are skilled fighters with both hand-to-hand combat and magic wielding.

Sweat pores down my back and chills my skin further in the bite of the wintry wind. I run across the lines to where a surge of the strange creatures threatens to break through to the core of our army. Teeth and claws, screams and shouts. More warriors fall. More bodies litter the ground, adding obstacles to an already treacherous situation.

I jump into the fray, bumping into another Myzonian. I grab his arm to steady him before swinging my sword into another creature's neck.

"I knew you'd try to take all the glory in battle again."

I bark a laugh, not expecting Adrian to be the person I collided with.

"You know me, always seeking more glory for myself."

We press our backs to each other, fighting off the creatures wanting to box us in.

"I think it might be time for some magic, Marcus."

I don't want to use any. Not when Khitaen himself hasn't joined the battle yet. Magic is our only weapon against him. But the fallen

Myzonians increase in number, and we need to make some headway. Adrian is right.

"I'm ready when you are."

Without pausing our movements, we both call forth magic to our hands and unleash it on the surrounding monsters. Blue and green light clash with the creatures, dropping them quickly and without warning. The magic draws the attention of more Myzonians, who notice that only Adrian and I protect the breach in defenses against Khitaen's men.

We gain a few moments to breathe before more of the enemy fill the hole left by the fallen creatures, but it's enough time for Myzonia's warriors to pour into the space, too. The next wave of enemy clashes with dozens of Myzonian swords.

I jerk backwards as Adrian drags me through the midst of our fighters toward the camp, away from the fighting. We get far enough from the battle before I yank my arm out of his grip.

"What are you doing?" I demand. "We need to stay in the fight."

"You're injured, Marcus! Come with me so I can heal you." Concern etches my friend's face.

"What are you talking about? I..." I pause.

The energy in my veins lets up enough for me to feel what he had already seen. I look down at my stomach and see a slash in the leather armor and tunic where a sword or claw cut across me. I touch the wound with my free hand, pulling it back sticky with blood.

Adrian grabs my forearm and pulls me farther from the front lines. Nobody notices us—the battle holds everyone's attention with absolute power.

"I can heal you if I can get enough time to do so. You were caught up in battle and must not have felt the creature's claws."

He's right, but I feel them now. I stumble a little. There's a lot of blood. How did he know? Our leathers and tunics are black. It's dark out. I'm covered in the blood of others. The tear is not so noticeable that one could see it without looking for it.

He pushes me down to sit on a log. He leaves my tunic and leathers on, wasting no time before kneeling in front of me and shoving his hands through the slit in the fabric onto my wound. I hiss from the pain, and black dots fill my vision for a moment. I watch as green, shadowy light leaves Adrian's hands and disappears into my body.

If he uses magic to heal me, he might not have enough to fight.

"Wait! You can't waste your power on me. We'll need it later."

"Be quiet, let me concentrate."

I feel the skin mending and stitching together. It gives me enough clarity, as some of the pain subsides, to shove Adrian backwards onto the ground.

"Why did you do that?" He stands quickly and steps toward me, but I rise from the log and hold my sword in front of me, pointed at his chest.

"You will waste no more magic on me. It is enough."

He shakes his head. "It wasn't enough. I barely got the skin back together. It could come apart easily."

I don't lower my sword. Adrian stands there with his hands clenched in tight fists, glowering at me.

"How did you know I was injured? You couldn't have seen it."

He closes his eyes for a moment before opening them again, a green glow filling them once more. "I felt it. I felt the death upon me. I have felt death greet every soldier, both ours and his, who has fallen in this field tonight. Not one on either side has fallen that I did not sense. You were going to bleed out from it if I didn't do something."

My mouth gapes open as I stare in wonder at him. It's more of Darci's magic. How has he been able to stand with all this death happening around him? How has he kept his head? But I see it now.

The tremor in his fingers, the tightness of his shoulders, the darkness forming under his eyes. He's felt it all and is barely hanging on.

I nod and lower my sword. "It is enough, Adrian. If I am to fall today, then I will. But you must fight for all Myzonia, not just me."

He clenches his eyes closed; his jaw tightens.

I repeat. "It is enough, Adrian." My voice is barely above a whisper.

Meiora sweeps in across the ground and wraps its shadows around Adrian. Some of the tension leaves his body. I had forgotten the cryarsh was battling with us.

"We have to go back into the battle."

Adrian nods and bends to pick up his sword. Together, we turn and run to where the fighting is most intense.

Meiora spreads out in front of us, flying past our people and colliding with the front line of the enemy. The shadow creature covers the space of ten men, and soon the line is engulfed in darkness. Screams of agony and torment reach out of the inky black, but no one caught in the cryarsh's power can be saved. When Meiora moves away to the next line, it leaves behind a dozen bodies of bone. A female fighter steps on one in her effort to follow the cryarsh into battle, and the bone disintegrates into ash.

The power of the shadow creature rallies the Myzonian army as they charge into the battle, following the path Meiora carves through the enemy's forces. I'm grateful for its help. Maybe we do have a reason to hope.

THE HOPE IS SHORT-LIVED as the night carries on. Staying near Adrian, I attempt to keep an eye on him while fighting alongside others. He conserves a lot of magic, but I see the strain on him from the fallen bodies. The death that moves like a living entity around us.

I run to his side when I see him stumble under the pressure of it. "Adrian!" He steadies himself before I have a chance to reach him.

We need to know how it is faring, but it's the middle of the night now. Seeing isn't possible, but I have an idea.

"Adrian, can Meiora see what our numbers are?"

Adrian doesn't say a word; he simply twists his wrist and the cryarsh appears. After a silent conversation lasting mere moments, Meiora vanishes again.

Within minutes, it returns and communicates silently with Adrian once more. His eyes widen, and my instinct knows the answer isn't good.

"What is it?" I block an attack from the left as I stand with Adrian to my right.

"Half."

"Us or them?"

"Us."

Half of our army has fallen. We need to fall back. We need to rest and regroup. We need to use magic.

"We need to do something big to gain enough time to fall back," I shout over the madness.

"There is nothing to fall back to! We're too far from the city. The Plain offers zero protection." I know what he's saying is true, but I don't want to give in to the hopelessness that threatens me.

"Let's give them all we have in magic. Have Meiora join us. Maybe we can give our people time to reform lines."

Grunting, Adrian stabs a creature in the chest and pulls his blade free.

"Okay."

I find the nearest captain and order him to fall back and spread the news. He never hesitates, only obeys. I return to Adrian, and together we unleash as much magic as we can. Waves and waves of blue and green light plow through Khitaen's ranks. Adrian's power drops them quickly, some even turning to dust. He is using too much of it, but it doesn't seem to lessen.

My magic will be spent soon, but I still pour it out. Hundreds of the enemy fall before our wrath. When I'm spent, I see Adrian's magic prevailing. He's never been this powerful. Meiora aids us by taking out dozens at a time, too. A horn blasts in the depths of Khitaen's army. He's pulling his creatures and men back.

"Adrian!" I grab his shoulder, breaking his concentration. "Fall back!"

He nods, though I see he wants to stay and pursue. Maybe we'll give ourselves enough time.

We run back toward the camp following the Myzonian soldiers into the fray, eliminating monsters and navy-clad men along the way. When space forms between our armies, Adrian summons Meiora. When the cryarsh appears, it isn't alone. Four other cryarsh appear alongside it. Five shadow creatures to aid us in battle. Hope flickers to life in my chest for the first time in a while.

Adrian points and the cryarsh move spreading outward and forming a black wall between our camp and Khitaen. It's not perfect, but it may give us time to breathe.

My wound has pulled apart some, but I don't think it's bad enough that I'll bleed out.

"James! Tell everyone to drink and eat whatever they can. The line will be breached again soon." I'm grateful to see the commander still alive.

The sky remains a strange, dark color. I wonder if Adrian still sees the glow on the eastern horizon. I look for the moon, desperate to see where it is in the night sky.

When I spot it, I can't help the relief washing over me. It sits low in the sky. Dawn must only be an hour away. If we can see, we might be able to fight better.

I find Adrian drinking from a ladle of water. His dark skin is speckled with blood, and a sheen of sweat coats his brow. He offers me the ladle, and I take it gratefully.

"She's not coming, is she?" I ask after I gulp down the cold liquid.

He shakes his head. "I don't know. But we did gain four more cryarsh."

"Dawn is coming." I nod toward the sky and specifically toward the moon. He faces the east, and his eyes narrow.

"Do you still see the glow?" I ask.

"Yes. It's still there. It's getting brighter."

"We're almost to the end, aren't we?" He doesn't answer me right away. I wonder how the death toll is weighing on him now, if he can feel the losses even with some separation between them and us.

"I think it might be. But better to face the end fighting for what is good and right in this world, than to face it in silence and cowardice."

I nod. "For Myzonia. And after, to Arawnia."

A sad smile passes over his face. There and gone again.

A STRANGE HUM FILLS the air. Men and women clasp their hands over their ears, the sound pierces everything it touches. Adrian and I turn around searching for any source of the sound. The earth quivers beneath our feet, and I run in the direction of the cryarsh wall. Only the cryarsh aren't there. The creatures have pulled back.

Adrian jogs up next to me and points to the east. The glow of dawn creeps over the horizon, casting the Plain in faint light. Meiora appears at Adrian's side, and his head tilts as he listens to whatever it is the creature says.

His gaze snaps in the direction of Khitaen's army, and I follow his stare.

What in the name of Araina is that?

In front of the line of our enemy, another line has formed of shadowy monsters full of claws and teeth and golden eyes. Their large bodies are shifting and shapeless. They appear to have four legs, but their form changes as if blown by a wind none of us feels. I have seen these creatures only once when they destroyed Adrian's house in Zaiven.

Every fiber of my being trembles with terror. I grab Adrian's shoulder. His eyes never leave the monsters, but I see his head tilt toward me.

"Adrian, those are the creatures that destroyed your house." The words come out choked.

His shoulders tense up at the revelation. There is no way we can stand against this enemy. The sun continues its ascent over the horizon, bathing the world in golden hues. Gasps and worried murmurs reach my ears. The monsters have been seen by my people.

"Marcus! What do we do?" James stands trembling next to me. His body is stiff from battle.

"Tell everyone with magic to come. We're going to pour everything we have into them."

He nods before running down the line, barking commands along the way.

Aella jogs toward me from the left. She must have arrived with her contingent sometime in the night.

"High Commander," she nods.

"What news is there of your contingent?"

"Most are gone. We have fifty left." Many more dead than should be.

"I need you here at the front. Magic is our only defense now."

"I'm here, sir. We are with you. Until there is nothing left."

Hearing the words I spoke to her earlier repeated back to us fills me with sorrow and resolve. We will fight until we cannot give anymore. The creatures before us move restlessly, waiting for command from their leader. I spot Khitaen standing behind the line of his monsters, a smile on his face.

Meiora and the other cryarsh appear at our feet, spreading out and preparing to intervene. I have no idea if this will work. Will the shadows be able to stand against these monsters, or will more of our allies fall today?

Faster than I could have predicted, a group of the monsters seems to transform into black fire and launch toward the far western portion of our line—the line least protected against an attack. Within moments, dozens of those soldiers are simply gone. Nothing but ash is left behind. Someone screams, and I understand the feeling.

"NOW!" I yell. We cannot wait for them to make the first move. They are too fast. Magic streaks out and collides with the monsters as they charge toward us. It seems to keep them from turning into black fire, but it doesn't slow them. Their unholy eyes glow as they approach undaunted.

This may very well be the end. Sweat pours down my face as I put every ounce of power I have left into the attack. Our magic is weak, and the sun reveals to us the size of the army seeking to destroy us.

Right before the monsters collide with us, a roar rattles the ground beneath our feet, and a great shadow soars over our heads. A dragon breathes black fire into the line of monsters, instantly destroying every remnant of them before they connect with our line.

The great beast lands silently on the battlefield before Khitaen's army, lowering his head and roaring as shadows drift lazily off his body, his rider dressed in black leathers and a black cloak, green light surrounding her, dismounts.

She came.

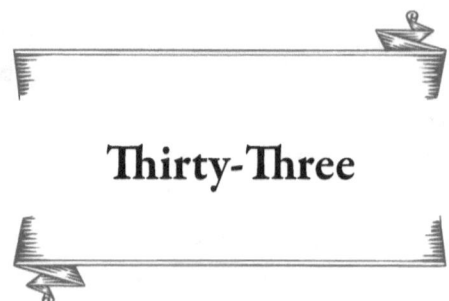

Thirty-Three

"The only way to destroy great evil is to stand against it no matter the cost."
—Adrian, Sovereign of Myzonia
Speech before the final
battle of the Throne War

Darci

Khitaen glares at me as I drop to the ground next to Ryuzio. Malice seeps out of his very essence. The scene around me is catastrophic. Bodies litter the earth, the snow a nauseating blend of mud and crimson. I know Khitaen brought more shadow abominations with him than what we've seen. I sense their magic from behind his lines.

The Myzonian army stands battered and broken, but still present. They should have retreated, but I knew Adrian and Marcus wouldn't go down without a fight. Death calls out to me from all around the Plain. The sensation is overwhelming.

"Enough, Khitaen! This is between you and me!" I shout it across the monsters and the men he has assembled. The creatures quiver in my presence, knowing judgment comes for them for their disobedience to me, their true maker.

He says nothing. With a flick of his wrist, his army shouts and charges toward Ryuzio and me. I think the command, and the air fills with the sounds of wingbeats as thousands of dragons darken the sky.

Gasps and shouts sound behind me. Khitaen's army hesitates, and a few stumble as they look to the skies.

Ryuzio takes flight and joins the others as they dodge blasts of magic from Khitaen and swoop down, picking up soldiers and crushing them before they can advance. I turn and run toward the Myzonian line, locking eyes with Marcus. He stands open-mouthed, staring at me, and Adrian steps up next to him. They both look exhausted and battered.

My chest aches briefly at the sight, but I push the feeling down into the depths of my soul. When I reach their line, the exhaustion on every face becomes more apparent. Their strength is waning along with their numbers.

I stop in front of Marcus, and he stares intensely into my eyes, penetrating my essence. A memory of blue eyes, light brown skin, and a quirky smile flashes in my mind. I don't think I ever thought long and hard about how much Marcus reminds me of Kiran. Kiran, whom I killed to prevent Khitaen from getting my magic and destroying the world. Kiran—the man I loved more than life itself. The sorrow tears at my chest, my heart struggling to pound against the grief that rises inside of me.

That's not happening this time. I will end Khitaen once and for all, and Marcus will be safe, as will Adrian.

"It's almost finished," I whisper the words.

Both men watch me a moment longer before shifting their eyes to the enemy pressing past the line of dragons. Cryarsh have joined in the attack, but they won't keep everyone at bay.

"Steady!" Marcus shouts as nervous shuffling fills the air. The line of Myzonian warriors holds. Even in their fear, in their doubt, in the knowledge that the end is coming, they stand.

Adrian regrips his sword, casting his eyes quickly toward me before focusing again.

"Now!" Marcus roars, and the host of soldiers echoes the call. I join the line in their final push and run to the front. I will pave as much of a way as I can, but I intend to find Khitaen and to fight him myself.

Magic sparks from my fingers, and soon shadows stretch out from my body, blasting through the lines of monsters and men that managed to slip past the dragons. The hiss of more shadow creatures is met with roars as Ryuzio finds their hiding place. It all only does so much, and soon the clash of bodies and swords reverberates in the air.

The essence of death begins to reach out for me. Its presence makes itself known as monsters and men alike fall on both sides of this war. I use as little of my magic as I can because I want all of it for Khitaen. He is strong, but I'm hoping he's spent some of his strength by this point.

Adrian slices flesh and bone, his weariness making him sloppy but not reckless yet. He's watching me. I feel his eyes on me constantly. It's distracting. I've lost my sense of where Marcus is. He must have been separated from us during the struggle.

"Adrian, if you have something to say, now would be a good time." Another shadow of mine slices through the monster, lunging toward me.

"I... don't... have... anything... to... say..." Each word is broken by a swing or jab of his sword as he parries with a man marked by Khitaen.

I send a plume of shadows over, and the man drops instantly. Sending a wave of shadows into the air, I form a wall around us that will hold for a short while. He pivots in a circle, looking for an opening.

"Adrian, what do you want to say?"

Finally, he stops and locks eyes with me. My magic flares to life at the sight.

"Why are you doing this?"

"Helping you? Why wouldn't I?"

"What do you plan on doing to stop Khitaen?" There's an edge to his voice. He senses something. There's an awareness that wasn't there before. Needles flare across my skin.

"I'll do what I have to do to stop a monster from controlling all the worlds." With that, I drop the shield and step back into the fray, hearing Adrian's sword clash with another's.

As time creeps by, I hear from Meiora that Khitaen has moved toward the back eastern flank of his army. Myzonia is holding its own against the enemy. My dragons are making progress through the shadow monsters and quelling the attack of the others, but it won't be enough. Khitaen has been planning this for years.

I decide to go with my instinct and shift to where I picture Khitaen to be. There he is. Strange, glowing white eyes snag on my sudden appearance. A wicked smile forms on his face, and I can't help but mirror it.

Magic strikes out toward me, but my shadows are quick and slam into the wave. We parry like this, back and forth, shadows and light pounding into one another. I become single-minded, nothing else entering my periphery.

His power strikes, but it also searches, seeking an opening where he can find a weakness in me. He won't. I'm too strong now, too powerful. But I would be foolish to allow myself to be distracted. Sweat beads on my brow and trickles down my temples. I summon a cryarsh and one slides behind Khitaen, knocking him off balance slightly. It gives me enough time to strike him hard with a shadow that twists into his chest.

His eyes widen, and he drops to his knees. I stride toward him, holding the shadow tight. I form a sword of black fire out of my magic and use one hand to hold it to his throat.

"DARCI, NO!" Adrian's voice pierces my ears and breaks my concentration enough that the shadow slips and Khitaen rises again. I refocus when I hear a shriek, the sound only a cryarsh gives when it dies, shredding through the air around me.

The sound tears through me, and I fall backward. Scrambling to my feet, all eyes lift to the skies to see a different kind of monster gliding through the air on waves of light. Myrukim—their bodies writhe and twist like serpents through the air, harnessing light as their weapon instead of shadows. No, no, no, no!

My sister Araina has sent her creatures, and their focus turns to my shadows—the dragons and the cryarsh—and the shadow creatures Khitaen brought with him. Light slices through their essence, and more shrieks and roars begin to fill the air.

I scream at the skies and order my shadows to retreat, but I know they won't all do it. My eyes find Khitaen again, and I barely have time to react when he attacks again. Magic bombarding me and knocking me backward step by step. I gather every ounce of strength I have and pour it into my hands. Shadows erupt and writhe out of me, wrapping around his legs and forcing him to fight to stand.

Rage controls my every breath now. Araina would kill my creatures, my dragons. She would aid Khitaen! Khitaen fights to stand against the shadows. I almost have him subdued when I hear him again.

"Darci, you can't! You can't kill him!" Adrian shouts at me. He's getting closer. I need to finish this now.

"Darci! Enough!" Marcus's voice joins Adrian's, and my soul tears open a little more.

But they don't understand. I can't stop. Not now. Khitaen is no fool. He sees the turmoil in my eyes, and I feel the blood drain from my face as I see his eyes flick over my shoulder toward one of them.

"NO!" I scream, but it's too late.

A lightning bolt of magic strikes past me, and I hear the moment of contact. I hear the body hit the ground. I hear the grunt of pain, and my soul knows. Adrian.

"NO, ADRIAN!" Marcus's voice twists in anguish, and I know he's running to Adrian's side. Seeing what I already know. The blow was a promise of death. Adrian cannot survive this.

Death seeps out of him into the ground, reaching for me, showing me what has happened. I roar in rage and draw my hand back, plunging the shadow sword into Khitaen's chest. Surprise dances across his face for a moment. He didn't think I could do it. He didn't think I would stay on task when my friend fell. If I can even call him a friend.

The cacophony of shrieks and roars as more myrukim destroy more of my creatures smothers me. Meiora. Ryuzio. They are not safe, but I will not be stopped. Not this time. I twist the sword in Khitaen's chest and pour shadows into him along the wound.

"You should never have done this, Death Goddess." The words sound tight, strained, as they slip from his lips.

"You must pay for your sins against the mortals, God of War." I grit my teeth, bracing against the power surging in protest at my presence.

Slowly, the power weakens. Slowly, the magic wanes. I hear the beating of his heart stutter before I lean forward and whisper into his ear only.

"It is finished."

I rip the sword out and let his body collapse to the ground. The monsters he created die instantly, and the men and creatures stutter at the strange change in the air, not knowing what to do now that their leader has fallen.

Tears stream down my cheeks. I wobble on my feet; almost spent from the power it took to finish Khitaen. Grief taints the moment. I turn my gaze to the skies and watch as more dragons are destroyed by the myrukim's unrelenting power. A few myrukim fell, but my dragons were surprised. They have no advantage here.

I stagger backward and move away from Khitaen's body. I feel the worlds crack at the loss of another god. The groaning of faraway places that have lost their life-force. I don't care about his world, though. He broke the rules. He violated the trust of mortals, and he would have stopped at nothing to take my power for his own and rule all the worlds. It had to be done. I was right. I was...

My thoughts are choked off. Marcus cradles Adrian's body, whispering something to his friend. He's not dead yet. I can sense the life still in him, but he's close. The piece of my soul buried within him is the only reason he didn't die instantly from Khitaen's power.

I take faltering steps toward them, getting close enough to hear the whispered pleas of Marcus. Chills run down my spine. A great chasm forms in my soul where connection and life should be. My tears never stop, though I cry not for him. I cry for my worlds. For the death that was carelessly strewn about. I mourn for the souls stolen too soon, the creatures I imbued with my magic who have fallen under the power of Araina. All of it for what? She didn't stop me. I still killed Khitaen exactly as I planned to.

"Mar... cus..." Adrian's breathing is strained.

"Shhh... Don't talk. I'll get a healer." The field of combat has grown strangely quiet. The enemy has retreated, and those who stayed are bound by the Myzonian soldiers.

"Somebody, get me a healer! NOW!" Marcus's voice shakes with emotion. A young woman standing nearby runs toward the camp searching for any help.

"It's... okay..."

"Shut up, Adrian. You need to conserve your energy." Marcus presses a palm flat on Adrian's chest and attempts to pour magic into him, but Marcus is spent, and he can't heal. It's not his gift. Healing Adrian isn't possible now anyway.

"Please..." I sense what Adrian wants to say, but he doesn't have the energy to.

I step closer and feel my magic reach for Adrian. Meiora appears and glides its velvety body across Adrian's broken one. Ryuzio lands featherlight on the ground behind me. Relief cascades through my bones. They haven't been killed. I stare at the skies for another moment and see the myrukim vanishing, called back to wherever Araina hides them, except for one. A beautiful pink myrukim lingers in the air nearby. Light and magic give it the appearance of a sea serpent floating in water. Most of my dragons are gone. Their absence is keenly felt in my soul as my magic tethering them to this world comes back to me instead.

I know, Meiora. The cryarsh is right, and only one clear path lies before me.

I come to Adrian's side, and I don't miss the way Marcus pulls him tighter to himself as if he's afraid I will steal his friend away. Adrian's eyes slowly slide to me. The connection, no matter how faint, thrums between us still.

Clarity passes into his deep brown irises. He feels it.

"You. It's... you."

I smile sadly at his effort before answering. "Yeah, it's me."

"I'm sorry, Shadow." The words come out choked like a broken promise between us. There could never be any broken promises here, though.

His eyes glaze over, and Marcus's shoulders tremble with the effort to control his emotions.

"No apologies this time," I whisper.

This world doesn't need me. It needs him.

He smiles softly, a peace settling into his features.

"To Arawnia," he murmurs.

I shake my head. "Not anymore."

Confusion floods his eyes, and Marcus shouts as I reconjure my shadow sword as a dagger this time, violet wisps twining around the black blade.

"What are you doing?!" Marcus throws himself backward, dragging Adrian with him.

I lock eyes with Marcus, an apology painted there, though I doubt he'll care. He won't even remember. Every apology I can breathe to Meiora and Ryuzio and every creation I've made with shadows and magic, I send into our connections. No one can kill a god. No one but me.

Then, I plunge the blade into my chest.

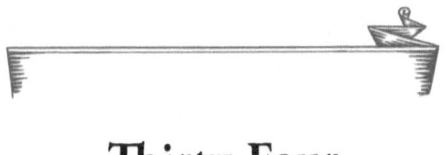

Thirty-Four

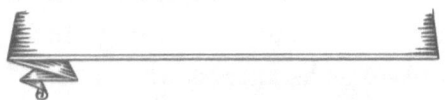

"There is balance in all things, even in death. In death, the balance is made whole, absolute, complete. In death, there is peace when Arawnia greets the soul."

—*Scroll of Arawnia,*
passage 130

Darci

It stings. Marcus reaches for me, but realizes he still cradles Adrian's almost lifeless body and shifts back onto his heels. A roar shakes the air around me, and Meiora trembles across Adrian. I focus my mind on the blade and force shadows to pour into my body. The pain of battling my instincts, of turning my magic against myself, threatens to rip me apart. I fight the desire to wrench the blade out.

Tears pour down my face. One part from the pain, the other because of the man lying before me. His eyes flutter closed, his breathing becoming ragged.

"What are you doing?" Marcus shifts again before slowly lowering Adrian to the ground. His body language suggests he wants to snatch the blade out of my chest.

"Don't." I grit out through clenched teeth. The shadows flood my veins, swarming my essence, my soul, my lifeblood. In their path, nothing is safe. I didn't intend for this to happen. I didn't intend for it to go wrong, but I did have a plan for it if anything were to go off the expected path.

The pink myrukim lets out a strangled cry, a strange sound like water and wind combined. I realize then it must have stayed back to communicate with Araina. It is her eyes and ears here. The turmoil it feels is hers.

I have one consolation in this. My sister grieves the loss of me.

"Darci, please! We need to use your magic to save him." Marcus begs, walking forward on his knees slowly.

I shake my head. "I am." Speaking is difficult.

Meiora trembles more violently and struggles to get to me. It slides with difficulty across the ground, wrapping its body around my knees. I'm sorry. I'm sorry for doing this to you, Shadow. I plead for it to hear my thoughts because I can't get words out anymore.

Marcus's eyes frantically search my face for any understanding. A flash of deep sorrow passes through them, and I think for a moment he might have loved me. He might still. This is for his good, then.

Shouts echo around me as the sound of Ryuzio collapsing to the ground with the remaining dragons shakes the earth. My soul tears in two. Everything in me feels weak, breaking, and falling to pieces. It's only as I get to the edge of darkness that I risk removing one hand from the blade.

My fingers shake as I reach for Adrian. I fall forward, my outstretched hand landing hard against his chest. He lets out a strained gasp, and Marcus reaches for me. His hand brushes my shoulder, but he watches as green magic slips out of my fingers into Adrian. He doesn't push me away and instead waits, breathless.

"What's happening?" He whispers. His eyes dart to Meiora, whose movements slow moment by moment.

It's dying. The loss is too much, too unbearable. *I'm sorry*. My lips move, but no sound comes out. As if Marcus can read my mind, his eyes widen as he looks at me and back to Meiora. The realization dawning in his icy blue gaze. The cryarsh, the dragons, they all need me.

Adrian's eyes widen slightly, a spark of life awakening within them. The shadow dagger dissolves, the rest of the shadows seeping into the wound I made, and the green light that was escaping my fingers and slipping into Adrian goes dim. My other hand holding the dagger goes limp, and I collapse toward Adrian.

Strong arms catch me before I hit Adrian's body. Marcus drags me away from the Sovereign into his lap, cradling me. All the hurt that was there, all the pain from my lies and the truths he discovered, dissipates. I feel his warmth, but it's not enough to banish the cold spreading throughout my body.

"Darci, I..."

My body is limp against his; my head falling backward to look up at the sky. The myrukim glides through the air again, circling overhead before vanishing. The thumping of my heart slows. A single tear slips down my cheek, the coolness of it a balm to my aching skin. A hand brushes strands of hair away from my eyes, but I can't see who it is. Kiran? I can't remember. The touch is soft, loving, almost. It must be Kiran.

My thoughts turn fuzzy, twining around each other, memories flashing through my mind, a conglomeration of millennia. I can't feel the warmth anymore. I can't feel Meiora anymore. A ragged breath escapes me.

I wish I could close my eyes, for only a moment, a breath, an eternity.

Darkness welcomes me, creeping along the edges of my vision. My chest tightens, and then all the tension releases, trickling out of me like a stream skipping down a mountain. Effortless, undaunted, easy. Free.

Shadows engulf me one last time.

I WATCH HIM AS HE LIES in the middle of a quiet wood, waiting for him to move, to shift, to open his eyes. Scanning my surroundings, a soft smile graces my lips as I see the shadows in the trees, the stars in the sky, the dancing flakes of snow as they drift to the forest floor.

Finally, he stirs. My eyes slide back to him, and I take in his beauty. The deep ebony of his skin, the strong jaw, and the peace etched into his features. A faint green glow emanates from him. My smile widens at the sight.

When he opens his eyes, I wait for him to sit up and soak up the calm of the forest. Surprise, followed by wonder, lights up his eyes. Those deep brown eyes, almost black, find me sitting cross-legged on the ground only a short distance away.

"Where are we?" His voice is light, full of life and joy.

I look around, taking in my surroundings.

"We're wherever you want us to be."

Confusion furrows his brow. "I... I think I'm dying. Did I die?"

"No, you didn't."

He stares, captivated by me for a moment.

"I feel... I feel okay. Is this what Marcus saw? When he almost died, that is?"

I look around the glen and hold my fingers out to catch a few snowflakes on my skin. They are cool, but not cold.

"Marcus was given the choice to walk into Arawnia with his family or return to you and your world."

He tilts his head inquiringly at me. "Is this not the entrance, then? Is this the way into Arawnia?"

A soft ache enters my chest. A throb warning me that time is limited.

"No, it's not. You are not dying, Adrian. I am giving you something."

He pushes to his feet and spins in a circle, marveling at the beauty here, at the peace that floods every aspect of his being.

"What are you giving me? A second chance? I felt your magic coming into me, tying together the frayed ends of existence. Are you healing me the way that you healed Marcus?"

I look down at the snow-dusted ground before dragging my eyes back up to his.

"Not exactly. There's a lot I did wrong in this world. There's a lot of darkness in me that I could not banish. You are the best of me, Adrian. I didn't plan for all of this. This death, chaos, and destruction of worlds. I guess I should have. I am Death after all. I was."

I rise to my feet and step toward him, holding out a hand for him to take. He narrows his eyes and then places his hand in my mine. I turn his palm over and trace the lines etched there. Green light and shadows twine together in a beautiful thread on his palm.

"It's your magic, isn't it?"

I look up to see him watching me closely.

He continues, "It's your magic that's growing in me. I think mine has always been like yours, but I can tell—it's different. You're different."

"Adrian, I cannot save you."

He frowns and pulls his hand from my grasp. Coldness seeps into my fingers.

"But what does all this mean then? Do I not get to choose? The way that Marcus did?"

The ache in my chest grows, but I ignore it.

"I cannot save you, Adrian. Khitaen struck you with a powerful magic. The only reason you didn't die immediately is because a part of my soul lives in you."

He nods his head slowly. Understanding, but only in part.

"But you... You can't save me?"

I shake my head and step away from him toward the shadows tangled in the trees. My feet feel numb. A tingling grows up my legs into my spine.

"I told you once I wanted only to be loved. To be remembered. To not be erased from history and the world." I smile, but it's painful. Maybe he can sense it. I feel his eyes boring into my back. I know the crack in my voice wasn't hidden as well as I was hoping it would be.

"Yes, I remember you telling me that. You found love. You lost it, and we know your name now. The histories will be corrected. We can't deny it was your presence that saved us today. You saved my people, my world."

I close my eyes, a traitorous tear escaping my eye. I feel his presence at my back. His warmth and life radiate into me.

"Darci, it's okay. I am ready to go on. It's okay," he whispers.

He places a hand on my shoulder. I see it from the corner of my eye, but I can't feel it anymore. The ache turns into a throb, into a tearing. Still, I ignore it.

Turning to face him, I draw in a deep breath, reveling in the smells of the wood. The cool damp of dead leaves underfoot being slowly buried by snow. It smells of earth and smoke. For some reason, it reminds me of Marcus. It reminds me of Kiran. Their names are getting harder to pull from my memory.

His eyes glow a lovely green around the outside of his beautiful, dark brown irises. The light is stronger now. Concern settles within them when he sees the watery state of my own eyes.

"I can't save you, but I can let you be more. I can give you one last gift."

"What are you talking about?"

"Myzonia lost its god, but your magic can sustain. Khitaen's world..." A derisive laugh escapes my mouth. "I don't really care what happens to it. It's a cruel world. If it falls, I'm not sure any will mourn it. I think that makes me a villain, doesn't it?"

He remains quiet, waiting for some clarity.

"Oria will be without one too, but maybe someone can do something about that."

"What are you talking about?"

The numbness grows in my body. My mind turns a little fuzzy.

"I'm giving you everything, Adrian. I see this is the way it was meant to be. You are so much more than I could ever be. There is a lot more goodness in you. You are the best of me. I wish I could have seen everything you would become."

He laughs softly, in disbelief. "Darci, what are you talking about? You're not making sense."

"I'm giving you the rest of me. No one can kill a god, remember? Except for me. I... I think it's time for my name to be forgotten. Not that I can do much about that now anyway."

I step away from him, or I try to. My legs don't seem to be working very well. I collapse, but Adrian catches me before I hit the ground. He lowers us together, searching my body for injuries.

"What's going on, Darci? What's happening to you?" He brushes my hair from my eyes.

"I'm dying, Adrian. The only way I could save you was if I died."

He shakes his head. "No. You can't die. You're the Goddess of Death. Who will care for their souls?"

I smile softly up at him. Soft, wispy shadows seep from my skin, drifting between us until they find solace in his presence, sinking into him.

"I'm sorry... I didn't mean to burden you with this."

His brow furrows before clarity brightens his eyes. I watch as he observes the shadows drifting toward him. His eyes are almost frantic, darting back and forth, watching as the world changes for him.

"What did you mean, Darci? What did you mean when you said we were wherever I wanted us to be?" His voice is tight.

One side of my mouth barely tilts up. I can't feel much now.

"You know."

"Will I find you? In Arawnia? Please? I don't know how to do all of this."

My eyes dim. Shadows and darkness greet me. Oblivion awaits.
"No, Adrian. You won't... You won't remember me."

It's the most painful thing. To be forgotten. Or maybe it's not. I won't know either way.

He shakes his head. Denial eclipses the light in his eyes for a moment.

"I've always been connected to you. I've always felt you. I won't forget. You're the shadow on the wall. Always."

I let my eyes drink him up.

"I... just... wanted... something... beautiful."

"Shh... save your energy." *He runs his hands down my arms. Sparks of magic flaring from him, but they reflect off me. The shadows slow to a trickle now.*

"Adrian..."

He stops his desperate attempts. I know the ache he feels, the tearing apart of his soul. Our connection was strong. It will be painful for it to be severed, but only for a short time.

"Tell him..." *The words die on my lips. The effort is too much.*

"Marcus? Tell him what? Darci? Please! Darci... Arawna."

A light flickers in my chest. It's nice to hear that name one more time. Then, there is nothing left. I am nothing. I am darkness. I am shadows.

Thirty-Five

"In long times past, before all that is
Death walked hand in hand with Life.
When time ran out, at the end of all things,
Death surrendered, that Life may persist.
The God of Death brought life and peace.
His reign is eternal. Forever and ever."
—*The Account of Death and Life*,
page 1

Marcus

I grip her in my arms, gently shaking her, desperate to get her eyes to open. Adrian's skin flushes with life, and green light emanates from him. Murmurs fill the air around me as soldiers talk to one another, curious about the events taking place. No one truly understands who she is, but I do. I regret not telling her how I felt. It made no sense, but I can't control what she became to me.

Her skin is cold now. The great black dragon she flew in on lies still, faint slivers of shadows escaping its nostrils. Meiora has faded away, and I can't see it anymore. Araina, what's happening? She can't do this.

"Darci, please." The ache in my chest deepens.

A gasp startles me, and I look toward Adrian, finding him breathing hard, staring at the sky. He sits up abruptly and looks at me before his eyes trail down to Darci in my arms. I'm covered in blood and mud, snow soaking my pants, but I don't care. I hold her, and I plead with my eyes for Adrian to help.

He notices the crowd around us.

"Leave! Tend to the wounded. Go, now!" He barks. They scramble away, and I see him looking at his hands, turning them over and back again.

He twists his wrists, and plumes of shadows erupt around us, forming a barrier between us and the armies. He maneuvers onto his knees and shuffles toward me. His eyes fill with tears, and screams fill my head. No, I won't believe it.

"Marcus."

He drops his eyes to Darci and reaches a shaky hand out to touch her cheek. I want to tell him to stop. I want to beg him to do something, to use his magic to make her wake up.

I clutch her tighter to my chest, but she feels different. Panicking, I scan her face for life, for something.

"Please, wake up. Please, don't leave me."

Adrian's warm hand presses into my shoulder. I try to avoid his gaze. I try to see only her, but then I see the shadows drifting off her body, leaving her and floating in the air toward him. *No.* I watch, helpless, as they abandon her.

"Marcus." His voice cracks, and it takes everything inside of me not to break down right there. Walls. I need walls around me.

Finally, I force myself to meet his eyes. They glow a soft green, a light reminding me of her.

"She's not coming back, Marcus. She...she saved me instead."

How am I in this impossible position? Of course, I want my best friend, my brother, here with me. This world, this kingdom, needs him. I need him. He's the only family I have left. But a part of me needs her. I need her here with me. I'd even go to her house in Oria and live my days out, however long they would be with her.

I'm bleeding out on the inside.

"You can save her, though, right? You have magic. Strong like her." I realize it now. Every moment these past months has led to this. This change coming over him is from her. She gave herself to him, and now, it seems her magic is no longer hers either.

"I can't, Marcus. I saw her in a different place. She said..." He looks down, avoiding my eyes. I don't think I want to hear what she said.

I look at her in my arms and notice shadows spreading out from her in every direction. She gets lighter, and I try to hold her, but it's like grains of sand slipping through my fingers. Darkness swells around us, and the only light I can see is the soft green light of Adrian's magic pulsing from him. A faint glow fails to dispel the darkness that has fallen completely over us.

I plead. I beg. It is not enough.

When the shadows dissipate, my arms are empty. She's gone.

"Marcus, I think I took her place. I think I am now the God of Death."

Confusion floods my mind. What is Adrian talking about?

I rub my face with my hands before I lift my eyes to Adrian's. He looks different, changed. I think I should be sad. There's a strange ache in my chest, but it dulls moment by moment, becoming faint, barely a memory.

"Did you hear me, Marcus? I think I took her place." Adrian watches me closely. He looks desperate, like he wants me to understand something.

"Who are you talking about, Adrian?"

My friend's eyes widen with shock and a deep sorrow. Of course, he's upset. We just fought a war. A lot of good people died. My body is bone tired. The cold has seeped into every inch of me. I want to go home. I want to rest. I want peace.

"You don't—you don't remember her? Darci?"

"Adrian, I think you're as exhausted as I am. I've never heard of a Darci." I sigh, "I just want to go home." I push to my feet, brushing snow off my pants. All my muscles ache, and my joints complain. I reach a hand down to Adrian, pulling him to his feet. Unshed tears fill his eyes.

He looks different. Shadows creep along the ground at his feet. Is that a cryarsh? The walls of shadows that were around us only moments ago have vanished, and a loud snort draws my attention. I turn around to find a great black dragon standing before us, watching carefully. I vaguely remember dragons joining the battle with us. I can't remember why, though. Instinctively, I stand between the monster and Adrian. Protecting the sovereign is what I do best.

"It's okay, friend." Adrian pulls me back a step and walks to the dragon. His eyes are full of wonder. A shadow follows him along the ground. A cryarsh winding its way around his legs. It seems familiar. A name I should know, but I can't grasp it.

Adrian reaches up and gently touches the dragon, wisps of shadows twirling along the surface of its body. I follow him slowly until I stand a few feet away. He's murmuring something to the beast, talking to it like it's a friend.

I catch only a couple of words. Something about a woman and promises to keep the dragon safe. The dragon snorts, and shadows spread out on its breath. I step back, avoiding the darkness.

"Adrian, what's going on?"

He hangs his head, pressing a hand into the center of the dragon's head. Then, he faces me.

"I think we need to change things, friend. I think it's time for me to step down as Sovereign."

I can't hide the shock on my face. "You're crazy. Why would you do that? Who will serve in your place?"

He smiles. "I have an idea, but first, let's help the wounded. Then, let's go home."

He walks away from the dragon, which spreads its massive wings and lifts into the air, flying somewhere to the south. A few other dragons rise in the air and follow him. However, the cryarsh lingers with Adrian, draping itself like a cloak across his back. I can't do anything but follow, wondering why the shadow feels familiar, a memory from another life.

WE SPENT THE NEXT SEVERAL hours walking through the remnants of our army. Too many fell. James is gone. Others I called friends, men and women I served with for years, who fought with me and Adrian in the Throne War. Death taints every surface. Adrian walks from injured soldier to injured soldier, healing them as best as he can. A few who are too close to death, he kneels over, placing his hands gently on them, a strange peace settling into their eyes as they breathe their last breaths.

I help carry the dead to multiple pyres scattered throughout the field. Enemy and comrade alike share the same burial. We all bleed the same. We all die the same. None of us is immortal.

Exhaustion weighs heavily on us all. The night creeps in, and shadows loom over the Plain. When the last of the bodies are placed on a pyre, I summon the little bit of magic still in my veins, and let fire lick the fabrics and wood intermingled with our fallen. Others light the remaining pyres scattered throughout the Plain.

The glow of the fires creates an eerie display in the dark. Dancing flames light up the surroundings, and the mutual exhaustion and sorrow on everyone's faces weigh heavily in the air. I haven't seen Adrian in a couple of hours. A change is in the air. The earth feels settled, the air a tinge warmer than it was at the start of the snowstorm.

After all this, perhaps we will experience some beauty and peace in this world. A chance to breathe after so much turmoil. The god we defeated in battle was the one stirring up strife in the capital time after time. He's gone now, and the world has a chance to recover from all the death.

The murmuring of prayers to Araina fills the air as people say goodbye to friends and comrades. Whispering quiet encouragement that they will find rest somewhere else. A memory flashes through my mind of a forest in the fall and a sky full of stars overhead. The musty scent of dead leaves, crisp air, and voices bickering playfully on the wind touches my senses. It's a strange feeling, this memory passing before my eyes. A part of me feels something is missing. *Someone* is missing from it, but I can't place their name.

It's probably the stress of the battle getting to me now. I probably dreamed it a long time ago.

I scan the faces of the gathered, watching as people wipe tears from their eyes, fling arms over shoulders, hug, laugh, mourn—-a strange blending of loss and relief, of life and death in this place. I stop when I notice Adrian standing in the shadows. He doesn't look as tired as the rest of us, but a different weariness shadows his face. A darkness never leaving his eyes, marking him in grief. He closes his eyes and prays, I think.

I make my way toward him, slowly maneuvering around the pyre and the others. His lips continue to move, and as I draw near, I hear the fervent prayer on his lips more clearly.

"May they find rest in Arawnia."

Arawnia? I feel I should recognize that word, but it's strange. A different way of praying for the dead than I remember.

I wait in silence for him to finish. Eventually, his eyes open, and the sorrow revealed in them stuns me. I didn't expect him to feel so deeply about the losses. Of course, we all feel the death surrounding us, but he seems more torn, more broken than the rest of us.

"You should rest, Adrian."

A sad smile flits across his features for a moment. "You're probably right. Let's go find a tent. Tomorrow, we'll head back to Rizyrk."

As we walk through the camp or what's left of it, I can't keep my thoughts to myself.

"What is Arawnia?"

Adrian looks over at me quickly, and if I'm not mistaken, deep sorrow etches his skin. He focuses again on the path before us as we draw near the end of the camp, farthest from the battlefield.

"It's paradise. A place of peace for the souls that have passed on. I think it should stay that way."

I nod. "That makes sense. Why does that name sound familiar?" Why does it make me feel safe and hopeful? I don't voice those thoughts.

"We used to know it, a long time ago."

He leaves it at that and steps into a tent. I should follow, but I don't want to. Instead, I move over to the other tent nearby, peeking in to find it empty. Perhaps peace is what is coming for the world now.

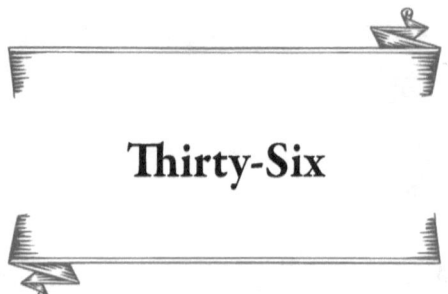

Thirty-Six

"Death is not the end. It is only the beginning."
—Airos, the Immortal

Adrian

The world has changed. I have changed. I don't understand why, but I remember Darci. I still hear her voice, and I can still picture her face. Her magic courses through me, and perhaps the tiny sliver of her soul embedded in mine holds her memory closer than the others. The pain of seeing Marcus forget her almost ruined me. In a way, it was a gift. He loved her. He didn't want to, but he did, and the loss of her was tearing him apart. Until it wasn't anymore.

I realize now the voice I kept hearing in my strange dreams was her speaking to me. She was with me every step of the way. I was never truly alone. I couldn't figure out that it was her at first, but it was because she appeared to me stripped down of all the strange components of humanity, leaving only her divine nature before me. The other voices, the ones whispering on the breeze, they meant something too. On the battlefield, I realized it. The whispers are souls as the bodies perish in this mortal realm. It felt heavy, knowing death bombarded me effortlessly. I think of it now as an honor. To hear them. To know them.

I stand on the balcony overlooking the courtyard. It's been a week since the battle ended—the losses causing a painful ripple across the world. Aella was killed during the battle. I had forgotten about her arrival, and the final stand against the enemy proved to be too much.

The moon casts a blue tinge on everything. An ethereal glow on a world in transition, making everything feel calm. The opposite of my soul now. I feel restless, uncertain about the coming days. Plans must be made, but I'm not sure how to execute them. I don't even know what I am supposed to do anymore.

Sighing, I rest my hands on the railing, focusing on the cold stone beneath my palms. A shift in the air causes the hair on my arms to stand up. The sensation of someone watching me from inside my chambers leaves my skin feeling itchy. My thoughts drift to my cryarsh lingering in the shadows, and instantly it twines itself around my legs.

"It's good to see not everything was lost." The voice is warm and soft, caressing my back like fingers.

I face the unexpected visitor, finding a stunning woman dressed in a vibrant green dress with long sleeves. Her mahogany skin emits a soft light, and countless braids drape down her body to her waist. A spark of something flares to life in my chest. A piece of me recognizes this woman.

I should be bothered that someone made it into my chambers unnoticed, but I have the feeling this woman could not have been stopped.

I clasp my hands behind my back. "Who are you? If you don't mind my asking."

She smiles, and the light on her skin intensifies.

"I believe you knew my sister."

I'm confused and unsure of how that's possible. She doesn't look familiar, despite my heart pounding harder in my chest, the depths of me calling out to her.

"I think you might be mistaken."

"No. No, I'm not. It won't be long now. Your memory of her will fade. It's already started fading, hasn't it? All our memories will change."

Her words ignite a fire in my chest, one seeking to destroy these words, to deny the truth of them.

"Darci," I whisper.

She nods. "Yes, I believe that's what you called her."

"I won't forget." I deny, but I can already feel the traces of her name beginning to fade. It's slippery, harder to hold onto. The last couple of days, I've found myself forgetting her face. If I'm honest, I can't remember her voice at all.

"You will, Adrian. You will forget. We all will. It was the price she paid to spare your life."

Guilt gnaws at me.

"Do not feel guilty, Adrian. It was her choice."

I think about that for a moment before responding. "You're Araina, aren't you?"

Her eyes sparkle with light before she subdues it. "I have come because what Arawna started must be finished. I did a lot of things wrong when it came to my sister. I won't deny that. And she did make a mess of things in her quest for vengeance, but she tried to make it right with you."

I think I know what she means, but I don't want to accept it. I need to hear her say it; I need to hear her confirm my fears.

"What am I now?" *Who am I now?*

She tilts her head and glides closer. Her eyes trace my face; if she's searching for something, she doesn't tell me what it is.

"A void exists where a guardian once stood. A shepherd to care for the lost and abandoned. One to welcome home the wanderer."

She moves past me and stands on the balcony facing the kingdom. I'm terrified I'll fail.

"My sister was that guardian. I denied it for a long time, but she was good at caring for the forgotten and broken. She broke the rules herself when she created Oria, but those actions cannot be undone now. Not without destroying innocent lives." She pauses, and I take the moment to face the courtyard with her.

"You cannot help all the worlds, but this one could use your magic."

I stare at my hands for a moment, watching as shadows and green light dance together.

"You still didn't answer my question." Am I still me, or did something else happen when Darci died?

She lifts a single eyebrow before dropping her eyes to my hands.

"You were given a gift, Adrian. No, you are not the same. You are not mortal anymore. I am here to bestow on you the name of the God of Death. A new shepherd is needed, and she chose you."

My skin feels too tight. A part of me knew this was going to be the case—the actions Darci took would lead to me becoming more than I ever thought I was meant to be. I still don't want it. How can I live forever and watch my friends, my comrades, die?

"What if I say no?"

She offers me a sad smile. "You cannot say no. It is given to you whether you want to have it or not. A part of her soul remains with you, and you exist the way you are because of her. We don't always get to choose the path our lives take, but we can choose who we impact along that road."

The tightness in my chest intensifies, but Meiora senses my distress and spreads its warmth over my back.

"The cryarsh, the dragons—they all exist because of the magic in your blood. When Arawna died, they began to die too. The only reason they did not vanish is because you were tied closely enough to her to have her magic spill out toward them, holding their lifeforces in place until you recovered."

I nod, understanding their connection to me. I sense their thoughts, their feelings, their presence, the same way I have sensed the dying in this city and even farther out into the stretches of the world.

"This world also needs you. Arawna destroyed Markyr because he failed to protect this world from Khitaen. We cannot interfere in matters of mortals, but we are to protect our worlds from each other. Markyr failed to obey that command, and Arawna brought judgment to him. But now your world needs a new god. You can be that for this place."

I ponder that for a moment. "What about Oria, though? And what about Khitaen's world?"

"We will have to see what comes of those worlds on their own. Magic has a way of choosing for us." She murmurs the last part, thoughtful.

I face her, pulling my shoulders back and making myself resolute. "What do I need to do?"

She smiles and faces me. "Kneel, Adrian." She must see the skepticism on my face. "It's okay. I will not harm you."

I kneel before the Goddess of Light, my heart pounding in my chest. Meiora pools around me, a shimmering blanket of shadows at my knees.

Araina extends a hand toward me, and a soft light plumes in it. The tendrils reach for me and mingle with my shadows. A greeting of sorts, or a welcoming. I'm not sure.

"By the power of Endeilo, I welcome you into the circle of shepherds. Caretakers of the worlds. Guardians of the magic within. May your power be infinite, your honor never-ending. You are sworn to guide the souls of those greeted by death, for you are He who greets them. The world you welcome them to will be called the name you wish it. And all will cherish it if you remain faithful to the role you serve."

Magic swells in my chest. Her light magic flares bright, blinding me momentarily. Then, like a great wave, power rushes through my veins, and shadows erupt into the air around me. Every question I've ever had gains an answer. A veil is pulled back, revealing truths about all the events leading up to this moment. It's overwhelming in the best way possible. As quickly as those truths play out before my eyes, they fade away like wisps of smoke on the air. A roar in the distance reaches my ears, and my heart soars knowing the dragons feel my presence as deeply as I feel theirs.

The ground trembles for only a moment before settling, and a warmth trickles into the air that wasn't there before. The world feels more alive now. I press my hands into the stone at my knees and pour magic into it, marveling as I watch the light race down the side of the balcony and dissipate into the earth below. There is so much of it. I am overflowing with power. I give as much as the earth cries for, and even then, I feel full.

I stand and find the space in front of me empty. Araina is gone. Meiora nudges me toward the room, to my desk that rests under the window. I follow its prodding, curious to know what it wants me to do. A random thought enters my mind as I reach for a quill and parchment to write a word down on.

Dipping the tip into the ink, I quickly scratch out the word that the cryarsh pushes into my head. When I see it, I'm not fully aware of why this word fits just right, but it is the name I choose for paradise, for the souls that leave this realm to enter another. Another name slips into my mind, and I record it on the same parchment as well.

When I finish, I grab the parchment, blowing on the ink to help it dry before folding it carefully.

My new role weighs heavily on my mind, and I have many places I need to go, people I need to care for. First, I have to find Marcus. He won't be happy about this, but I know he's perfect for this part. This role must be filled, and I won't leave here until it is.

MARCUS LEAPS OUT OF bed, pulling a dagger out from under his pillow at the same time. He lands light on his feet, blinking against the light emanating from my hands.

"Sorry." I dim the light and raise my hands. "I didn't mean to startle you. I guess I got a little enthusiastic."

"What in Araina's name are you doing here in the middle of the night, Adrian?" He lowers the dagger, but the scowl on his face remains. Typical Marcus.

"Well, I—-" How do I tell my closest friend I'm not the same person anymore? I'm not even mortal. I spoke my suspicions on the battlefield after Darci disappeared from Marcus's arms. But the loss of her and the memories associated with her led Marcus to forget much of our exchange. Even I wasn't certain about who I was or who I was going to be then.

Meiora slides across the floor toward Marcus, and I watch as his shoulders tighten slightly at the sight. I watch it for a moment before remembering I came in here for a reason.

"Marcus, I need to talk to you. Things have changed. Everything actually. Can you feel it?"

Marcus sets his dagger on the side table next to his bed before sitting down on the side. The scars marring his back and chest appear more stark than usual in the strange greenish light coming from my hands. He fumbles around with something, and soon a flame sparks to life. He lights the lantern next to his bed, and the room is bathed in a warmer light.

"Why don't you have a fire going?" The room is chilled.

He stares at me for a moment before drawing in a deep breath. "I can't stand the smell. The fire, the smoke—it reminds me of the pyres in the Plain."

War leaves its mark on all of us.

I nod. "Understandable." I move toward the armchair sitting vacant near the empty fireplace.

Sitting down, I clutch the folded parchment tightly in my hands, calming my frantic heart.

"I cannot be the Sovereign of Myzonia anymore." I couldn't think of another way to broach the topic. It feels better to simply throw it out there between us.

His eyes widen, and his mouth opens and closes a couple of times without a sound escaping.

"I know this comes as a shock, but I think you can sense something different about me. I'm not the same person I was before the war. I don't think I've been the same person for a while. Something happened during the battle, and it changed me forever."

He stands abruptly and strides toward me. "Yeah, you almost died! But you lived. Araina spared you." Something settles strangely in my stomach at this statement, but I can't figure out why. For some reason, I believe someone else spared me, but I can't remember who it was. My heart says Araina explained it to me, but the memories are gone.

"She did, and she was here in the castle, in my chambers only moments ago."

If possible, my friend is even more stunned by the revelation. I chuckle. "My feelings were the same as yours. But she was here. I don't really have a choice in the matter—the work she told me I must do."

"What work is that? Haven't you done enough?" Anger slips into his tone, but he simply wants freedom from war and sacrifice. We all do.

"I have been gifted immortality." I press on before he can interrupt. "With that gift comes a responsibility to care for those who are mortals. Those who are broken and in need of protection."

"You're...immortal?" He whispers. "This is madness." I don't let his unbelief dissuade me, though.

"I need to do this. It's my duty now." I send out shadows from around my body, letting the green light I have become accustomed to glow brighter as well.

The shadows reach out for Marcus, and at first, I see fear in his eyes. He waits, though, reaching for the tendril that is extended before him. When the shadow touches his hand, his eyes widen in wonder. The cryarsh joins my shadows and slides around his legs like a cat. He chuckles at the warm sensation I know he feels.

"You have a cryarsh and you summon shadows and light."

"Its name is Meiora."

An odd look comes over Marcus's face. He looks the way I feel when I say the name, like it's an old familiar friend from a time long ago. He shakes his head, clearing the odd sensation away.

"That's a strange name."

I shrug. "I can't explain it. It's the name I associate with this one. It doesn't seem to mind." The cryarsh comes back to me as if in confirmation.

"Now, for the most important part." I draw in a deep breath, bringing my eyes back to my friend. "I think you should be the Sovereign of Myzonia."

He shakes his head. "You are mad. There is no way I can take that role."

I hold my hands up to stop his protests. "Marcus, you have walked side by side with me all these years. We have grown up together. You know as much about ruling this world as I do. I could never have ruled these past years without you by my side."

He opens his mouth to argue, but I press on. "You helped me in the Throne War. You helped me overthrow my father, and together we started to build a new world founded on goodness and fairness and justice."

I pause, scanning the room for a moment, and drawing the shadows back into my body. "I can think of no better man to rule this world than you."

He rubs his face with his hands before dropping them limp at his side. "Adrian, I don't want this. I'm your High Commander. I lead your armies. How am I supposed to be..." He swallows like it is physically painful for him to say the next part. "Nice to people."

I drop my head back and laugh. "Marcus, you'll do just fine! I don't know what you're worried about."

"I can't be diplomatic and negotiate with people." I try to suppress my laughter, but I'm doing a poor job of it. "Quit laughing! People *like* you, Adrian. They don't like me!"

He crosses his arms, brow furrowed, as I make every effort to compose myself.

"I'm sorry. Listen, I don't know how to be immortal, but here we are. We don't always get to choose the road we must walk. We only get to choose what we do along the way."

He takes a deep breath. A sadness sinks into his posture. "Will you leave? Will I never see you again?"

I become somber as I think. "I think I *need* to leave. Something is calling me away. I need to do some things, but I also think I can come back. I think I'll get to see you again, and someday, maybe I'll lead you to rest." I didn't tell him I was the God of Death. I don't know how you are supposed to reveal that sort of thing to your friends.

He remains quiet. "Okay, but you better come back for me. If not for me, you'd better come back to make sure I haven't ruined the entire world."

A soft chuckle escapes me. Sadness makes my throat tight. If I don't see him again in this life, I'll be there at the end of his, to lead him home. "I promise. I'll come back for you."

I stand and walk toward him, holding the parchment out for him to take.

"What's this?" He asks, confusion on his face.

"I get to choose the name of paradise. The name of the place where all things end and begin, and peace reigns eternal. I choose the first one."

He looks down at the parchment in his hands. Slowly, he unfolds it and leans toward the lantern to read the name I wrote there.

"I'm not sure why, but I wanted to make sure that our histories record this name as paradise. It seems ridiculous now, but at the time, it felt important." I reason.

He stares at the name before looking up toward me again.

"Arawna? Why is that name familiar?"

I shake my head. "That was my thought, too. I feel like it's a name I've known my whole life, but I can't remember where I heard it."

"Well, if it's the name you want recorded, then I'll make sure it happens."

I smile, though it feels strained.

Meiora tightens around my ankles for a moment, sending a warm sensation up my back. Happiness, contentment, and a tiny trace of sorrow in the gesture. What the cryarsh could be sad about, I don't know.

"Oh, and Marcus? The other name I wrote there? I think that needs to be mine. I need to separate myself from this mortal plane. I don't want people recognizing me. I think they'll already begin to forget who I was to them. Now that I'm different."

He glances back down before looking up at me. Emotion swells in his eyes, but he restrains himself. He nods; no other words needed.

This may be the end of one era, but I think I'm ready to see what the world has to offer. Maybe I can even see what I can offer the worlds. No matter how far we part, Marcus will always be like a brother to me. I'll find him again. Hopefully, before death calls for him, but if not, I'll lead him to Arawna myself.

Epilogue

"At the end of the journey, all mortals face death. Some face it in fear. Some face it in anger. Some are forced to face it too soon. But for some, Death comes for them like an old familiar friend, welcoming them into paradise, into Arawna, into peace."

—High Priestess of Luna's Temple
The God War Annals

Marcus
Three Years Later

"Your Majesty, the council is ready to meet."

I straighten from my position leaning against the balcony railing. The sun casts warm beams across the courtyard below, and birds sing merrily in the branches of the trees.

"Thank you, Noe. I'll be there in a moment." She nods, curtsying quickly before walking out of my chambers.

There's no rush. The council will wait for me. I close my eyes, breathing deeply of the fresh spring air. It's hard to believe we've had three years of peace. Three years since Adrian, I'm sorry, Airos stepped down as Sovereign. I'm the only one who remembers he didn't die in The God War.

It must be some immortal trick of the mind—how the collective consciousness simply remembered a different outcome—their sovereign slain on the battlefield, and my taking his place on the throne. The world is strange.

I haven't seen him in three years, but I guess I can't expect the immortal God of Death to visit often. He must stay busy, caring for all the souls lost to this realm. I'm finally getting the hang of it—this position of power and leadership. I don't feel as out of place as I once did, finding my position with the others, working to rebuild what was broken and destroyed.

A warm breeze blows across my skin, and I am grateful that winter's grip on us has finally ceased. Fewer fires will be burning throughout the castle today, and I won't have to stay warm by wearing an ungodly number of layers. I still can't stand the smell of fire.

The God War remains a strange mystery to our scribes today. I cannot fully recall what spurred a battle between Araina and Khitaen. I only know our world was caught in the middle. Adrian almost died, but Araina was gracious enough to give him life. Now, he's the God of Death and protector of Arawna, the afterworld. Perhaps, it isn't meant for us to know the movements of the divine, to understand the choices they make, or the paths they set us on.

I stretch my arms over my head and slowly turn to walk inside when I notice a shadow in the corner of my vision. It startles me in part because it conjures a vague memory of something from my past. I recognize it. A memory flashes through my mind fast enough that I can't grasp it. My heart responds to its presence, though, and pounds in my chest.

Do I look toward it? Do I dare face the shadow that feels like more than a mere trick of the light? If I look, will it still be there? Do I want to know who watches me from the dark?

I clench my hands into fists, but ultimately, I decide to ignore its presence for the moment. Walking toward my desk, I gather a few parchments of notes and stop when I come across his handwriting. A pang of sorrow makes my chest ache, but I ignore it, reaching for the note that caught my eye.

My heart beats faster. I don't remember leaving that note here, but there it sits, waiting for me to pick up again.

Two words. Two names. Arawna. Airos.

"I was wondering if you'd finally say hello."

I jump, turning toward the voice. I can't stop the smile planting itself on my face. He's here. My closest friend has finally come back. Shadows swirl around him, and a cryarsh takes up residence on my bed, an inky pool of black on the green blankets.

"I didn't expect to ever see you again."

He smiles in return before closing the space between us and embracing me. It's felt like a lifetime since we last spoke.

"Well, I'm here now. I told you I'd come back to visit." He releases me before turning into the room, taking note of the empty hearth. "Still bothered by fire?"

I shrug. "I've never been able to get past it, honestly. I sound crazy."

He shakes his head. "No, there are still things about death that don't sit well with me. Yet, I am the shepherd of it." He continues perusing the space, even stepping out onto the balcony to observe Myzonia in all its brilliance. "It's beautiful."

I join him at the stone railing. "Yes, it is." Silence fills the space between us. Unspoken words we can never quite force out.

"I've been here often. You just haven't seen me."

I laugh. "Well, I've been a bit busy taking care of everything you left behind. Besides, I thought I did see you from time to time."

He turns his head toward me with a curious look on his face. "And when was that?"

I gesture aimlessly with my hands. "You're the God of Death. Shadows and darkness are sort of your thing, am I right? Every once in a while, I thought I saw a shadow in the corner of my eye. The slightest movement drew my attention, but every time I looked over, it was gone. To be honest, I kind of thought I was going mad."

He never revealed the truth about himself at first. It didn't take long for me to figure out his role amongst the divine though.

My eyes meet his now, and I'm surprised to find confusion there.

"What? You're telling me it wasn't you or one of your shadows?" My tone is light, but I feel anything but calm now.

"I—-" He pauses, pursing his lips together for a moment. "I'm sorry. What you're saying reminds me of something from a long time ago. It sounds familiar, like from another life." He shakes his head and leads the way back inside.

"We're rebuilding the house in Zaiven." It's abrupt, but I get the feeling he won't stay long.

His features soften. "That's good. I'm glad to hear that. Do you have big plans for it?"

I nod, patting the stack of notes on my desk I had been riffling through before he arrived.

"Yes, I want to make a shelter for families still trying to find their place in the world. Specifically for children with special abilities."

"Like Risa?"

I nod. "Like Risa. The world is better than it was, but it's not perfect. There are still those who wish to exploit the innocent. We've also discovered some new continents in the far west. We hope to explore them further as well."

He gives a knowing smile, one that seems to say he knows more than I but isn't telling. I scowl back, which makes him laugh.

"You're as fun as you always were, Marcus."

"Yeah, yeah, I get it. You're a god. You know things now." I wave him off.

"Meiora, tell Marcus I'm only serving the people the way I was meant to."

The cryarsh stretches its shape outward before curling up even tighter on the bed. It looks cozy and content, a cat happily snoozing the day away.

"Your shadow doesn't seem too impressed by you." I raise an eyebrow.

He rolls his eyes. "Well, Ryuzio listens to me still. Some of the time."

"Who's Ryuzio?" The name is another chime pestering me to remember something important.

"My dragon. Well, one of them." A dragon named Ryuzio.

"I, I think I know him. Maybe I dreamed of him." His eyes lock onto mine, seeing into the depths of my soul.

"You dream of dragons, Marcus?" He crosses his arms, and a faint green glow fills his eyes.

"I have strange dreams. Dreams of a forest in the fall. It's peaceful there, I never want to wake up. I never want to leave. Then, there are strange dreams of a person with green eyes, but maybe I'm only dreaming about you." I pause, thinking. "I don't think so, though. Your eyes may glow green, but they are most assuredly the color of dirt."

"Hey!"

I smirk and ignore him. "These eyes are brilliant green. I catch glimpses of shadows, dragons, and flying. I feel like I'm watching someone else's life." I look down at the parchments in my hands. "It sounds foolish."

When I lift my gaze, I'm surprised to see him looking pensive, as if the things I have spoken to him remind him of another life as well.

"I don't think it's foolish, Marcus. Who can understand the vastness of the mortal's mind? Besides, you have lived through enough major events to last many lifetimes. I'm sure your mind is simply trying to process it all."

I nod, letting his words sink in.

"Adrian, come back for me in the end, okay?"

His expression grows serious, but he doesn't brush off my thoughts, my fears. "Always, Marcus. I'll always come back for you. From now until I bring you into Arawna."

"Thank you."

His eyes grow distant for a heartbeat, and when they refocus, I know he's about to leave again.

"Go on, you have people to shepherd and all that nonsense."

He laughs, and I can't stop my own from joining his.

"Alright, but you better get the house approved and built. Maybe find someone to love, too." He wiggles his eyebrows, and the scowl on my face appears out of habit.

"I don't need to find anyone to love." Except my heart says I already did, but I think that is from another life.

"I'll see you again. Whenever that happens to be." He grasps my shoulder, and shadows curl around his fingers onto my skin.

I nod. "Oh, and Adrian, quit hanging out as a shadow, okay? You never answered me when I said I saw you at times. I assume that means you're being a creep and following me around."

He releases me, stepping back and flicking his wrist to summon Meiora to him. "I told you; I believe you're remembering something else. All I know is it's not me, my friend."

I furrow my brow and open my mouth to ask another question, but he vanishes in a plume of shadows and darkness.

I drum my fingers along the back of the parchment. When I've had a chance to compose myself, I turn to leave the room and head to the council meeting. A shadow flickers in the corner of my eye. Perhaps I am going mad. I close my eyes, forcing my heart to beat slower, willing for the shadow to be gone when I open them.

Instead, I hear a strange scratching noise coming from the direction I had seen the shadow. The sound reminds me of something Adrian had confided to me a long time ago. My heart races as the image of a person flashes through my mind. My memories forcing to the surface someone I don't remember but feel like I should. My skin crawls with goosebumps. The scratching persists until silence settles in its wake.

I open my eyes, and the darkness taunting me from the corner of my eye is gone. Something calls to me from the wall next to the door, though. Something draws me to it. Or maybe it's someone.

I walk slowly toward the wall, reaching up to grab the lantern hanging next to the door and shining it across the surface of the wood.

Two words are scratched into it. The words lure me into an ocean of memories. A name I cannot place. A person I once knew. A friend I found and lost.

I reach up, brushing my fingers across the letters. They're as cold as ice, stinging the tips enough to cause pain, but I can't look away.

I may not remember, but if I wait a moment, maybe it will all become clear. Either way, the message sparks a warm glow of something in my chest. Chills run down my spine, and my skin feels tingly and warm.

The smile forming on my lips can't be helped as I murmur the words aloud to myself.

Hello, Shadow.

The End

More Books by Olivia

Of Gods and War Duology
House of Death and Shadow
War of Shadow and Bone

Acknowledgments

I'm deeply grateful to everyone who has helped me along the way. It's amazing the power that readers have on an author's motivation. Having people read my book and truly enjoy it has been encouraging to me in this endeavor.

Thank you to each one of you who picks up my book and takes a chance on a new author.

To all my beta readers: thank you for your input and encouragement. It was invaluable insight! Thank you to my family for not thinking I'm a completely crazy person writing these stories.

To my husband, Colin: thank you for standing by me and marketing my book to random people when you get the chance.

To my girls: thank you for your silliness and thoughts and patience as I write, edit, and format in the pockets of time throughout the day.

To Cheryl, thank you for being my biggest cheerleader in the background. Reading all the roughest parts of my book and still enjoying it.

For more from Olivia

Follow on Socials
Instagram @oliviagoldwrites
Threads @oliviagoldwrites
TikTok @author.o.gold
Bluesky ☐@authorolgold.bsky.social☐☐☐☐☐
Visit my Website
https://lifewiththegolds.wordpress.com/
Subscribe to my newsletter
https://oliviagold.substack.com/

About the Author

Hi! I'm Olivia, and I have had a deep love of reading and all things books pretty much my entire life. I grew up on fantasy and magic, and the fact that I get to write stories full of those things boggles my mind. I hope to continue to grow as a writer and reader every year.

I love a variety of genres and consume a diverse range of books. I was born and raised in Kentucky, and I spend a lot of my time outside with my family, enjoying our garden and nature.

My horses, cats, and dog also hold a dear place in my heart.

Thank you to every person who takes a chance on my book. I hope you like it, and even if you didn't, I'm still grateful you tried it out!

Happy Reading!

www.ingramcontent.com/pod-product-compliance
Lightning Source LLC
Chambersburg PA
CBHW030651260626
47157CB00007B/2591